# THE IMMORTAL COIL

# THE IMMORTAL COIL

*Short Stories*

by

## PETER VAN GREENAWAY

LONDON
VICTOR GOLLANCZ LTD
1985

First published in Great Britain 1985
by Victor Gollancz Ltd,
14 Henrietta Street, London WC2E 8QJ

*British Library Cataloguing in Publication Data*
Van Greenaway, Peter
  The immortal coil.
  I. Title
  823'.914[F]    PR6072.A65
  ISBN  0-575-03577-3

Typeset by Centracet
and printed in Great Britain
by St Edmundsbury Press, Bury St Edmunds, Suffolk

# CONTENTS

# INDEFINITE ARTICLE

THE LITTLE TOWN of Knockmealldown is not to be confused with the mountains of a similar designation. I say 'similar' because that extra 'L' makes a divil of contrarity. And wouldn't I know what I'm talking about as being born, baptised and bred up in as God forsaken a hole as never makes a difference how you spell the name of it?

By now, everyone's heard of it; by now, nobody remembers the place. Except your humble chronicler.

Oh God, when I think on the starkened beauty of the town of my dawning, I thank Him or his nominees for being where I am else; but fate it was that brought me back for a spell without enchantment not a month since, and my Aunt Sophie pining for a last sight of me before she took a running kick at the bucket that puts paid to a second opportunity.

Sure, I found my last surviving relative on my mother's side as hale as a parrot with a Linguaphone degree in Arabic and half as intelligible as usual. But those are her derogatory words, not mine.

It seems I was reeled in from Dublin because I'd been overworking, though she covered with a pretext of wanting to tell me I was the sole beneficiary of her will; and when I asked her why couldn't she have told me so by telegram, if she felt it was that late, she accused my face of bare ingratitude. There's no understanding the logic of a testatrix.

Howsomever, it's not of my personal affairs I wish to tell. My part in the proceedings is no more than that of an innocent bystander who gets drawn into a street brawl and not the slightest interest either way until the outset shows signs of having an outcome.

First, then, I'll make my apologies for the town.

There's a saying among its younger folk that God must've been wearing dark glasses when he made Knockmealldown, and while I don't altogether agree, I'll concede somebody must've distracted the divine concentration at the crucial.

I'm not the hand for making a description fit to electrify the tour operators into packaging a holiday for the blind but, like Hilarity, the celebrated undertaker of Cork, I promise to make the most of what there is.

The town trickles down a hill, but, God forgive me, the more I think of it, the more I reckon someone tried to knock most of it off when no one was looking. The houses and all tumble down in such a way as defies tongue to tell or pen to record.

'A watering place,' says the only guide-book I ever knew to mention it. A watering place!

Almighty God, the sea got tired of visiting long ago and left off ebbing and flowing to go elsewhere, and with the everlasting silt in a moderate-sized estuary the waters grew stagnant till never a coaster could ply to the warehouses for commerce and mutual prosperity.

Knockmealldown was left high and dry till the now of things is such, you can step off the end of the High Street and go up to your waist in mud and a tangle of discarded bedsteads, and there's nowhere else in all Ireland where you can do that. Again I'm quoting from the guide-book which it was obviously desperate to find an outstanding feature or a peculiar leisure activity, so you'll understand me being at the same wits' end.

The railway comes in from Limerick and gladly goes back again. Its station is behind the hill and at the bottom as you'd expect. The Railway Hotel is at the top. Many years ago Councillor Sweeney campaigned for to have the railway at the top and the hotel shifted to the bottom, 'to give the weary traveller a better impression of the town, presently nowhere in sight, on his instant arrival.'

There's no other statue in Knockmealldown but the one in the town square. It's a bronze of Sweeney, bent as a beachcomber, looking for the brains he never had to start with, and that's as near an act of vicious judgment as our townsfolk ever came to.

Plentiful, the colonial properties hereabouts as befitted the officermen and their wives who retired to live as cheap as church mice within sight of the sea or what was left of it. Many of the fine old houses are derelict now but my Auntie still occupies one as she has for all her seventy-five years, and as I did for some of my own.

'Tis a grand old Georgic house, built in Victoria's day and modernised in Edward's time, with a fine flowing stairway, and my auntie flies down the banister rail every morning at seven, regular as clockwork, to keep herself healthy; and if that's eccentricity I'll tell you she has the best youth of her age in the town. From a bowed window on the raised ground floor you can look up the High Street to O'Dwyer's surgery and the hotel and down to the slough of wallowing bedsteads.

To the left of her is a pub, to the right of her is another, and on milder evenings she opens the window in the long, side passage and the door on the right-side to let the fumes mingle in the middle and soothe her nerves. *Stet fortuna domus*.

There's the school across the way, inset and out of sight. A two-piece academy for infants and juniors run by Mr and Mrs Rafferty, the pair of young immigrants who wander about the town like a brace of pheasants who didn't know what hit them in the close season.

Into Furnell Place is the church of Father Mahoney first, and St Thomas a poor second. And down with the railway is the convent of the Little Sisters of Big Brother as the rascally youth of Knockmealldown will tell you, and as they told the good Mother Superior; and when they looked disappointed with her laughter, she laughed again.

If it hadn't been for Mahoney's sister Molly, there'd not be a decent hall of temperance in the town. Long ago he gave her a new interest in life with opening a comfortable tea-room in the lower High Street.

A tea-room! the dazed inhabitants had exclaimed. Why the Jesus do we need a tea-room? Sure, Mulligan sells it by the pound.

For the young! Mahoney thundered. Somewhere they can indulge in refined discourse over tea and—and an innocent crumpet. No one knew why this shocked Postmaster Hogan who'd knocked about the world a bit what with a fortnight in Torquay and a cross-channel voyage to Jersey.

'Oh, Father!' he could get no further with the shock of God knows what.

'Oh, Father!' Mahoney summoned an echo. 'Why shouldn't they have a place of resort like their beer-swilling elders!'

'It isn't that, so it is, Father. But didn't you know the youngsters only drink the coffee and Cola and Rory O'Neill's Scintillating Suds?'

But Knockmealldown got its cafe and the leading citizens now use it as a matter of course and with civical pride for having something to contribute to Egon O'Ronay's *All Ireland Good Food Guide.*

What else do we have apart from the Warehouse cinema which Mahoney says is the divil's own work but Clancy McGee swears is all his own and the two men at daggers drawn because Clancy slipped in *The Blue Angel* when Mahoney wasn't looking thirty years ago? There's a billiard hall for non-residents at the Railway, a youth club in one of Knockdown's many redundant warehouses, and shops enough to keep twenty-three hundred inhabitants in all they need without bothering Dublin for a light.

I have heard tell how the celebrated Paul Henry came down to paint one of his inimitable scenes of Ireland many years ago. He took a squint from the summit, disagreed with what he saw, turned round, took one disbelieving step after another down the drunken High Street until, at last, he took a step too many and fell arse over tip into the mud lapping the side wall of Macey's Boot and Shoe Emporium.

Apparently he daubed his Whatman's with suggestible browning and pissed on it before donating the impromptu to the municipal library and him shaking the dust of Knockdown off his feet for evermore. But never believe all you hear in a town that doesn't have a municipal library to start with.

Not that I'd have you think the folks here are too thick in the head to go chasing print. Mick Mulligan's super-store boasts as fine a circulating library as you'd hope to meet anywhere in Ireland. One of those beautiful wire contraptions packed with Romances and Westerns and suchlike, and all you need do is spin the doings with a finger and there's the literature of the world passing before your very eyes. Show me anywhere in the country a public library that can offer as much *and* a packet of Sweet Afton at the same counter.

Where did I get to and where am I going? 'Tis the age-old cry of the chronicler and, at the end of a Guinness, as Dubliners say, you've still to make up your mind and come to the point.

Touching my forelock to you I'll confide: is it credible, in this day and age of moonshot and cavorting particles of molybdenum, selenium and soluble Disprin, such a thing as came to pass could happen at all, making a mountain out of the molehill of Knockme-down?

If only one could begin at the beginning and manage without the ending. . .

Some say it was found before six o'clock mass, others between six and seven, and the rest, between seven and eight. In fact it was ten past, and for sure it was Dimmy Boyd the sacristan who bent down to inspect the steps of the church itself for all the world like he's taking the mike out of Sweeney round the corner, doubled up in green bronze.

Dimmy looks at the object from every angle then asks himself a question: what's this doin' here? Being weak in the head he forgets the question before he's on to looking for the answer and slopes off to find out Father Mahoney who's divesting in the vestry between sips of something hot out of the classical Thermos. Not the man to be trifled with and, wedded to the daily routine, he's none too pleased to see Dimmy's fishy eyes swimming round the door's edge where none should be.

'Did you blow out the candles?'

'I did, Father.'

'Then go back to your bed and be done wid you!'

'Father—'

'Did you hear me now!'

'Father, I hear you, but there's news I'd be tellin'.'

'News! At this time of the mornin'!' Mahoney glared suspiciously, but remarked no more softening of the brain than was usual. 'Well!'

You'll observe he seldom asked questions so much as fired interrogative missiles.

'Father, there's a ballewn on the church steps.'

For once in his natural the poor simpleton got the better of his intellectual and spiritual superior. Mahoney gave back a look Boyd never ever could have beaten for daftness.

'A ballewn!'

''Tis sittin' white as a ghost wid th'anaemics out there now, Father.'

A long glare, another sip from the comforting flask and then, with an impulse born of his known temperament, Mahoney makes a dash out of the vestry, down the side aisle and through the tallowstink to the door itself.

He saw nothing at first, until, his eye chancing to the right, he spies a white object draped over the third step as graceful as Madam Recumbancy reclining in a deserted saloon. He bends to it, hands on knees, walks down a step or two, goes up the other side, and tries a new point of view.

Dimmy Boyd hoves into sight, little more than a pair of bulging optics hovering in the gloom spilt from the interior.

'How long is it here!' roars Mahoney.

'Divil a bit I'd know, Father. No one's after tellin' me.'

'Will you leave off invokin' the Prince of Darkness in the outside of me own church ye heathen bog-squatter! Come down to me side . . . now, who told ye 'twas a ballewn!'

'Me own intimate experience of th' darlins, Father. Sure don't I be blowin' up fifty-two of the craithers for the children's party every December of the year?'

Mahoney peered narrowly at the man beside him, and doubted. Dimmy Boyd was never the one for a madcap caper of this hue. He looked up at the last brush-strokes of night sweeping out to the west and tried to visualise—now, that's how it was, no one would have seen it with the morning darkness, so there was no way of telling when . . . the priest blundered from perplexity to anger, from anger to blind fury, and all of it gone to his head.

'Off wid ye and ring the bell!'

'Ring d'bell? Now, Father?'

'Now!'

'Did I forget to ring d'bell then, Father?'

'Will you do as I'm tellin' you! I want the whole town to know. I'm blowin' a tocsin so I am, to ring in all the quarters of iniquity!'

For the blatancy and the enormity of the thing he stared upon began to pull at his heartstrings, one after the other, and he saw no way to break the silence of his anguish but by noise and the summons of all with ears to hear, and eyes to see. Oh, the first words of a fine Sabbath sermon were already writ large and the greatest of these was 'sinners', with 'messengers of lust' thundering up for the photo-finish.

A word about Father Mahoney while Dimmy Boyd fumbles for the bell-pull in the dusk-laden porch.

Mahoney is a waning power in the land: about two square miles of it not counting the built-up area. He's held the sway now for close on forty years so you'll deduce him not in the first flush of his youth. Well, age can be a useful thing, inversely ratio'd to the utility of a pyramid balanced on its apex. You start, like an American president, with nothing but a pokey point of view and end up with a power base big enough to grow your own vegetables *and* have space over for the compost heap.

So it was, or used to be, with Mahoney. His word came near to being law in his allotment and the garda was left in peace to work the most exquisite tapestry known to man since the Goblins.

A kindly man, an irascible man, he was tolerant to the foibles of the flock and a scourge to the vices of the strays—within the meaning of the Acts. But, as the local paper said when once it made a rare appearance:

'Of course he's brought peace and stability to Knockmealldown. Who's arguing? If a car's standing tip-toe on one wheel in the knacker's yard, where's the fines for speeding, the head-on collisions, the casualties and the divine divvying up with the insurance man? That's the peace and stability of death passing all understanding. Especially mine.'

From which you'll gather Phelim Felocity, the publisher, editor, printer down to a menial's responsibility for putting out the dustbin at the premises of the *Knockmealldown Occasional*, is a burnt-out radical.

A word as to the grand Fleet Street sounding monniker of our organ of spasmodic dissemination. It's simplicity itself. The *K.O.* appears on the streets after Rogan's fish parlour shuts down for the night, or in Mulligan's newsagents and tobacconist, when Phelim's in the mood or some burning issue of the day tickles his fancy. It's then you'll see the sparks fly in the Vulcanic stithy he maintains down at the old corn respository as he hammers the type into total compliance with no other's will but his own.

But that's from my direct purpose which is to characterise the good Father in his living colours, for thereby I'm hanging on to the very shirt-tail of my story.

Now the good Saint Euphemismos never had half the job fated to me for making the unmentionable—mentionable; so difficult it is, I'm taking the coward's way out by letting you figure out for yourselves what I'm going to say.

Many were the worldly things abhorrent to Mahoney but none more so, and naturally so, considering his cloth, than the mechanical interception of all that's crucial in the act of procreation—I strike out the term 'mechanical' as suggesting the cogs and pistons of some almighty clap hammer which, by its nature, can go berserk enough to macerate unwary fornicators into affectionate mince-meat.

Fortunately or not, there are other ways, and some of them

Brannigan, Mahoney's bugbear, keeps under his counter for those legally entitled to dodge the issue.

With the divil's luck you'll begin to understand what an offence was created by the debut of a 'ballewn' on God's own doorstep, and you'll maybe deduce some of Father Mahoney's thinking as he peers in outraged perplexity at this sudden sully.

The bell's scarcely been clapped for two minutes when Mahoney comes belated to his senses and careers back into the church with the agitated conviction of a man who knows he's done wrong.

'Stop the bell, y'natural son of a polterghost! Is it the whole of Ireland you'd be rousing to witness our shame!'

Poor Dimmy dropped the rope and crossed himself with his eyes. 'Divil a bit would I, but y'told me—'

'I'm not in command of me faculties at all and youse the best judge of a simpleton to tell me the error of me ways. Where's your hat!'

'Me hat, Father?'

'Your hat! The Black Death of a bowler you screw on for funerals and holy days.'

The Boyd's eyes widened all the way round at sight and sound of a man bellowing for his own hat with ringing of bells, and all for an auld ballewn.

''Tis in the vestry on the hook you gi'ed me five years ago.' Dimmy was overweening proud of his hook.

'Get it!'

No sooner repeated than Dimmy's there and back with a rim surrounding nothing so like a pitch-black skull that passed for the poor simpleton's headgear.

To do him some credit it was all Mahoney could devise in the fever of the moment, and he *was* thinking of the children soon to be on their way to school and them spotting the ballewn on the steps and the maidens of Knockdown glimpsing it and both nudging each other in stupefied horror. So he snatches the hat from Dimmy and claps it over the offending object before it can jump up and twist around like a roller-skater doing the Bolero.

Satisfied all had been done that could be done Mahoney stumped off to the nearby presbytery for breakfast and to work out what next to do, leaving the sacristan to lock up and wonder about his hat.

Now, whether Mahoney acted wisely or no, the fact is, he acted.

By ringing the bell in his utter state he advertised to the town the anomaly that no bell should be ringing at all at the time; so naturally, the inquisitives were bound to sally forth and inspect the damage. Which they did, in their ones and twos.

If you ask why didn't he just remove the ballewn there and then, I can only refer you to his aforementioned state of utterness.

While he brooded over his bacon along comes Seamus Mac-Donagh, the butcher of Knockdown, a forty-fiver, red-faced as his own sirloins and only twice their age some say. He seldom has a word for anyone.

Turning the corner he goes up to the church and stops dead at the foot of the wide splaying steps. The first thing he sees is the bowler, the second is its owner hovering round the church corner as one reluctant to leave his property unaccompanied and naked to the public gaze.

A dozen times the butcher's eye travelled from the hat to a sacristan unsure about wanting to avoid publicity, but never a word did he speak though you could see him sweating with the effort of putting two and two together.

Then Mother Jackson who runs the other tobacconist comes scurrying round the corner and she too stops dead as if she's met with a cannon ball on a two-inch fuse.

A few shawlies appear, followed by Duffy, the builder and undertaker; a more inquisitive, gossiping rumourmonger you'll not find in the Republic.

'What's that then?' he calls aloud in his squeaky falsetto.

Nobody replies. It's obvious to a congenital what it is.

Duffy contemplates the object with blank amazement and by the time he can find other words, there's another dozen or more turn-ups staring at the scene.

Apart from the obvious, no one, including Duffy, can think what to ask. There's the hat balanced on the steps and there's Dimmy's moon-face keeping goal while the rest of him's round the corner.

It's about this time I arrived on the scene. My aunt Sophie, flying down the banister rail like a fireman answering the call says will I go see what all the ringing's about when there's naught down in *Radio Eirean Times*. With nothing better to do I go round the corner and there's half the town staring at—well you know what they're staring at.

'What's the ringing for, Dimmy?' someone calls.

'I had me orders—toll for the iniquity, said Father Mahoney.'

'What iniquity?' says someone else.

'Keep it onder your hat says he.'

This stunned everybody into silence but Duffy.

'What iniquity?' he squeaks.

'Take your hat from your hook and hide the shame of the world says he.'

We all look at each other. No ones goes near the hat. Some of the shawlies even take a step backwards.

'Dimmy Boyd, will you come to your senses and tell us what's _onder_ the hat!' shouts Mrs Jackson, for she dimly sees the bell wasn't tolled for nothing.

'I can't,' says the sacristan mysteriously, 'or why would me hat be there at all?'

I applauded the logic and wondered had they done the first Irish brain transplant on Dimmy when he wasn't looking?

'If you won't tell us, I'll look for meself,' yelled Duffy. ''Tis a free country for investigatin onder things when they're open to the public skies!'

This got a murmur of approval and the face from round the corner looked concerned, conscious of itself as the guardian of its hat and Father Mahoney's dearest wishes.

'Will you please leave me hat and the ballewn alone or I'll be off to tell the Father I'm beleaguered and no way of reachin' him.'

The mention of Mahoney yet again sobered them all. No one was anxious to get on the wrong side of his wrath so, for the moment, they turned to each other and demanded didn't the (dimwit) mention a ballewn?

I was near enough to say I thought he had and unwittingly helped to spread a rumour that went four times round the world, and with so much broderie even the Russians were accusing the Americans of test firing a new inflatable weapon for nervous gas on a New Mexico range called Pknockledown.

That's what it says in Pravda.

Puzzlement kept the crowd rooted to the spot. As Duffy said, 'Why the Jasus would anybody clap a bowler on a ballewn?' At which a thought occurred.

'Dimmy Boyd!' he called, 'is it blown up at all?'

'It's flatter than a tyre on a dead bicycle,' reported the sacristan and that, for some reason, brought all eyes to rest in uneasy peace on the cover-all. (hat)

Seeing no reason to stay longer I decided to go back and enliven aunt Sophie's day with an account of how things stood; so far as they were standing at all.

Meantime, Father Mahoney fretted over his second cup of coffee, wondering how to proceed with the unprecedented. His sister, gentle Molly Mahoney with the brown eyes you'd never think were sixty-five years in the world, dances a discreet two-feet in expectation of a revelation. She knows her cherished brother too well not to know something is amiss, but she'd never ask.

Suddenly Mahoney looks up as being smote with a decision. 'I'll get to the bottom of this so I will, Molly. I'll come to it.'

She nodded with his certainty. 'Sure you will, Michael.'

'I'll hold a disquisition in the vestry and I'll start right here.'

She nodded again, a little less certainly.

'What time does Dusty O'Hara pass by?'

'The street-cleaner, Michael?'

'Unless there's another I know nothing of.'

'About now. He'll be draggin' the High Street.'

'Run down now and tell him I want a word with him.'

'Dusty O'Hara?'

'And why not?'

She viewed the nice, neat parlour, clean as a paper of pins, and thought of O'Hara in his filthy cords and blue linen jacket flecked with the fruits of his industry.

'D'you think he'd be hurt if I ran Bathwick's germicidal aerosol over his person?'

He smiled a little. 'Just be fetchin' him here and discuss your hygienic requirements on the way back.'

She left him to his melancholy reflections on the ways of the wicked, and how best to stem the rising tide of filth already lapping at the foot of Knockmealldown; at the very steps of the church itself.

Not for the first time his eyes lit on the polished brass fire-irons set in the grate before him, and didn't the tongs suggest to him the dramatic gesture best calculated to fit a purpose and his own histrionic talents? Darting from the chair he seized the ponderous tongs and brandished them mightily, and that was the stuffed birds on the mantelshelf gone for a Burton. A good rehearsal for smiting the enemies of the people.

Five minutes later Molly returned with Dusty O'Hara, the man with the two bicycle wheels escorting a dustbin and him paid to keep the town free from spicks and spans.

With a bit of handkerchief to her nose Molly let O'Hara in and gently closed the door in his indignant face. O'Hara was as pugnacious as the next man who happened to be Mahoney.

'She's after hintin' to fumigate me. I didn't come here to be insulted.'

'Sit down, O'Hara, and leave me to tell you what you did come for.'

So O'Hara took a chair wondering what for was the tongs in the Father's hand. He was more than ready to take umbrage if a tass of tea came at him from the ends of them so he was. But Mahoney had no intention of offering refreshment.

'Now, O'Hara, I want God's truth here and now. Did you find anything disgusting on your rounds last night or early this mornin'?'

O'Hara opened his face—and shut it. Then he did it again, blinked a bit, took out the handkerchief his mother gave him thirty years ago for his first communion, and blew his nose to gain time.

'Would you mind axing me that again, Father?'

With patience ill-disguised, but not before asking had he ever considered putting his nose rag on to boil, Mahoney did so.

O'Hara considered the question from a philosophical not to mention diplomatic point of view. He saw straight off there was no money in it. 'It depends what y'mean by disgostin',' he temporised.

'Lewd, filthy, obnoxious to the mind!' Mahoney had no doubts, but that didn't slow down O'Hara from scratching his barely shaven chin and pondering.

'Let me see. Would the wrapper off a Mars bar do ye, Father?'

Mahoney squinted in surprise. 'What's lewd about the Mars bar!' He sounded like someone genuinely in search of enlightenment.

'Well, you're strippin' it naked after a fashion and all. And there's the banana skin . . . it makes you wonder,' he said hopelessly, then tailed off at a total loss.

'Are you laughing at me, O'Hara!'

'You axed me. I'm tellin' ye! How the Jasus do I know what you're lookin' for? If I find it I'll give it straight back to ye if you'll only come straight out wid describing the details.'

It was Mahoney's turn to stare back in blank disbelief and horror. 'Are you accusin' my face of—! Give it *back*! I'll tell ye somethin'! You'll be punished upside down and sideways in purgatory for the contents of your filthy mind, O'Hara, and that's a promise!'

The sweeper felt he had a right to be aggrieved and said so. 'I come in here to do ye a favour and I'm threatened with me afterlife. I axe ye, is that fair, Father?'

The priest was in no mood to be fair to anyone; but he did perceive the need to re-phrase his question if he was to get anywhere. 'Did you find any *article* of a dubious nature such as might be calculated to put sinful thoughts into a weak body's mind?'

A look of misery stole over O'Hara's gravelly face as he reflected how bloody boring a street-cleaner's life could be.

'Savin' y'cloth, Father, the dogshit doesn't exactly raise a man's expectations regarding a sinful blow-out anymore than Rogan's fish n'chip parlour at—'

'Did you ever come across a ballewn!'

'. . . ba . . . llewn?'

'What are y'lookin' at me like that for!'

'Did ye say a ballewn, Father?'

'Ah!' triumphantly. 'I see you know what I'm talking about!'

'Yes, Father,' said O'Hara shaking his head violently. 'A bal- lewn.'

'You've found one!'

'No.'

'On the church steps.'

'You did say a—'

'A ballewn. Now, are you, the lawfully appointed streetduster of Knockmealldown, goin' to deny you left a receptacle of the divil on me very own steps and not a swipe of your broom.'

'I'm not paid to sweep the divil's reciprocals off the steps of y'church—that's Dimmy Boyd's obligation!'

'Ah! So you saw it there and left it there to bring shame and disgrace on the community!'

'What the blody hell is a ballewn got to do with Sodom and Glockamorra! And if I want insults I can get me own brand at the Four Feathers *and* drown 'em in a pint o' stout so I will! Good day to ye, Father!'

The door slammed violently and Mahoney was left listening to O'Hara's self-righteous volubility being let out at the front entrance by Molly.

Who reappeared moments later.

'You've upset him, Michael.'

'I'll upset a few more before they drive me to me grave,' he muttered through the twitching of his every facial muscle.

'And they with nothing to patch the hole you'd make with your going,' simply as a matter of pure fact. 'D'you know there's a crowd outside the church and Dimmy Boyd up there with his bowler on the steps . . . is something wrong, Michael?'

He broke off from his gnashing to look at her innocence, and some of his time-worn kindness came up to refresh his eyes till he sighed, half doubting if the battle was worth the effort that no longer came so easy. But, of all the humours, the choleric lasts longest and he was soon in war-horse harness again.

'Go down now and open up your tea-rooms, Molly, and you'll have the business of y'life this day. Be off wid ye, for I've much to do.'

He kissed her cheek and she went, submissive to her cherished brother as ever, and they orphans too soon with no other flesh and blood to put them a bit righter with the world though they almost perfection in each other's eyes.

Meantime I'd taken myself back to Auntie's round the corner, and I'll admit my step was a mort jauntier than when first I set out, or for many day past. I began to speculate that this boring place of my childhood and early youth was livelier than I'd had eyes to see. For sure, the sight of a bowler in strange circumstances was a dramatic departure from the unmitigated sameness of life in the air apparent of Knockdown.

Aunt Sophie had the bacon and eggs ready in the pan and the coffee bubbling on the hob when I got to the kitchen. She never failed to surprise me first thing in the morning, washed, combed and looking fresher than many a younger woman of my acquaintance. Being a sensible body she left me to take the edge off a healthy man's appetite before I told her all I'd seen.

'And the last I saw was Felocity, notebook in hand, taking statements from everybody including the hat. There'll be an *Occasional* this week for sure.'

'But what's under the hat Father Mahoney's so anxious to hide?'

I shrugged and reached for the soda bread. 'All I heard was Dimmy talk of a balloon.'

'A ballewn!'

'That's what I thought he said.'

My auntie isn't the kind of woman to take a bombshell lying down. At least, she'll pick herself up so soon as it's flattened her. Which she did.

'There's more in this than meets the eye,' she announced, looking straight into mine.

I'll allow I flushed a bit under the collar and I didn't exactly know why. After all, it amounted to no more than a peculiar practical joke having no better object than to assemble the townsfolk for Till Eulenspiegel's rendering of the raspberry. And it's worth mentioning, I had no sure idea just then what exactly *was* under the hat since Dimmy Boyd was not of a mind you'd give the credence to. As I pointed out to my mother's eldest sister.

'True enough,' assented she, 'but the more reason to wonder. For Dimmy's not the man to invent what isn't there.'

Now that did set me thinking. Aunt Sophie, I had to admit, demolished my theory of a jape very neatly *and* provided a vacuum for filling with some new thoughts.

'Do you volunteer any theories of your own?'

Again the shrewdness in the eye of a woman who'd travelled further and wider than postmaster Hogan. 'Father Mahoney found something more than a joke outside his church. It threw him to the four winds . . . there was panic in the ringing of the bell—'

'To tell the world,' I supposed.

'A cry for help.'

'Since when did he need help! The iron heel of Knockdown,' but she wasn't chuckling with me.

'Times have changed, Patrick. The good Father's no friend of mine, but it's not a whit less sad to watch a man losing the battle—'

'To what?'

'Oh!' she waved a hand vaguely. 'To superior knowledge, I suppose. Knowledge at any rate. Science, technology, the flight to the stars. If heaven's up there, we won't need to earn what we can occupy . . .'

'Then it's high time he lost.'

She smiled a little. 'You're young enough to say so. But time does funny things to some people . . . they begin to see both points of view.'

'Both! There's a thousand.' Even so, I lit my first cigarette of the day and thought about it. 'So the hat's no joke?'

'That, nephew, depends on which you choose of your thousand points of view.'

Which resolved me to act before her wicked humour demolished me entirely.

'In that case, I'm going back to see which one comes out on top. Are you coming?'

'I've to wash the dishes, my dear. Just to prove it's a man's world.'

'Only in Ireland,' I promised, and set off once more, at about the same time, probably, as Father Mahoney strode out of his house armed with the tongs.

When I got to the tiny square before St Thomas's it was crowdier than ever and I had to view the proceedings from afar, which wasn't that far.

I could see Brannigan deep in converse with Mother Jackson. Duffy was here, there and everywhere, circulating faster than Mulligan's library and spreading about as much fiction. Clancy, aloof and sombre, likely wishing he could charge a punt for admission. And he'd have doubled it had he known it would turn out the equivalent of an XYZ fillum. Felocity was busy taking snapshots of everything, immortalising the doings of Knockdown by the light of the celestial Polaroid.

I'd never seen so many nobodies who weren't just anybody gathered together at a swoop. Even Doc' O'Dwyer stood discreetly by, sardonic-seeming even at this distance. But, wherever all eyes turned, they came back to roost, like spent carrier-pigeons, on the hat.

Dimmy Boyd still ducked and bobbed round the side of the church and, over all, the air was festooned with expectancy. Not an animated scene, exactly, but you could tell the sludge was bubbling under, better than the Bog of Ceoinagh, and almost it heaved a little at sight of Father Mahoney, erect in every one of his sixty-eight years, striding into the picture clutching, God Almighty, the fire tongs?

A great sigh went up the multitude at sight of them.

'What's he doin' wid the fuel-grippers?' was heard on all sides.

I heard old gentlemen swear they'd never seen the like since the Taoiseach caught the wrong train to Limerick in 1937 and landed in Knockdown in 1938 . . . that would've been New Year's Day.

'Sure his grey matter's turnin' black,' said one.

'I wouldn't say it at all,' doubted another. 'Who'd be touching Dimmy's hat without the grippers and him as lousy as a hedgehog?'

Such were the comments undertowing the massive silence come down as Mahoney took his stand by the headpiece.

'I'm glad you've come, and I wish you hadn't.' Loud and clear the pulpitating voice of him as he gazed about with more than a touch of distaste.

'I'll pick me words carefully, for there's women among ye, and I'll not offend their ears with the language of the day. Now! at some time of the night or early this mornin' someone of the town put down on the steps of our church Satan's own callin' card such as was never seen in our public places since the light of the world. Before I go further I'll ask all the members of the other sex to withdraw about their business.'

Not a bit of the other sex made a stir.

'Unless,' said cunning Mahoney after a pause, 'there's whores among ye on speakin' terms with the divil's own dirt.'

Forty seconds later there's not a bit of the fair sex left in the place.

'None of this is woman's work, so now we come to it . . . I'm going to pluck off the hat and show youse men the symbol of y'degradation.'

Silence reached fever pitch. If there's one thing the men of the world can't wait to see, 'tis the palpable, tangible signs of their utter degradation. I never beheld such tipping of toes and craning of necks. Felicity was scribbing in his little black book fit to bust, and all eyes, even O'Dwyer's, were intent on Mahoney: you'd have thought a conjuror in priest's clothing was after extracting a bloody elephant from under that gruesome reminder of the dead, for did I forget to tell you the headgear once belonged to Dimmy's father?

It came at last. Mahoney crossed himself and muttered a 'Hail Mary' or maybe 'abracadabra' before tweaking the hat with the tongs and deftly whisking it away—to reveal 'the divil's own callin' card'.

Somehow, the turn didn't go down like a glass of Guinness. Perhaps the lassoon in sequins, hands on provocating hips and a rallentando on the drums was missing but, whatever, you could feel the dampness of a squib cooling the air.

''Tis only an auld ballewn like Dimmy said,' piped up an old fellow nearby.

Well, there was it, draped coyly over the riser, and all eyes waiting to see if it would get up and take a bow. Otherwise, nothing to clap hands for, and, for a wonder, none could find a word to say.

Mahoney made the grievous mistake of turning from a conjuror into a quiz-master.

'Do any of youse know what that is!' he bellowed.

''Tis Rory Shane's changed out of his long winter underwear at last!' someone obliged.

That got the roar since Rory is the pokiest man known to every clachan in the district. I won't repeat the lewder observations of some of our younger fry but, if I say 80 per cent recognised the article for what it was, that left a sizeable minority convinced it wasn't, and then only for the sake of argument.

'Eh, Father, you had us fooled entirely. Certain I was ye'd clapped Dimmy's auld hat over Mary Donnelly's drawers and she never in 'em so they go off for the neglect of 'em.'

Mahoney eyed the speaker and the crowd's delight with a terrible contempt. 'You disgust me,' he let out, but quiet-like, and all the more effective for being out of his ranting style. 'The signs of the times is writ clear on every brow in the pack of ye, and you'll scrape your wit from the barrel's bottom to make jots and tittles for an act of desecration. Now, I'm giving you the chance of a lifetime to defuse the collective sin. Let the owner step forth this minute now, and wipe out the shame of all by proclaiming his to the world.'

'And suppose, Father, the world isn't interested.'

Mahoney turned his head sharp enough for dislocation to set in. 'Ah! Is it you, Brannigan! Wouldn't I know the purveyor of murderous weapons would be defending his own!'

At which Brannigan came out of the crowd to confront Mahoney, and impressive he looked for sternness. A quiet man, scholarly and stooped with years of learning on his back, he reminded of a patriarch, washed, shaved and on a strict diet. Some said he was ascetic, others said that was the acid of the vinegar in him, and mayhap both sides were in the right.

'Have a care, Father. You're not beyond the laws of slander if I forgot the law of tolerance. And why this clatter? D'you be making a fool of yourself or the firetongs, or the bowler? In ten seconds you could have turned your mountain into a nothing for a miracle, but you choose to do the opposite. For what? Publicity for your cause? What difference to you whether 'tis a balloon, a contraceptive or a sausage-skin?'

Mahoney made hard work of breathing owing to his wrath, for if there was a man in Knockdown who could put out the fire of his vehemence with the cold water of reason, it had to be Brannigan himself.

'Try it! Take me to the highest court, yea, sue me at the Seat of Judgment itself . . . I'll tell them to your face what you are—a curse on the act of creation!'

Unmistaking, the sudden tension. Not a man of us didn't lean forward in his mind at this display of hostile, irreconcilable forces for, however you worded it, it was no other.

Historically, it may not amount to much; but the history of the world is nothing but yesterday's doings in today's neck of it wherever.

Shortly to say: however much the one's intellectual agnostic rationalism tormented the other's dogmatic romanticism over the years, matters never boiled higher till the progressives made legal the right of married couples to plan their families in such a way as to put 'almighty Stopes before God Almighty'.

From that time the gloves were off. The good Father lost no occasion to embarrass Brannigan with spiritual sideswipes, and the apothecary fought back with as icy a display of contempt as ever hemmed a red rag.

'You'll not have the last word on this, Father. Till now you could avoid egg on your face. A balloon could have got you off your hook. But there's Felicity running about like spilt quicksilver, snapping, talking, noting and all for to blow up your *bête blanche* till, I'm warning you, it'll burst in your face—'

'Get out of my sight y'heathen!'

'. . . *you* know why I'm advising you, Mahoney. If this doesn't turn out to be a judgment on you then the powers of darkness are not what I took them to be.'

And Felicity had that down in short-hand before Brannigan had finished striding out of the concourse back to his shop.

\* \* \*

You could say that, from that moment, things took an ugly turn. For sure they created the biggest thirst for many a day in our town. And didn't the men recognise their moral duty to argue the pros and cons over the glass that clears? The publicans did, and all four inns were open before the last stragglers had left the little square to Father Mahoney, the sacristan and the doctor who still held his ground with a quizzical eye to the priest now dividing his dejective attention between the tongs and the article in question.

As if with mind made up after self-consultation, O'Dwyer jerked into motion, briskly crossed the space from the old Music Rooms and went up the steps sufficient to face Mahoney.

'Too much wasted effort, Father. I'd advise you to—rest awhile—from your labours.'

Pugnacious ever, Mahoney scowled mightily. 'You're shy enough of takin' my advice. I'd be ashamed to take yours.'

The doctor's long-ago divorce still rankled, and I'll say no more of that old history. But O'Dwyer smiled, the comfortable smile of a professional man who knows that all must come to him later, if not sooner.

'Amateur dramatics won't further your cause.'

'And what's that supposed to mean!'

'I saw an amateur production of *Romeo and Juliet* once in Dublin—my final year . . . now you remind me of the Romeo, shinning up the lath and plaster tree like a real trouper, and passing the time agreeably with his intended. All very dramatic till he's meant to swing a leg over the balcony and rejoin the *terra firma*. Half-way down he catches his sixteenth-century trousers on a projection till he can't get up or down whatever the sticks poking out from the wings to help him off. He'd be there now if they hadn't rung down the curtain.'

'What's that to me!'

'Amateurs, Father. They know fine how to stoke up a blaze of glory, but devil a bit can they sustain it—or extinguish it.'

'You maybe don't have much cause for professional outrage, but you'll do me the favour of recognising vocational indignation.'

'Of course. And I'd never doubt you meant well; but so did Friar Laurence . . . and that was the tragedy of it.'

Mahoney peered a little closer at the physician, unsure for once as to which side of the fence he stood, unsure even of the fence's very existence.

'Whit are ye tryin' to tell me!'

O'Dwyer shrugged and pursed his lips in one. 'Tenesmus, I think. Progress cloys and retrogression clogs, more's the pity. And if you were another man I'd pity you; for the world has none for a fighter.'

The doctor departed in a way that somehow suggested he meant no malice though Mahoney looking after him was strangely bothered in half his understanding. The good doctor was almost out of earshot when the priest suffered an impulsion.

'Loyalties, O'Dwyer! Would you leave those out of the reckonin'!'

The doctor turned, intrigued as much by a note in the voice as by the words themselves. Was it something like the inexplicable ringing of the bell, with the same faint echo of an S.O.S.?

Whatever, O'Dwyer retraced enough steps to meet his old agonistes part way. 'D'you recall St Kieran and the Dun Cow?'

'I do.'

'Was the servant of St Kieran true to his faith?'

'Never doubt it!'

'. . . then why did they bury him in unholy ground?'

'You know as well as I do, he made a stupid mistake.'

'Losing a manuscript.'

'What then!'

'A *material* error?'

'Will you say what y'mean!'

'Easily, Father. If you can pay a high price for losing something, you can pay as much for finding—something.'

This time the doctor made no concessions but went straight off to his daily rounds leaving Mahoney a prey to mankind's greatest predator: mixed feelings.

Moments later he trailed his tongs back to the presbytery leaving Dimmy to make a decent burial of the *corpus delicti* in the first piece of wasteland he came to.

'Whit shall I do wid me hat, Father?'

'You can bury that too! And if there's room in the hole you can throw ye'self after!'

God help us, I'm glad I missed sight of the loneliness leap in poor Dimmy's eyes at those words, and the instant act of contrition blinding the sight of Mahoney. He fumbled uncertainly for his pocket and stepped to the sadness that would have died for him at a word.

'Dimmy, boyo, they promised ye the earth for your meekness. Some day we'll tell 'em you deserved better . . . go on now, take this and buy yourself your favourite coke when you're shot of this and hung up your own hat on your own bit of hook.'

Sometimes, the harsh word is worth all for the smile that comes after. A coke! Of all the treasures of this world. Sure and it doesn't take much.

I had no inclination to share tavern talk and hear a multitude of opinions growing more exotic by the pint. Besides, I was become a stranger in my home town insofar that gossip would mean little. There's a kind of code informing local talk that you needs must live with for longer than a now-and-again sojourn.

But gleanings enough were there prompting a desire for facts. As I wandered down a High Street struggling to go up the other way, an eye to the blue breaks in the Atlantic high-fliers, I concluded Mahoney had reason for waxing so wrath. And I conceded through his smouldering eyes the deliberate care with which someone had left—a message.

Leaving aside the farce of it, an object is just that: someone is trying to say something, unless it be a trifle dropped from carelessness, thoughtlessness or plain stupidity. Remembering Felocity's fussing over an ostensible nothing and the depths of Brannigan's upbraidings, I felt it was none of these and concluded Aunt Sophie hadn't strayed far with her tincture of misgivings.

I hadn't strayed far myself from my purpose since a sight of the old gilt pestle and mortar above his premises told of Brannigan's near presence and my best recourse. Throwing a glance over my shoulder as I turned into the recessed doorway, I noticed there were more little huddles of the other sex than usual, twos and threes of shawlies and the rest all along the straggling hill and I'll swear 'ballewns' were floating in the air above from out the holes in their heads. Ah well! it must make a change to the loaves and fishes of the daily errands, so why begrudge them their tongues when novelty strikes?

Brannigan's pharmacy is a broth of a Boots. For nostalgia he leaves his competitors at the post. Not stuffed alligators and oil of mandrake exactly but all else is there, from the great globosities of jewel-hued liquids to the brass scales and mahogany drawers filled with wicked-sounding ammunition for the everlasting chemical warfare against man's eternal aches and pains.

Such a surround of officials made a cavern of treasures enough to put God's fear into an hypochondriac that He might be afflicted too soon with perfect health.

At the bell's jangle Brannigan appeared from the rear quarter where he ground and rolled and scrupled and sugared and boxed and bottled his pills and his potions.

The fine face of a fine man never to be discounted in any society, Brannigan preached in life the practice of his craft. As he distilled ingredients to the perfection of elixir, so he pounded the coarse materials of the town's opinions, prejudices, foibles and conceits and brought all to a quintessential wisdom against which even a Mahoney was sore put to argue.

Reason enough and because I loved the man, to be at the counter, invited to take the old bentwood chair we call 'the rickets' and a pinch of the violet cachous he kept on a plate for the public refreshment.

'A week you're home, Patrick, and I've seen five minutes of you. Young solicitor at the counter, how say you—?'

'Guilty all the way up and down, your honour, but I've three weeks to while away yet—'

'So you drop in on Brannigan this day of all.'

He sat at his own chair behind the mahogany and smiled knowingly, knowing I knew he knew why I'd come.

Too old to blush, too young to care, I smiled 'guilty' again, with the ease of complacency.

'Is it Mahoney you've come about?'

'It is.'

'And you're wondering in the mind's eye how much I've to do with it?'

I deprecated with a cough and he nodded as if I'd replied in plain words.

'Believe me, it's none of my wanting.' He paused to find the right beginning. 'You heard our clash just now?'

'I did.'

'Aye, it's buried in that somehow. That, and what he couldn't stomach the sight of.'

'I can't altogether blame him.'

'No more can I. There's nothing pleasant about the calculated insult . . . if I seem to be feeling my way forward, you'll understand it's because there's no naming of names for the sake of ethics.'

I nodded amen to that.

'Now the Church,' he continued, 'is worldly-wise enough to know when it's beaten on a fundamental such as birth control. You know the twists and turns as well as I, and how eventually it makes the qualified concession. The trouble comes from the faithful who don't know or won't accept they're beaten.'

'And Father Mahoney is one of them.'

'The more I reverence him for it—let there be no mistake in that quarter . . . I'd rather ten of his ilk than a sneering liberal like Brady or Felocity.'

'Though they hold your views?'

'Wrong, Patrick. None but their own. You saw the lengths they went to; not drawing attention to the situation, but to the part they'd elected to play in it. They're like non-smokers persecuting the smokers for *their* righteousness' sake. A new generation of hypocrites who look for a Puritan pretext first and the agnostic argument second.'

'Concern for other people's health?' I demurred.

'Camouflage for a deep sense of guilt. Over the water they wrinkle their noses at the filter tip and despise those who think nuclear missiles are a danger to health. But that's their business. My point is, Mahoney's in trouble. Now why is that? Because someone flings down a challenge, a gauntlet—a "ballewn"? Or an accusation?'

I looked blankly at this renewed threat of more than could meet the eye. . .

'What should anyone accuse Mahoney of?'

He took time to reply and, even then, it came reluctantly.

'Murder.'

More indeed than I'd bargained for; more than would get my tongue into first gear.

'It was well said: there are crimes and tendencies—depending on your point of view . . . take this for a supposition, Patrick. A young fellow goes overboard for a lassie in the next town. They can't marry but they can't wait. Youth doesn't last as long as it did before the means to everlasting perdition became "fully operational". O'Dwyer can't help him—and I dare not. So the inevitable happens and they too tostified to do anything about it till the evidence shows. There isn't time or know-how to get to England, but there's the Dublin backstreet she hears about in the food-processing plant where she works.

'Two hopeful, guilty innocents ... he takes out his savings and they go off to Dublin. He waits outside till she comes away, pale and slim-seeming and they smile ruefully at thought of narrow squeaks instead of lusty cries for the milk of human kindness ground to powder. Before they reach the train for home she collapses in Capel Street and he's with her in the ambulance to St Bricin's and, after a little fight with septicaemia, she dies ... and he comes back to Knockmealldown as silent as the one that goes home in a coffin.'

One doesn't dash into speech after revelations; there's much to digest, more to regret.

'"A judgment on you" isn't that what you said?'

He nodded. 'The young man went to confession—for advice as much as anything. Mahoney said "come back when you're married and we'll talk about it". He left, feeling lost, bewildered.'

'It wasn't bad advice.'

'It was good advice if the parents would have it so, and if the couple had been sure themselves. They were honest enough to know a strong physical passion may be no more than that.'

'How did you hear of it?'

'He came here one day—afterwards. Suffering tells. I hardly recognised the boy dressed in the face of a man. Bitterness. I listened, and felt unclean. Worse than it felt to be branded a purveyor of murderous weapons.'

'Why!'

'Sure if I'd done a bit of gun-running the girl might be living now.'

Which raised a point of law. 'Then who—?' I broke off, not a little confused. 'Somebody must have done a little "gun-running".'

Brannigan looked into a distance filled, it seemed, with perpetrations: a landscape of sordid hills, rent with defiles and passions that came down to the valley of the shadows and a river polluted with nothing but life everlasting.

'Not to be caught out again, he went shopping before the girl began to bleed in that back-street, went to a merchant devoid of qualms ... bitterness. To come home with the dead, the parents, and Durex forgotten in his pocket. All this he told me.'

'So it's an act of revenge?'

Again he nodded. 'You could say so.'

'I still don't see why Mahoney should blame you.'

Brannigan heaved a sigh and tried to explain, how he was part and parcel of a system loathed and execrated by the good Father.

'What he found on his steps was a symbol—lust, promiscuity, loose-living—a permit for those things.'

'Points of view,' I murmured.

'Was there ever a thing in the world that didn't cut both ways?'

Another thought occurred. 'He must know who's responsible?'

'Why? I told you, Patrick. Mahoney is a good man. Too honest to suspect people. Too straight to accept the validity of moral transgression . . . there's little room for such in a half-and-half world.'

We talked a bit of other things, but it didn't last long. I left feeling a degree less enamoured of life than heretofore and took a thoughtful way home.

Aunt Sophie listened to my recital as she peeled the potatoes for the evening meal. I omitted no warts in the telling. There was no way I could, in the nature of things; but age can face much without flinching.

'So that's the whole of it,' I concluded.

'"Little room for such".' She quoted reflectively. 'I wish it were, Patrick. But there's Felocity to begin with.'

Which reminded me. 'Wouldn't everybody know the boy at least? It must've been reported.'

'Why? D'you think the parents would advertise their shame?'

'Not if they'd no social conscience at all!'

She regarded her nephew as he remembered from his later schooldays, and him using fine, big words fresh-culled from the dictionary.


She was right about Felocity.

The following morning everybody was reading the local rag-bag for the one item that figured. Felocity had made more than the most of it.

'Mystery Balloon in Knockmealldown.

'Yesterday morning exhibited the biggest mystery seen in our town for many a year. An unidentified lying object was found on St Thomas's steps by a church official and was instantly blacked out with his bowler in the interests of national security.

'Further investigations revealed a deflated inflatable of a kind not normally associated with juvenile jollity, and we understand the Reverend Mahoney, on whose territory this object materialised, is forwarding it by today's post to the Defence Ministry for ballistic tests.'

Heavy-handed humour; not to my liking, and probably not to yours. But the sensation came at the end of more of the same.

'The mystery took a new turn only hours before we went to press, when we were advised that yet another of these abominables had been identified on the plinth of Councillor Sweeney's statue in Mostyn Square. The defunct dignitary appeared to be bending forward examining the thing with great and nostalgic interest. Indeed, when I went to confirm the intelligence I was struck by the similarity of his pose to that of Father Mahoney at the time of *his* discovery.

'The garda say there is no way of knowing who or what is responsible for this phenomenal irruption of latex but the editor of your local organ has, with an eye to the well-being of all, furnished the press agencies with the salient facts which, hopefully, may provide an elucidation of the conundrum. It may be that this sort of thing is going on in other parts of the world.'

I groaned inwardly and, if I remember aright, outwardly as well. Aunt Sophie reacted with more than usual vigour.

'The man's a bloody fool!' tossing the paper on the table with force enough to knock over the milk jug. Spilt milk seemed about right in the circumstances. If Felocity had planned to make Mahoney and the town a laughing-stock in Ireland's Eye or anywhere else, he was on the way to succeeding.

I thought about it as she mopped up the milk with grim purpose, then made some sort of decision. 'I've a mind to go over to Mostyn Square.'

'To join the rubbernecks! Haven't you seen enough of the things?'

'That's not my purpose. I'll tell you later.'

Nor was it.

I took a short cut through Back Street and Liam's Lane with a detective's intent and, as you might expect, came out on a square already full enough of ones and twos 'just passing through' to see if the *Occasional* spoke true.

Sad to say, it had; and nothing done about it. There was the bronze moron, bent as a banana, examining the evidence of his eyes. Everywhere about me was the sound of giggles, from grown men, shawlies and ancients no less than the colleens and gossoons hurrying by or lounging mesmerised.

As I walked slowly round the square with senses alert for I knew not what, I heard someone demanding where would the mad balloonist strike next? I was looking for someone, I kept reminding myself, and I had no idea whom.

There's a happy factor about comedy in the theatre. It never changes character in mid-stream. Life alas, sticks to no rules. In real life, comedy is the ill-fitting mask that slips to reveal that tragedy is, after all, the ugly, unacceptable face of existentialism.

What role I'd cast for myself in this souring farce I'm uncertain to this day. I think I was eye-bright and fool enough to believe I could avert—single-handed—the consequences of everybody else's folly threatening to get out of hand.

But, for the moment, as I say, I could do no better than play the Sherlock and discover, if I could, the man who had to be responsible for this unnatural—mementum.

I shouldn't have been too surprised that, five minutes after leaving the house, my Aunt Sophie put on her best hat and Ulster and toddled off to the presbytery with the *Occasional* in her hand and a purpose running through her head.

Mahoney opened the door himself and her quick eye caught at the small signs of neglect in him, unshaven as he was.

'You!' he greeted her effusively with a scowl.

'Yes me, Mahoney,' and without by-your-leave she brushed past him to make her way straight to the parlour.

'I won't ask you to sit down,' he said to her back. 'I've a funeral today.'

She sat down and eyed him sourly. 'Your own, by the reports I'm getting. Read this.' Meaning the paper she'd slapped down on the table.

'I never touch it and well you know.'

'You don't have to. I hear you play the tongs like a professional. Not another word from me till you've conned it.'

'It's soakin' wet!'

'A slight difference of opinion with the milk jug.'

Half rebelling he hesitated, then read it, and didn't look up till he could have read it two or three times more.

'What's it to do wid me—or you—what are you here for with your plaguing!'

'I'll tell you what I'm here for, Mahoney. I'm here because it has to do, not with you, or me, but us.'

'You'll know what you're talkin' about, for it's God's truth I don't.'

'Us, Mahoney. Not priest and spinster of this parish but us—the oldest generation in the town, very nearly in the world.'

He looked at her oddly but held his peace.

'Was there ever a time when the oldsters haven't made a mess of things, then blamed the young for making it worse, for not clearing it up?'

'I tried!' he snapped.

'With the tongs?' she wondered. 'What's a pathetic gesture to do with solving problems?'

'All right! I lost my head. If that's what you're after I'll admit it. Then what?'

'Do you know who's behind all this?'

'Brannigan for sure. Him and his creature Felocity.'

She shook her head. 'You're wrong, Mahoney, and you know it.'

'I know you're meddlin' in what's none of your concern.'

'I stayed away from your church for ten years because you told me family planning was a sin, was none of my concern.'

'My right as a priest caring in the pulpit for his congregation, *Miss* O'Neill!'

'Against my right, married or no, as a woman. No, Mahoney, it won't wash, any more than it'll bring back that girl from the grave.'

And there was half the fight leaving him—visibly. 'I'll not ask how you heard.'

'I wouldn't tell you if you did.'

He glanced sharply at her, ready with a retort, then something happened inside the man, dulling his eye, draining the redness of his choler to leave the hue of fuller's powder, blunting, visibily, the keen edge of his love for life. He turned away and lowered into a chair, old and defeated, with an eye to the cold fan of paper set in the grate.

'What am I to do, Sophie?'

'Retire, before it's too late. Let others do the fighting, if there's fighting to be done.'

'Retire . . . like a coward . . . that's as good as saying I killed her.'

'Could you face another coming to you with the same story?'

He stood, not renewed, but with an awesome blaze of energy.

'D'ye think I've never faced it before—and won! It's unfair! What do they want of me! They said . . . go forth and preach the sanctity of love in God's eyes, nothing about the availability of a cheap thrill in Brannigan's sight; from the top of a ladder, tell of the perfectibility of two souls through the divine ordinance of marriage vows. They never told how to reconcile the take of sex with the give of love!

'Doctrine I know about, scandals I know about, but a girl with child almost five months—what was I to advise him? Have done with it! 'Tis only a life! Oh God . . . there's no mother of animals in the world would rip an unborn from its belly with the ravening fangs! And am I to say go, and sin once more . . . our mother died with the bearing of Molly, gave me the best and only remembrance of childhood a man could . . . go off with you, Sophie O'Neill . . . go back to your progressives who long to cut down the human race to their size and image . . .'

Large and beautiful are the eyes of my auntie, brown as youth, and all the more radiant from filling with tears. She paused a moment, long enough to see clearly when a man is best left to bear his anguish, and she went, letting herself quietly out of the door.

A long time he stared at nothing much, head askew as if listening for the word, hoping it would come at last, willing it into existence, till come it did, and him breathing it aloud.

'Tenesmus.'

Hurriedly he sought and found an old, worn dictionary, feverishly burrowed in the book of words for understanding—and there, above a tremulous forefinger, was his very own diagnosis.

'—a painful and ineffectual straining to relieve the bowels, an equivalent condition of the mind (fig.)'

He closed the book and his eyes for the comfort of darkness.

There isn't a deal more to tell.

While Aunt Sophie was wrestling with her brand of futility, I followed my own useless intention of playing the sleuth. I'd not been in the square more than two minutes before I marked him; a young man in blue denims and an old windcheater standing at the window of Moore's haberdashers, staring with the idle pose of one choosing a pair of socks, but every so often casting a quick glance at the larger scene at his back.

There's nothing so obvious as the man who pretends he's elsewhere or perfectly unnoticed and I knew to a certainty that the features etched in acid, the eyes dark-rimmed with the shades of hindsight, were those of one bowed under the weight of a grudge.

I'll never know with clearness why I stepped up to him, for I'd little in my repertoire to fit the case. He turned and frowned as I approached, much as if he expected what he couldn't welcome, and for a few seconds we simply regarded each other.

'Are you the man?' was all I could ask.

'I'm the man,' he replied after a pause. Then he spat to one side and, as if satisfied by a single act of recognition, he stepped away and went out of my sight, leaving me with no other purpose but to take a walk down and along the deserted strand to digest my inadequacy.

That same day I heard the bishop of the diocese had called incognito on Father Mahoney. I've no way of knowing what passed between them, but I took out pencil and paper that evening and essayed how I thought the duologue might have ensued.

'Father, I hear you do be making a fool of yourself.'

'And why not? Since when was it the prerogative of me superiors!'

'I'll buy ye a bell, a book and a candle if you'll promise to give up the tongs.'

'An aberration! Sure I'm entitled to an aberration once in my days!'

'I feel for you, Michael. I understand you and I share your convictions as we shared the tea chest they called a room at Maynooth years since, but *suaviter modo* now. There's more to winning the war than losing a battle.'

'*Fortiter in re!*'

'Certainly *fortiter in re*, but *suaviter in modo* first.'

'Losing a battle . . . but on the steps of the church!'

'In the church itself. If, to vandalise a divine ordinance, if what thine eye seest offends thee, pluck up and cast it away. For there's no offence in the eye, Michael.'

'So much for the divine ordinance.'

'Ah! I said nothing about what lies behind the eye, interpreting and magnifying all it looks upon. You flourished a shadow in the eyes of the world instead of throwing away the substance. Now, I'll tell you how it is. I hear from Dublin you can expect a television team tomorrow. After the six o'clock angelus there'll be a news in which Knockmealldown will receive the imprimatur of national renown. London is on to it, and there'll be others, ready to profit from a nine days' wonder. And all because you rang a bell and turned wine into water for a miracle that's cheaper by the dozen. Ah, Michael, there's nothing so definite as the indefinite article.'

'I'll fight them as I ever did!'

'Who? With what? The world's turning to water. Fight it and you'll drown, go with the current and you'll last.'

'You mean I should've left the tongs at home and gone out there in me bathing costume?'

'God, how you take the pomposity out of a man's words with y'bit of ridicule! I mean, it's an indefinite world, filling with desires, the cupidity and the wants, the must-have-at-all-costs . . . sometimes I think our world is over unless—'

'Unless?'

'Unless we scour abroad enough to find examples, no, that's not what I mean . . . I suppose I wish Christ would come again to clear up a few points.'

All that his Lordship promised came to pass, and more than he or anyone in Knockmealldown could have wished or bargained for.

There's quiet in the town these days; Felocity is silent for many a day, Brannigan grieves as he grinds, and even ubiquitous Duffy's jaws do no more than keep his teeth in place.

Heart-harrowing, to see Dimmy meander like a sudden orphan, too miserable to take folks' pennies for the coke.

Quiet it is, and only half alive since . . .

She came home at six, the cafe closed and the till locked for the day. And sick she looked in his searching eyes, though she smiled as always, glad to see the brother of her life once more.

'How—was the funeral?'

'Molly . . . what's wrong now?'

She took off her coat and hat, laid them carefully on a chair by the door.

'Tell me, Molly.'

A hand through her hair as he'd never seen before, and she

wan-faced and trouble-eyed. 'Michael,' quietly, and a flow of tears
between close-packed fingers as she spoke, standing like a penitent
in need of a stool.

'Those people—in the teashop . . . all day . . . laughing at you,
and saying such things—women too . . . I didn't rightly understand
and yet I could tell somehow, it had to do with—'

She looked up suddenly. 'Michael, what did they mean with all
the laughing . . . what *is* a French letter?'

Will you find your own words to depict the look of a man who
fights the years, the mob, the times brought low, to protect the
great and only love of his life, and sees all collapse in a brace of
words, each as innocent apart as both are guilty together?

Or can you swear without a snigger, there *cannot* be people on
our Olympian mudball who've never heard of the one piece, see-
through, extra smooth raiment of the great god Priapus?

Well, here was one who hadn't.

Being comforted by a terrible emptiness who listened acutely to
his world, their world, fragmenting like a distant battle of wind-
bells, as surely as impotent birds listen to protecting glass shiver
under the casual blow from—for example—the fire tongs.

'Come, Molly, let's take a walk and see a bit of the world they're
always on about.'

As they often did, when the day was done, fine or fair, walking
hand in hand always, to the same end, down the back of the hill,
past the railway station, across the estuary bridge and almost to the
foothills of the Clonach barrier, then left to the sudden upturn of
Columb's cliffs where they thrust out to give a peep of the town not
a mile distant as the gull goes.

And he most like singing to her their favourite ditty, though
Yeats forgive me for calling it so.

> When I play on me fiddle in Dooney
> Folk dance like a wave of the sea.

For sure, he sang it that night, since the station-master swears he
heard and, for sure, he talked long of the auld days, and of nothing
but humour and happiness till he had her eyes shining once more
and she full of a sister's love for the brother who'd cared for her
since she couldn't remember when.

They're buried in holy ground, so it was never suicide . . . the

Columb cliffs are almost four hundred feet above a rocky fore-shore, and the false step is as good as a flying leap.

But this I know: when search was made in time, they were found with hands still clasped as by a miracle; and there's not a soul, easy or uneasy, in Knockmealldown, who doesn't 'know', and not one would tell tho' they were threatened with those tiresome inconveniences sometimes referred to as the torments of the damned.

# JANUS

I'M PENCILLING THIS by the light of an ounce of wax melted in a foil cup—a feeble glimmer floats off the wick and I gaze on it with that especial affection we reserve for dependence.

They're called 'nite-lites' these things. Very useful, very cheap.

So, it has come to pass. I'm here, which is nowhere, nowhere known to me, and I feel safe till daylight comes, and then, the proximity of my species will force me into—awareness.

My possessions surround me, more perhaps than I can comfortably carry; but it suits me well and draws from my very depths a breath of satisfaction. Frequently, I gaze round on my little home and experience the content of one who hasn't much at last, but has enough at least.

Hard to know how or where to begin though I feel, truly, this is my beginning. More than half a lifetime spent on pleasing others, now I have no one to please—not even myself. Laid to rest, the pleasure principle! And I certainly don't write for posterity.

These words will be my reminder, a prayer posted in an unaddressed envelope, advantageous to none.

There's plenty of time to live in the moment. Opportunity too. Of course, I'm too new to the game not to experience the pull of material possessions; but even now I can lie for hours and select of all I had, the objects I'd once handled with so much pleasure, feel them still, in imagination, under my touch.

The list grows shorter until, this moment, I can name each item on the fingers of a hand. Was it Horace who said the years as they pass take from us one damned thing after another? It doesn't take that long . . .

A favourite pipe, a niblick, Montaigne, a ragged cat that went with the chair I no longer miss, a tree in the garden.

Seven days or more to cast the shell I've dragged about on my back for too many times that number of years.

Not bad! No complaints. Well done and little else to do.

Not know where to begin! How wedded one becomes to the

concept of time . . . each moment is a beginning, each stroke of the
pen, the upward glance, each pause for thought. To live for the
moment, not *a* moment, is *summum bonum* as long as one is
unencumbered. Possessions do one's living for one—there now!
None to tell me I have written 'one' too many.

It's worth a chuckle, this having no one to please but my
indifferent self.

The first thing I jettisoned was a superb digital watch. It told me
everything I needed to know about the cancer of chronos, from the
second to the month. How I used to sit, trance-like, reading the
blow-by-blow print-out, marking the dead-lines . . . count-down
. . . mine . . .

Now, the sun, the moon, the stars. Daylight is the end of night
and the stubble on my chin makes calendar enough.

No man an island! What nonsense!

We are all islands, most of us connected by more or less
negotiable shallows but, if the waters are too deep, non-swimmers
stay home, the rest wave, invade or shout insults to the distant ones
. . . oh yes, we're islands all right. An accident of birth merely
dumps us on one archipelago or another.

But why did I feel the need to scribble the insular bit? Defending
my position already? Justifying myself to myself?

I think it goes back to the shedding of encumbrances—and the
greatest of these is loyalties. Allegiances, if that's preferable.

Yes. I've jettisoned everything. From then till now is the
inescapable undercurrent—I've eschewed loyalties.

Many and varied from 'loved ones' to one's building society; but
is that to confuse allegiance with vassalage?

To care for nobody like the miller, a supreme happiness?
Perhaps . . . if it's a positive doctrine and not a wasting of the will to
care, the will to fight for survival in a wall-to-wall context.

Robinson Crusoe. Poor Robinson Crusoe. How valiantly he
fought to recreate his former ambience. Without his guns, nails,
implements and utensils he'd have degenerated, become blood
brother to Caliban. But after all, it's comfortable to make all ship-
shape for one's self alone. And how could he cry out to God in
company? For that, Christ or Crusoe, there must be perfect
solitude or there's no hearing the reply . . . civilisation begins with
the footprint in the sand . . . I'll not look for one.

Ahead of me is a triangle of dusk. There's a star or two to the north-east and few clouds. They warn me it can be cold on the fells, even in late September. No matter.

The wind's rising and ploughing animate furrows across my roof. One can be entranced by the merest trifle . . . I broke off this rambling account to watch and wonder at so much happening. The rustling of insects under my floor, the chance creature scurrying over my pack by the entrance, a moth that visits each night—this is my third day here—the skivie flame of my candle, leaping and gyrating to the music of the wind.

My third. Fatigue, yes, but it's so easy to stay and appreciate the novel, desolate aspect of my surroundings. When I stand up at last in the morning, there's no life, no dwelling, no traffic, no traffic wardens, only the dip of my hollow, the rise of a hill, gorsed and hare-belled; the sheets and pillows and bolsters, a tumble of used linen: clouds.

Tomorrow I shall move on. Earlier I'd called at a farmstead not far back, begged some milk and satisfied their curiosity and maybe, a little apprehension. A camping holiday. They'd nodded, seemingly reassured. After all, I'm weighed down with a backpack, the tent and sleeping-bag, plus a haversack slung like a bandolier across my chest. To the most jaundiced idea I couldn't be other than an amateur in clumsy pursuit of a very temporary outdoor life.

'Yes, for sure. Everybody needs get away from it all,' the blue-eyed giant of a farmer agreed. He'd come to the door to support his wife, advertising his presence to an out-of-the-blue stranger.

'You'll find a bit of stream along the road, but call in and take what you want—there's a tap back of the house.'

I thanked him and felt I could stay awhile without fear of suspicion. That was important or there'd be no peace of mind in tainted solitude.

'Where d'you mean to go from here?'

'North,' I'd replied waving a hand vaguely, probably to the south. He'd laughed at my obvious lack of—preparedness?

I'll admit to cutting a strange figure. White shirt—tie, a short, fuscous-coloured raincoat—hardly the uniform of an outdoor type. No matter. After today I don't need, for example, to shave and retain a semblance of propriety. No wasting time on an empty ritual. Overboard with soap and razor . . .

I broke off once more to examine my store. Four pounds of cheese, four half-pound bars of chocolate, a left-over apple, which

I ate, and a small loaf of bread. A pound of instant coffee; as much sugar. Milk I shall miss once I move on. A pound of glucose sweets. Four canisters of gas. I'll go far on those—but no further. I have a map of the area, good enough for my purpose. I shall follow the stream, just the other side of a nearby road, then strike north. The map too will be a redundancy.

I have a book of crosswords. Each night I make coffee and complete a puzzle as I drink. That's the treat of the day, tho' there's so much to look forward to, to be thankful for.

And at the end, what's to be done when all runs out, coffee, cheese, gas, crossword puzzles . . .

The answer is: I don't know . . . that's the debatable point. The sudden bliss of ignorance, not to know where the next crust comes from, or even if there is one. To wear the mantle of Elijah and know that either a miracle will supply—or deliver me.

I believe in miracles: not the thimble-rigging tricks of the trade but something better. My miracle, the marvel that is, essentially, me—the one that almost died in my hands through neglect.

To rediscover some of one's original self. Won't that do for a marvel?

The cold begins to seep through. I'm wearing a thick sweater which I strike now and again, encouraging it to do better—and I swear it responds.

We, the animate, have lost the art and inclination to co-operate with the inanimate. Long ago the man who sat before a mass of metal would pray to it, to the forces within, coaxing aid in the great work of transformation. Now, we fight to overcome Nature, not because *she's* belligerent, but because *we* are grown aggressive, callously, mistakenly conscious of our superiority: phraseology for arrogance.

Yesterday, no, three days ago I suppose, I came by train to H——. I passed quickly through the town, stopping long enough to buy last provisions, but anxious to get away from the profusion of civilised merchandise clogging the windows of even the smallest towns. To stand for the last time ever at a checkout in a tiny supermarket; that comforted.

A minor, incidental ambition, to follow part of the Roman wall, had brought me this far. I found the small tourist office and learned I would have to take a lane leading out of the town and pass through a 'beauty spot' to reach the road running parallel with the Wall.

That was plain enough and I moved off at a good pace, anxious to gain solitude and avoid the curious stares of the local townsfolk. I seemed forever to be stopping, adjusting, picking up things fallen from my overfull baggage, presented a picture of total disarray, as indeed I suspect I have since I set out.

A good, thick pair of corduroys and the walking shoes I imagined to be enough to proclaim intentions. But the rest? More suitable for office wear! I should have thought of that perhaps—the total image. As an entity I don't, to the outward eye, hang together. Well, it's too late for redress!

I soon reached the 'beauty spot'; had no difficulty pausing to rest every hundred yards of a long sylvan glen, the perfect remnant of a vanishing English countryside.

At the last stretch I left the public footpath—obviously frequented by dog-owners—crossing a small bridge over a picture-book river, to examine a ruined tower-like structure. Less romantically it turned out to be a tumbledown chimney, probably for an engine-house nearby.

Within this stack was a sort of cavern that had once been the 'stokehole', large enough to crawl into and rest among the granite shards. Burnt twigs and a tin or two were sure signs of an earlier occupation by Man.

The sky had grown overcast and rain was falling, not hard, but soakingly persistent. I had time to rest for an hour and nothing lost if I stayed all night or forever. I was out of sight of the path at least, so I disburdened myself and dined off a glucose sweet, watching the rain with bovine equanimity.

More fatigued than I'd cared to admit I slept, woke with a start to absolute darkness. The scamperings and rustlings of creatures keeping a low profile melted into silence. Cramp and the ache of weariness had invaded by stealth as I slept and the chill night air mocked my carelessness. There was no going on till daylight came. I drank from my water bottle and fumbled in the haversack to find a match for the night light.

The smallest illumination defines home. In a trice the temporary shelter became just that, a cavern with walls, a floor, an indeterminate ceiling roofed with generations of nests.

I begrudged the necessity of venturing out to relieve myself before stumbling about long enough to ease my cramp. Safely home again I unrolled the sleeping-bag and crawled in, zipping it carefully as far as my chin, then curled, foetus fashion, close to the light, contentedly watching as it danced to the draught from my breath and the gentle currents of night air. I listened to the rain pattering and dripping beyond the golden circle and revelled in feeling warm and safe and everlasting.

With drowsiness my instinct for economy asserted itself and I blew out the light before drifting into a sound and dreamless slumber.

Time is become a question of adjectives, not numbers. I awoke early according to the greyness above and the monochromed trees; delayed to watch the day slowly gathering pace, revealing the true colours of all, then unrolled myself reluctantly from the haven of warmth. In five minutes my tiny stove had heated the coffee and I was breakfasting on a broken bit of bread and a square or two of chocolate.

I debated once again whether to stay a few days or forever in this delectable spot and then, firmly, I put the thought behind me. If I stayed too near civilisation I might well be tempted to go in search of a loaf of bread! Better to stick to my original intention . . .

Twenty minutes of strapping, tying and adjusting my paraphernalia and I set off, reasonably confident that I had, at last, mastered the art of marching in full kit.

Out of the glen and into a huge roadside field from which one toiled upwards, interminably, along a well-defined track, past a watchful herd of cows, and so to an iron gate in the hedge through which I had much ado to squeeze with all my goods. Breathless already! but out on the A69 road that went my way to W——.

I had it to myself until the turn-off leading to the Wall and I very nearly strode in a happy frame of mind, savouring my solitude and the crisp, morning air, watching the clouds bearing away to the east, colliding with the sun still somewhere over the horizon ahead of me.

Very soon I came to a little bridge. From there it was no distance to where the great petrifaction resumed its interrupted progress.

The map was right about an amenities area, and I couldn't resist a last opportunity to comb my hair and wash in the 'toilet facility'. I smile to think how I paid a little lip service to old habits. To wash in a stream, yes, but to give the Lord thanks for a wash-basin, taps, paper towels and a smitch of soap!

Refreshed, I sat at a rough wooden table in the picnic area thinking how it must be the last time I would do anything of the kind; but I rested there more from novelty than from lingering nostalgia.

Silence, better than soap and water, washes a man clean, so I bathed again and listened to the paradox of a single birdsong until the urge to push on spoiled the moment. Perhaps, imperceptibly, I was beginning to identify with animals, restless, snuffling, bristling as tho' to say, 'here be humans, let's off!'

Besides, I wanted the Wall to myself, simply to pace some of its length till I turned north toward Wark Forest skirting Simonburn and Wark itself, the long-ago capital of Tynedale when that area was part of Scotland.

Passing the sinister-seeming quarry lake on my right I climbed the slope for my first view of that magnificent stone outcrop pouring into the distance. All along, the eye constantly seeks out the far hills, the changing hues of fields and moorland as the light dims or dazzles. An ever moving picture without pall, as one dips down or climbs upward to new heights, and surveys ... the Wall itself is soon forgotten, taken for granted, as might be supposed. When all's said, and with a few reservations, a wall is merely a wall.

The sun was well up by the time I reached the end of that section where a road cuts across to the north. Tired as I felt I covered some of that too before I came to a junction and decided to 'rest my boots' as the vagrants say. I had one more village to pass through before the long trek to the great forests of Wark, Spadeadam and the rest.

Not entirely free of self-consciousness I sat at the roadside and watched the meagre traffic; a tractor, two private cars and a school bus. That told me I was in the vicinity of nine o'clock. The farmer scarcely glanced at me, but I never doubted he marked my presence. Nothing is taken for granted or for natural these days.

I'd wondered too about the car arriving in the picnic area when I'd turned back, as one does, to view my point of departure. Two men climbed out and began to stroll in my direction, but after an hour I saw no more of them. What were they doing so early out on the tourist trail? Then again, what was I myself doing?

Eventually, I passed through the village the name of which escapes me. I remember a garden filled with bushes cut and fashioned by a half-hearted topiarist, a public phone box and a country school converted to private use. The place was dead, meaningless, a mere collection of dwellings huddled under a name easily forgotten.

Beyond the village I saw not a soul but one shepherd on a motor cycle rounding up sheep.

Two or three miles brought me to an isolated farm, which I passed, following the road for another half mile, and I knew I could go no further . . .

And there I broke off, last night or early this morning for all I know or care.

To tell more: I spent an hour assembling my tent securely in a small hollow well clear of the road . . . I crawled in and slept as I was, for the effort of lumping so much doesn't come easily to a man of forty-five years and largely sedentary habits. When I awoke I judged by the sun it must be well after mid-day.

For the moment I had nothing to do but bestow my kit comfortably. Coffee and a bite of cheese satisfied thirst and appetite and I could laze as long as I chose contemplating nothing but the present.

Now, three days later is it? I'm ready to move on.

Have not been idle, have wandered to the top of the long sloping hill and down the other side toward my final destination, that forest fringe north-westward, so distant and so slightly menacing.

Also, I found what I was looking for among the strewn boulders. I selected one within my strength to move and rolled it with some effort to one side. I made a tight bundle of my raincoat, white shirt and tie and that I pushed into a scraped-out hollow, carefully rolling the stone back to its original position.

In their place an extra sweater and an old greyish topcoat for warmth. Thus, I've lightened my burden a little and buried the last of Joseph Winter. All that I possess, new and old, belongs to his successor. If I could rid myself of the shadow that belongs to us both I would do so.

I want nothing of any of it! Nothing!

And so, the time has passed in utmost tranquillity. Seldom that I can recall, have my thoughts ventured beyond the events of the last week.

I lived those days with an intensity of purpose such as I'd never experienced in my whole life. By training as well as temperament I'd mastered the art of observing in detail, but a fresh view of life, of everything about me, had grown microscopic. For example, I easily recall the colours, the very pattern of a sweater worn by the woman who sold me my camping equipment. I certainly remember her sceptical eye when I confessed it was my first venture. Obviously I didn't look the type to be trusted with outdoor matters for she kindly explained twice how to assemble the tent.

She'd asked where I was heading for? I told her the Northumbrian fells.

'That's a tall order,' she frowned. 'Getting late in the year for those parts.'

Apparently she knew the area well and mentioned the need for thermal underwear, even in the summer months! I was too amused to be annoyed at her insistence that I should purchase a more substantial sleeping-bag.

Her impression as far as I could gather was of bleak and scarcely inhabited country—'there's no kindness in the landscape.'

I thought those strange words to use at the time, but now I understand her meaning, I think. The land *is* indifferent. The velvety turf grudgingly conceals a Limestone substructure. It *is* hard country and a man must be in prime condition, without years of easy living behind him, to think of tackling it.

Well, I can reach my goal by easy stages. Once there, *j'y suis, j'y reste*, I don't have to return, have no intention of doing so. Mission completed with my last encampment. One more day, and I can rest forever.

Another crossword completed. These are pitifully simple. One piece of chocolate suffices for supper. I'm slowly waving goodbye to appetite.

I'd sleep now, but for some reason I'd rather not. Have an irrational fear of someone moving stealthily toward my flimsy stronghold.

At night when I step outside and go off to relieve myself, I turn and marvel at that tiny patch of bluish light set in the middle of nowhere.

Hard to visualise how it must have been for early Man. The inevitability of darkness, the creeping blindness; how, without words and unformulated thought, could it have seemed to them that night was blindness, blindness, night? Cured by the miracle of dawn.

And fire. When some shaggy Prometheus or proto-Priestley

snatched a brand from the burning tree, how they must have hoarded this great new supercure.

Mythologising in search of personal fear! What happens when my stock of matches and the candle cups run out? Well, I'll be in no worse straits than my desperately early ancestors, and I have the gift of hindsight. One who waits patiently—or fearfully—for darkness to pass. And anyway, by then, I constantly need to remind myself, it won't matter.

Nothing matters. Therefore, let those stealthy footsteps approach. Conscience, they say, makes cowards of us all. Quiescence, I declare, makes heroes of some . . . may I be of their number.

The new day brought a surprise. Stealthy footsteps there must have been at some time, for I found a bottle of milk at my doorway! From the blue-eyed farmer no doubt. Now that is an act of kindness.

I've managed not to bother them since I've been here, but there it is. Perhaps he left it on the way to his cows in the pasture across the road. In any one day I hear no more than three or four cars, one of which stops nearby and I assume he's checking the herd or shepherding them back to the milking parlour.

Or is he checking on me? Keeping an eye on the unknown by a simple expedient? And which is important—the motive or the milk?

Having boiled my mug of coffee with some of it I gladly concede—no matter. Royal repast, bread, a cut of cheese and two squares of chocolate. Who could want more?

Certainly I need the energy, if I lack the will, to break camp and move on. It's a wearisome business. Unless one rolls and folds and ties to pack all with care it's almost back to square one.

So I proceed methodically and by rote until, in less than half an hour, I'm ready to move on, looking considerably more the part than before.

The road, as I faced north, goes to the right, to Wark and Simonburn I suppose. I'd finished with roads. Henceforth my veer was to the northwest, towards the shadowy edge of the forest and distant Kielder.

I set off, skirting the hill to conserve my energy and gave thanks for a cold, crisp but incurably sunny day. Very little music on the air except the crested grebesong and the nearer croak of a raven.

Hours, many hours later, I ensconced myself at last. Have 'thirled' the forest, as they say.

It turned into a battle royal between failing energies, the coming of dusk and common sense which reminded constantly, my need to camp near a source of water.

The stream I mentioned earlier had long gone its own way to the north-east. I'd replenished my bottle, rested awhile under a huge rowan before parting company with the river Wayward as I apostrophised it.

Ever left I'd gone with misgivings. The forest, unlike Birnam, seemed to retreat with my advance and my spirits unaccountably drooped in spite of the buoyant weather and a wheel of kestrels stooping about their business.

The ground became more and more broken as I progressed and I suspected an ancient moraine underfoot. Plainly I was skirting the higher ground on my right in my impatience to reach the forest line. It would make more sense to climb boldly, even if it meant by-passing the point I'd set eyes and heart on.

And from a height I'd have a better sense of how the land lay, perhaps even catch sight of water: rill, rivulet or beck would serve.

Six hundred or more feet in the air I congratulated myself, silently, too breathless for vocal self-approbation. I should mention that I hold audible and reasonably intelligent conversation with *alter ego*—merely the rattle of a lone—not lonely—man. But not just then thanks.

I recall vividly how I flung myself down and lay for some while like any martyr splayed on a gridiron, too done up even to care about a powerful thirst.

Back on my feet I reviewed what Nature had in store for me. A vast plateau at first sight, but full of ups and downs. To the left were huge plantations of pines covering the hills but deeply fringed with a mix of great deciduous trees, beech, elm and even some oak. Spurs and outcrops of limestone made a fine contrast and, about a mile and a few degrees to the left, I fancied I caught a glint of water; a tarn or a large puddle. Either would do very well, and I decided to make that my lodestar.

A mouthful of chocolate helped fuel the last stage, for I was anxious to settle before the sun dropped too far too soon. The splendour of our intentions! I dozed off, defeated by warmth and weariness and came to with loudly expressed annoyance. The sun was well down and I still had a rugged mile to go.

Whether it was further than I supposed, or I'd stopped too often to recover breath, I'd lost most of the daylight's advantage by the time I reached what proved to be no more than a pond at the end of a precarious downward scramble. Scrub, gorse and treacherous roots of ling can make life difficult, but there were ferns enough and king-cup down there to suggest damp if not water, and so it turned out.

Two things rankled about this final stage of odyssey. Once, much earlier, a helicopter appeared to rise from the direction of Spadeadam forest, flying a few hundred feet above and toward me before hovering at a distance like a gigantic bird of prey. I had a distinct and uncomfortable impression of being observed as opposed to being noticed but, of course, that's the function of the beast; easily dismissed if another incident had not disconcerted enough to keep me on the move.

I'd looked back to mark my progress and enjoy the reversed prospect. My sight is not of the best but I could swear to two figures moving crab-wise in my direction. I noticed, by experiment, they'd stop and remain so for as long as I did.

Remembering the men I'd seen from the heights of the Wall I was bound to put two and two together in such a way that, against all the rules, they still made two.

The helicopter had sheered and clattered away after a bit, though surprisingly it made a large circular sweep before returning, as far as I could tell, back to where it had first appeared.

I saw no reason for concern. Down there I would be concealed and hard to find—assuming I was being sought for ... and why should I assume that?

For what it's worth, I remind myself that it happened.

At any rate, I dropped down by degrees toward the water watching for the likeliest spot to pitch my tent. Already I was among trees of considerable age and size; inexplicably, I felt relieved and I account for it now by supposing I'd come some way to perfect concealment. Almost immediately I found, in the fast waning light, a kind of grotto, framed rather than hidden by thicket and the coarser vegetation, knew at once I need search no further. It very nearly formed a cave, dry and room enough to pitch a small tent.

This, I assured myself, would be my home and, if the gods were kind, my eventual grave, or at least, a tented sepulchre!

No evidence of happy campers or itinerants, not a tin can in sight. No time to explore with dusk well on its way, so I set to and cleared the patch of loose rocks and pitched tent with some difficulty, there being little or no earth for the metal pegs. At best I could wedge them into crevices or tie the guy strings to scraps of vegetation thereabouts.

Exhausted, but happy with my situation I settled in for the night, warmed my coffee, ate sparingly and wondered quixotically how the forsaken world was getting on without me. Probably managing very well; better, with a complication the less!

I tried to think what I could be missing, and came to the immensely comforting conclusion that I missed nothing.

Wry, the remembrance how avidly I would read the newspapers. How I would impress on people how *vital* it was to know what's going on. And what a foolish notion.

Didn't my work tell me all I needed to know about the world?

Enough for the day. Writing reports was never so arduous as this profitless task I've set myself but, one must have a point of reference, a futile occupation concentrates the mind wonderfully—and there's no oakum to pick hereabouts. It's a companion of sorts: paper is tolerant, something to talk to without the disadvantage of answering back, arguing and disputing . . .

Today whatever the date, I awoke to the sound of heavy rain and a high wind; a glance was enough. Weather to keep one indoors if there's no necessity to venture out.

My time was my own. I felt warm and snug in my sleeping-bag and I could peer out comfortably at a damp, circumscribed world. The green-grey bole of a venerable beech tree pasted with yellowing leaves, a boulder, vestiges of Millstone grit and some minor vegetation. Plenty to look at, and that happy juxtaposition of tree stems and tangled branches suggesting an infinity of woodland beyond.

And so the day passed: dozing, watching, listening, day-dreaming and, for all I know, thinking; that couldn't have been to much purpose.

A sleepless night. Too much of it yesterday. No complaints, but an influx of premonitions was disturbing. Vague, formless, as I suppose these things always are, but they don't belong in my little scheme. On the other hand, I've chosen a life-style, half-way primeval, in which all is unknown.

The world outside is a frightening place, I know; as long as I remain here, I'm secure and beyond reach, but like any Neanderthal my ignorance knows there are monsters out there against which stones or a box of matches is no defence. The pterodactyl is an air-to-ground missile, the government machine is a brontosaurus, gigantic and all-crushing, and there are others, with or without labels. One is powerless—one is—primitive man . . .

To stay and fight with both hands tied behind one's back, receptive, taking in all they care to fling at one, those who create a weapon fashioned from—democracy . . . or do as I have done: abjure and abdicate—and *still* be vulnerable. That's hardly fair.

Tried a crossword but thoughts wouldn't go down or across. Backward, mostly . . . surely I'm not doubting!

The tiny flame comforts, but the wick will soon drown in its vital element. I make coffee—twice—for summat to do. For all I know the world's wrapped in an eternal slumber while I sip and ponder that little novelty.

Some of my misgivings dissolve in caffeine, and I slowly drift off to sleep with an eye to the greyness of dawn.

The end of a nightmare, or just the beginning? It's farewell to an idyllic dream for sure. And I'm not sure it wasn't already tainted . . .

At least they've left me with my belongings. And why not? I'm not a criminal. They won't say outright that I'm held for further questioning, but I'm here all the same. I was brought here. For what? The tale of abduction was a fiction, a pretext.

Tired. Damned exhausted in fact. But I can't sleep. I dare not sleep . . . of all things, to be sitting at a small, square table, writing God knows what.

I really don't know how to begin, except to say those premonitions were more than justified.

Let's see—I slept well into the morning. Woke with a bad taste in my mind, a sense of my destiny in a balance loaded with deadweights. That's not too strong in view of what happened.

With more than normal tardiness I struggled out of the tent and looked up and about me. A sky blue with contrition after yesterday's fit of the sulks, the earth still damp but drying in the sun's heat. Shrugging off my lethargy, if that's what it was, I began to explore the woodland ahead. I had need to stretch my legs after so much confinement.

I'd gone perhaps a hundred yards and was about to turn back when I saw, ahead of me, a fence. I knew there were such things to keep out marauding deer but, as I came closer, I wondered at this one's obvious strength and height. Nearer still, I found myself staring at the kind of chain-link fencing they'd never use to control animals. Left and right it ran, as far as one could see.

I stood blankly, idiotically absorbing this sudden unequivocal evidence of precisely that world I had no further use for. And I watched, in my mind's eye, a yellow helicopter rising from nowhere—which I now understood was somewhere.

Why should I hide from myself that I was close to tears? To shut my eyes seemed the next best thing, to turn and retreat, even better, straight to my . . . sanctuary!

There is no such redundancy in this world.

Portrait of a whipped dog crawling back into its kennel! I sat with legs drawn up, as if it mattered to make myself as small as possible, while I tried to work out the implications.

That fence had to mean an establishment of some kind, a helicopter suggested a large and highly security conscious complex; its isolation implied the need for maximum secrecy.

And I thought I knew them all . . .

Should I stay and risk discovery and the possibility of requests for an explanation, demands for identity, or better to find seclusion elsewhere to play out my time?

Paralysis of the will must have set in for I can't remember reaching a positive conclusion. My instinctive desire to quit was overpowered by a stronger compulsion to stay and not to make the kind of effort that had brought me, footsore, so far.

And after all, looking about me and listening to that utmost silence, was there any real need to flee? Who would be likely to come looking hereabouts and for what? I had little inclination to go near their damned fence again—and it *was* at a distance. We could surely live as neighbours, observing the unwritten rules defining benevolent neutrality.

And if there were hidden sensors activated by my presence, what then? Only trespassers risk prosecution—I never thought of persecution.

Is it our ridiculous logic that defeats us? This absurd need for sequence! Now I know better. Now I understand why my thoughts constantly swing back and forth between that chance discovery and this present and horrifying reality.

They have no right to detain me for further questioning! About what! But then—of course . . . I'm not being detained . . . am I?

It makes no difference. I arrived at my decision long ago. Since I've no intention of departing from it, there's little more to be said.

I'm curious naturally. For example, this change from ill- disguised truculence to official concern on my behalf? The one is as offensive to me as the other, and I made that clear. Even so— they'd deprecated with a calculated grin—for your own sake.

I—have broken the continuity. And after all, why not? I'm not forging a tale for posterity. This is my life, this bit of it, a concrete expression of what's lost forever without these symbols on paper. Not some televisual honkey-tonk, false smiles, false embraces before a non-stop lying camera.

I've no idea how long I sulked in my tent debating my best course. I felt drained of all that had sustained me this far and I couldn't understand why. Why should a fence raise fears and apprehensions? It created no bar to my freedom yet, looked at in another way, I'd escaped only as far as a barrier. Even as a symbol it seemed a mockery, a belittling of the great end I had in view.

Of course, gazing about this cell, I now know there was more to it than symbolism, but then everything tended to assist confusion. For example, what had my dilemma to do with the barking of a dog?

I heard before I listened. A natural sound, but not out here surely? I ran through the probabilities; the belling of a stag? or the baying of hounds? either seemed unlikely.

Whatever, the deep throated note grew louder until, somewhere behind me, I heard the pipe of men's voices in the clear morning air.

I listened with the conviction of one who knows he is dreaming.

'Down there!' Rich Northumberland dialect.

'Better wait till the others catch up!'

For some time I heard no more except briefly the crackle and distorted words one connects with Disney designated walkie-talkies. Then someone swore and yelled, 'Turn that thing off!'

Radio silence was being maintained.

And this is the twentieth century. A man, with no designs on the world and not much hope for the next, unfortified by democracy's greatest accolade—a criminal record—sat hunched in a tent, hands and mind trembling, while the guardians of the status quo prowled and prepared to swoop.

Orwell was a bloody fool. There are other, more subtle conceptions of 1984.

*This* is 1984!

Consider what followed.

'Okay. We'll take over. He may be armed.'

Nothing more for a fraught interval. Then I heard scrambling, as if they were deploying, giving me a wide berth because *I* might be armed? With what? I thought of my small pair of scissors . . .

A crackle of dead leaves, breaking twigs—forest sounds. I could sense the powerful forward thrust of—humans, a build up of menace ending in a distinct click . . . and a voice.

'Right, we know you're in there. Come out with your hands behind your head and no trouble.'

I sat tight, silent, my stomach churning, tried not to see into that woodland grown sinister. Grim humour reminded me I was not accustomed to this kind of thing.

'We can wait,' the same voice assured me.

'Who are you? What do you want?'

A pause. A dash of time suggesting surprise.

'Are you prepared to come out—or do you want fetched?'

They were edging nearer, watched by more of their number covering from above, as I supposed. Such fear as I had evaporated not in the fierce heat of anger, but with sudden realisation that I had nothing to lose. Wasn't that the whole point of my—defection?

I could break my silence—articulately—I could speak as I chose.

'You have a duty to identify yourself and require identification before giving reasons for your intrusion. You can fire away or I stay here till you do either!'

Another pause. My sense of humour resurfaced for a moment. There was Alice stuck in the chimney of a house too small for her, and two fellows outside pondering her robust threats in perplexed silence. And here was I.

'Police!' Tersely. 'We want to ask you a few questions in connection with a serious offence in Newcastle.'

'I know nothing of it.'

'I'm afraid that isn't satisfactory.'

'I can't help it.'

'It'd be more sensible if you came out and talked it over.'

'There's nothing to talk over. Just please go away.'

More silence. I assumed they were made uneasy by my complete lack of interest in their affairs.

They broke the deadlock in their own hustling style.

Quite abruptly the immediate area seemed to be full of uniforms, one of which was aiming a gun of some kind and sharply ordering me out. I saw no alternative if I was not to be hauled forth and the fragile tent torn and broken in the affray.

I crawled out, feeling ignominious, got to my feet and found myself facing five, maybe six officers. I made no attempt to raise my hands. I simply stared at them.

One, in plain clothes, nodded to the two armed men. They holstered their guns at once. Plainly, I posed no threat in that direction. He then came closer, confidentially so.

'Is your name George Henry Reid?'

'No.'

'Do you have any identification?'

'None.'

'Driving licence, credit card?'

'No.'

'You must have something.'

'Why?'

Nonplussed he glanced at his subordinates who kept their eyes on me.

'A man answering to your description was seen in the vicinity of H—— three days ago.'

'Well?'

'Subsequent enquiries show this man, carrying camping equipment but not dressed in usual camper's style, came into this area.'

'I did that, yes.'

'And buried a raincoat, a tie and a white shirt.'

. . . tracker dogs. Or a wily farmer.

'That isn't a crime.'

'I think you'd better come along with us. I don't mind lack of co-operation, but you're not giving a very satisfactory account of yourself.'

'Why should I? I've done nothing wrong.'

'We'll argue that on the drive back to headquarters. Don't worry about your gear. My men'll pack it up ship-shape for you.'

So that's what it was about. My innocence laboured under a severe attack of criminal tendencies.

It seems, about the time I was in Newcastle, two men had abducted a little girl. Chase was given and the men abandoned both car and the child, and ran off. A description of one included the details of a short raincoat, whitish shirt and tie. This had been circulated on local radio and TV.

Which I learned on the journey to somewhere. Information given voluntarily and in such a way I felt they were anxious to make some amends for troubling me. His questions and my indifferent replies made it apparent I could have no connection with the repugnant business.

But there were silences enough on that long journey giving me time to reflect on many things. Above all, why, if they knew I could not 'help them with their enquiries' were they taking me lock, stock and barrel, for further questioning? In every man there's a residue of guilt and I think I understood why; but I had to ask point blank, were they taking me into custody?

'No—no, no. Nothing like that.'

They wanted to clear up a few details.

About what? And why couldn't they have done so on the spot?

Silence.

Clearly, I'd been followed all the way, or at least from the town. When I'd felt I most belonged to myself, the reverse had been the case. They'd marked every step of my progress. The two men I'd seen earlier were probably in the crowded car with me, or in the second vehicle behind.

A few questions I recall. So casually framed that I was forced into guarded replies and a return of misgivings.

'On holiday up here?'

'Yes.'

'Not a young man for such a strenuous life.'

'Nobody told me there was an age limit.'

He smiled pleasantly. 'Right enough, and a bit tactless maybe. What I meant was, you don't seem kitted out right for the job. It can be a question of survival up there.' He glanced pointedly at my insubstantial footwear, and chuckled. 'We might've saved your life.'

I closed my eyes and felt sick, sick at heart. A quip filled with unintentional cruelty. How, I wondered, would he have reacted if I'd rounded on him and said . . .

But I didn't; saw instead *I* must maintain as much silence as I could gather round me if I was to survive long enough to go my own way to an ending.

Dispirited long before we reached *their* ending, I saw scarcely anything within my limited range of vision, certainly no exterior detail of the journey registered in my mind. I was aware of other questions, but I made no reply, knowing I wasn't obliged to.

Besides, latent suspicions had begun to surface, and I was too preoccupied in wrestling with unwelcome implications to feel obliged to anyone at that moment.

Now, of course, I know I was indelibly right.

Perhaps we were in Newcastle, are there now. It's unimportant. I only remember getting out of a car, traffic sounds, pavement, a blur of faces, a surround of uniforms, a freshly painted long passage with a shiny floor, then a room: small, bare, except for a table and two chairs. My travelling gear was brought in and left by the door. I was informed politely, I'd be attended to shortly. That seemed reassuring until I recalled executioners used to attend to the condemned—shortly.

Shortness stretched beyond the bounds of possibility. I could watch the sun's progress through the high small window facing me, remembered how firmly I'd been shown the chair in which I then sat and, on impulse, I decided to exercise my freedom of choice, got up and walked round the table to sit facing the door.

If there were psychological overtones to this long wait they'd wasted their time. I'm not naturally impatient and, moreover, I was tired. I know nothing of Buddhist doctrine but I can remain in totally negative contemplation for as long as it suits me.

This was, I comforted myself, 'not more than a curious but tiresome interlude on the Damascene road'.

Someone, a constable, has just brought hot, sweet tea and a cheese sandwich. He was the hearty type.

'Writing up your report, eh?'

I said yes, something like that, not doubting the fact would be noted—for future reference?

I might as well continue, tho' I feel sleepy and less enthusiastic about pencil and paper than before. Comfort myself that I'm providing reading matter to beguile the hours I'll yet spend in my sanctuary.

The waiting came to an end as one knows it must. Not even protracted, engineered delay lasts forever.

My escort appeared with profuse apologies—something about having kept me waiting. But I noticed his slightest check at discovering me in the chair facing him. In a single movement he switched on the fluorescent strip light and closed the door.

'Should've introduced myself. Detective-Inspector Ridley. CID.' He paused expectantly, but I merely nodded. He took the other chair.

'Now Mr—er—I'm afraid I don't have your name.'

'John Smith.'

The temperature dropped no more than a degree.

'Well, that's convenient . . . just one or two questions, Mr—er—'

'Smith.'

'Smith. Yes. You'll appreciate we have to cover all eventualities, and while it's evident you have no connection with the affair I mentioned—there are a few details—'

'I'm free to go?'

'You have been since you arrived. But as I say, we have to check—'

'I've done nothing wrong.'

'Of course. But it's not always that simple.'

'I don't understand.'

'Other people, Mr Smith. We know they have nothing to fear. *They* don't. They call their local station and tell of a man seen walking, not likely dressed for what he looks as if he's about, camping equipment and so on. See it from their viewpoint—a complete stranger in the district—end of the season—wearing a light mac' and other things . . . which he discards.'

'They didn't know that.'

'Don't underestimate country folk, Mr Smith. Farmers especially. They know every inch of their ground.'

'I see.'

'I thought you might. Now, if you'll excuse me saying so, to do that, is to lend weight to people's—suspicions, wouldn't you agree?'

'I had my reasons—innocent ones.'

'Ah but they don't know that do they? Or rather, they're more likely to put a different construction on a matter of complete indifference to you.'

'Perhaps.'

'And they'd know it isn't too lawful anyway, to litter the countryside with unwanted clothes.'

'. . . I forget your original question.'

The Inspector looked surprised. 'I don't recall asking one, Mr Smith. As a matter of fact, I think you asked the last. About your liberty to go.'

'Then I may?'

'Not immediately—unless you're in a hurry, Mr Smith. And I hope you'll accept we're acting in your interests.'

I remained silent for I simply could not see why, suddenly, they were so concerned for my welfare.

'Now,' he continued, 'I take it you're not a gentleman of the road?'

'A tramp?'

'Exactly.'

I pored over this utterly novel reading of my situation, my status, but resisted the temptation to say I was.

'Why should you think so?'

'Experience, Mr Smith. I once knew a company director who'd found the pressures too great for him—business, domestic problems, the usual thing. He just took off one day—let the company go bust. Lost and left everything including three cars—went to the road—corns instead of ulcers . . . well-educated chap too.'

'Unusual.'

'Not as uncommon as you might think. Anyway, I'll assume that's not your line.'

'Yes.'

'On the other hand . . . the clothes business, and you say you carry no means of identification?'

'I'm not required to.'

'No—of course you're not . . . but it's customary to—well, I imagine there are people who might be worried if you—failed to contact them by the way is it London you hail from?'

'. . . yes.'

'I ask because your discarded raincoat mentioned another place.'

'I—bought it there—on holiday. Some years ago.'

'Ah! I see . . . you'll be carrying quite a bit of money with you?'

'Ten pounds.'

'Is that all? Hope you've got a return ticket.'

'No.'

'. . . really? But you must have needs apart from the journey back? That alone'd take more than ten pounds. Silly of me.' (He'd shaken his head at his obvious stupidity.) 'You'll have an arrangement with a bank up here, eh? Wark or wherever.'

A little too obviously, I thought, my friend was prying mortar from the wall, some item of information that could verify my— exactly! one comes to realise in today's world, nobody exists without the trappings of existence.

I told him ten pounds was all I needed.

'Is that a fact?' He surveyed me intently, as if I had threatened to disappear before his very eyes. 'You mean to walk back to the south?'

'I doubt it. But does it matter?'

'Well, I suppose not . . . I think, Mr Smith, I'd better ask you to hang on a little longer while I work out what's best to be done. You see, if our enquiries are satisfactory—and of course they will be— we're obliged to return you—at public expense—to where we found you, so better for all concerned if we make absolutely sure.'

He stood and smiled affably. 'One of my men'll show you to a room where you can get some sleep. You look as if you could do with it. By the time you're awake we'll have everything sorted out.'

Very astute. Overtly I was still free to go. Covertly, he knew to a certainty I was in no state to begin all over again, knew I must accept, however churlishly, his invitation to return me to the forest. On his terms.

I agreed, with a pathetic condition that my belongings should go with me.

'Why not? Good heavens, man, you're not under arrest or anything like.'

He went to the door, called out to somebody who came with the alacrity of one who'd not been miles away.

'George, I want you to take Mr Smith's belongings to Room Six downstairs. More for his convenience. He can kip there, and if he wants tea or a bite to eat, just see to it.'

He turned to me, easy and affable as most of us are when we get what we want.

'Not quite Hilton standard, Mr Smith, but you'll not be disturbed and we shouldn't keep you long. I must emphasize, Mr Smith, if you take a notion to go, you're still free to do just that.'

Good thinking: reiteration creates cussedness.

I noticed too he shook his head at George's unspoken enquiry. It meant, as I later realised, there was to be no turn of the key.

They brought more tea just now.

No earthly use. I can't keep my eyes open, or my thoughts in consequence. I'm still here, still waiting. Seem to be writing in a thickening fog, and I—can't—really . . .

I've no way of telling how long I slept. The single light bulb under a very strong grille tells me nothing. I've slumbered under better suns, *and* felt less leaden, more refreshed.

Uncurled from the bed. Got to my feet. Waited for a touch of blackness to pass, but the throbbing in my head wouldn't go away . . . the tea!

The chipped enamel mug on the table, stared at by an idiot, all confusion, no comprehension. But they don't do things like that. This is the U.K. or something like it. So I refuse to believe in the likelihood. Besides, there's my little black note book, just as I'd left it, complete with a small indulgence, an expensive propelling pencil . . . I went to the table shaking my head foolishly, trying to emphasize the improbable.

Ridley's words came to mind. Free to go. But isn't truth made for testing? I gazed on the door, blatantly purpose built to contain. An eloquent piece of work, strident, assertive, a veritable Janus. Two sides to its nature. It kow-tows and pays deference to those outside, humiliates, disdains, mocks the—inmate.

To hell with theorising about a few planks! I've only to pull myself together, take a few steps, open it, and walk out.

I did—just that. At least, I moved as if afraid to disturb this god-like portal, laid a hand tentatively on the lever, pushed it up noiselessly—yes! furtively, and, hardly daring to breathe, slowly eased it open.

And can I believe even now, as I write? Not five minutes since, I couldn't bring myself to look out!

I closed the door again, a true believer, converted to the dogma of Janus, the omnipotent, two-faced god who could compel me, *by doing nothing*, command me: thus far—and no further.

So here I am, my eyes constantly straying to that door as I listen to a distant pounding on some portal in the mind . . . brain cells . . . some essential part of me, frenziedly beating to get out.

The exercise of self-anything debilitates; the facility to self-imprison is proven. I can think of no greater degradation.

I could *not* leave.

Self-deception followed. Bravo! How could I simply have walked out, leaving my traps behind!

Self-satisfaction superimposed itself on a heap of other selves for hadn't I demonstrated the fatuous solution to my dilemma?

Yet I sit, weak in will, too fluid to stand, confused as to purpose, or why do I not load up and go?

Because it was ordained, wasn't it, that the door would swing open once again before I could answer a stupid question!

I depend on first impressions. There's no intellectual reason known to me for rejecting them, though it's convenient to modify and qualify merely to oil the wheels of the daily social round. I was under no such compulsion—had done with my kind, had a right to face this fresh annoyance on my terms. That is, I took the newcomer at my valuation.

It wasn't high.

He had that variant of a bright and breezy façade *made* to hide something nasty. Clean and refreshing as a deodorant past its 'sell-by' date . . . the cut and hue of his tie suggested public school—Downmarket. Definitely tall, pale, thin-lipped and cold-eyed more or less menacing under heavy framed spectacles; he hinted at scholarliness as did the slight stoop and casually worn shabby raincoat. He had that ingratiatory knack against which one guards in the stock exchange or on a used car lot.

'Mr Smith isn't it? Sha'n't keep you long—oh d'you mind if I drop my raincoat on the bed? They keep these places deuced warm at any rate. I'll take this chair if I may.'

Amiability applied with a spray gun for a smooth finish—the smirky smile of his kind. And the brilliantly inflected rendering of 'raincoat'.

From that alone I knew I was dealing with no guardian of law and order in the familiar sense of the term. I watched, tensely or intently, as he settled himself comfortably, arm casually back of the chair, then frowning a shade too theatrically, as if he were thinking hard.

'You know, I'm sure I've seen you before, London?—let's see—Notting Hill maybe, the Kensington Gardens and I'm quite persuaded I asked you a direction—Pembridge Villas, Gardens or something like oh, not a month before.'

One of the East European embassies . . . wasn't that a bit too obvious? Instead, calmly:

'I've never seen you in my life before.'

'You're probably right. Someone else—similar appearance but I could've sworn—' he broke off, as if to concede defeat, but cheerfully. 'I'm *always* making that sort of mistake. No matter. Now, Mr Smith—'

'I don't have the advantage.'

'Eh? Oh I beg your pardon. One can carry informality too far— James Morell—a roving government employee with special responsibilities.'

'Such as?'

He leaned an inch or two, grinning like an hyena. 'You, Mr Smith. But I must assure you; no obligation. You're as free to walk out of that door now as when you first came in.'

'And if I had?'

He shrugged. 'Psychologically it proves nothing does it? Guilt to go—guilt to stay.'

'If there's guilt.'

'Quite so. Guilt and innocence—the feedback of opposites— how to reconcile terminological inexactitudes . . . without getting caught in the middle, eh? But the fact is, you're here and that makes life a lot easier.

'To be frank, Mr Smith, the powers that be are worried. It doesn't take much, and it doesn't take long nowadays for people to get the wind up at signs of inexplicable behaviour. And that's where I come in.'

I said nothing. It's for trouble-shooters to pull triggers.

He continued after an unproductive pause. 'I won't ask your name. For reasons of your own you prefer to be known as Smith. It'll do for the moment. But you must see that, coupled with other circumstances you may, at the least, arouse speculation?'

'That depends how you interpret freedom.'

'Oh dear,' mock wearily, 'the old, old chestnut. We could argue the definition for a whole week and still be sitting here, nothing gained or settled.'

'*What* are you trying to settle?'

Pointedly, he shifted his gaze to the little black book as though to focus an apparently wayward mind.

'About three weeks ago, an executive officer in a highly sensitive government establishment absented himself without leave. He has, I understand, scientific expertise enabling him to evaluate comparable weapons systems and so forth. Of those three weeks he'd obtained seven days' leave, which means two unaccounted for. Naturally, enquiries were made, his wife said he might be visiting relatives in Oxfordshire, though she gave the impression it was a matter of complete indifference . . . further enquiries were necessary, since it was known by those who must know all—no relative existed in Oxfordshire . . . the days of Bunbury are over, you know.'

The Janus symptom of our two-faced condition! I listened sourly to a man looking back and speaking forth, addressing to one what he knew of another. I saw no reason to interrupt.

'There was—concern—naturally. The man in question had an impeccable track record and splendid further prospects. Why should he disappear? Watch was kept at the likeliest places, but everything ended in the proverbial blank.'

'I'm trying hard to share your concern.'

'Nobody,' he eyed me like a schoolmaster using banter to soften reproof, 'thought of a camping holiday until some idiot goes off and parks himself close to another highly sensitive establishment in the Northumberland wilds. You follow me?' with an extension of that intolerable smile.

'I don't see where the idiocy comes in.'

'Well, my dear fellow! For some inexplicable reason he chose to walk, only half-prepared, on a gruelling expedition to some God-saken spot on the fells. He's seen, commented on, amateurishly conceals articles of clothing, *advertising* himself to the extent he was bound to raise more questions than answers.'

'Who? You seem to be implying I'm the man.'

'No, no—you provided the implications.'

'They can be false—even falsified.'

'Granted—but isn't it obvious in this case?'

'Not to me.'

'Even if proofs are forthcoming?'

'You can produce a wife, children, friends, colleagues, whomever you wish. I would deny them all.'

'Constructive amnesia?'

'Negative recall.'

'. . . why?'

'Because that's my free and unfettered choice.'

'Can it be that simple?'

'To me, yes.'

Attitude, responses, nothing like he'd expected or burrowed for. Some of the false bonhomie had peeled off during the last exchange and almost, one could see the wheels turning a little faster, hear the crash of changing gears.

'Can you explain further, Mr Smith?'

'I can explain this much: your hypothesis is nothing until you prove identity to *my* not *your* satisfaction. Mr Smith denies your claim because the man you speak of could be anyone.'

'That's correct—to a point but, confronted with hard evidence—I mean, the harsh realities of life?'

'For example?'

'Well, eventually, you'd require to draw on your account for the means to sustain—Mr Smith.'

'You mean money is the enemy of anonymity?'

'I couldn't put it better.'

'Then I still can't help you. I have none.'

'Family?'

'A denial based on that "harsh reality" would serve.'

It gave me some pleasure to watch him splashing about in a quandary. I noticed he eyed my belongings with the avidity of one who dearly wished for a voice within to denounce me as an imposter. Then, the loathsome smile returned. Man-to-man he offered this for my consideration.

'I really must put it to you that your name is James Edward Constance, an Executive Officer of the Mainwaring Weapons establishment and that his present address is—'

'Why must you?'

'Because I have to question someone on the sure and certain basis that he *is* James Edward Constance—'

'Wasting your time and mine.'

'—who is, of course, subject to the provisions of the Official Secrets Act.'

'Didn't your leaders teach you to raise your hand and say "heil" when you mention that?'

'Oh, come now!'

'And tell me, is your smile a natural acquisition, a learned response or a testamentary bequest?'

I don't think Mr Morell liked me very much after that. Plainly, he found it easier not to smile, and I'd achieved my objective—disarming the fellow of what he took to be a disarming feature.

'Attack isn't necessarily the best means of defence, Mr Smith. On the other hand I'll gladly bandy words with you if you'll accept the futility of the exercise.'

'You're still wasting your time.'

'. . . you know as well as I, proof of identity is a simple matter.'

'I know no such thing. Mothers have been known to repudiate their flesh and blood and call an imposter "son".'

'As to that, y'know, we've no objection to the pot calling itself a kettle . . . it's the blackness that counts.'

I said nothing.

'Every year, literally thousands of people go missing for one reason or another. But, unless the motive is criminal no one enquires too deeply; however, it can rather depend on who goes missing.'

'What can?'

'We're back to official concern, I'm afraid.'

'Forgive me, there's so much preamble that I quite forget the point of your last question—if there was one.'

'Forgive me also, Mr Smith, but a refusal to accept one's true identity can require an explanation of certain facts: the most important of these is motive. Bearing in mind his stake in national security, you'll understand how imperative is the need to know—'

'Know! Know what! You're eaten away with this need to know! Know what!'

'Why you are so anxious to get lost.'

'You're the quiz-master! Where's the question?'

'What, for example, do you mean by the shedding of loyalties?'

Aye, so that way goes the game. Not surprisingly, however involuntarily, I glanced at my notebook.

'Recap: make a pretext, keep him incommunicado until the higher lama appears, photostat his journal while he sleeps off the effects of tea, how crude can you people get!'

Morell considered the summary with ludicrously exaggerated interest. 'Well, you know, that's a very fair appraisal if the man in question happens to be James Constance.'

'What else are you trying to establish?'

'Not that you're not James Constance, but *are* Mr Smith. In your case—'

'Not at all in my case! I'm putting it to you that whoever I am, steps were taken *ultra vires* to—'

'La, la, Mr Smith, this is the phraseology of the law courts, but whether you're right or not—one is interested to know why you take pains to—to—'

'Renounce society?'

'As you please.'

'Because it's a crap society—paranoic—scared of the world, and scared most of all of itself. It's governed by what it deserved—rogues and scoundrels—perfect exponents of the lower middle-class death wish.'

'. . . I see . . . and so, a shedding of loyalties.'

'What else?'

'I don't know, Mr Smith. Suppose you tell me.'

'I'm tired of existing cheek by jowl with the living dead.' Definitely, he was not smiling now.

'Mr Smith—I recognise you as such for convenience' sake you understand. Joseph Winter is a clever ploy, but a ploy all the same, where evidence is irrefutable.

'In my circle, your type is common enough. The man in the glass suit, our soubriquet for him fits quite well I think. He is, after all, a naked man, apparently honest and open in his judgment, but he does wear a glass suit to cover but not hide his nakedness . . . our job, painful but regrettably necessary is to smash that suit to smithereens—d'you know I must look up the derivation of that word some day—perfect mystery—like yourself—derivation obscure eh?

'The man we're looking for thinks like you, Mr Smith. In the nature of things *he* will never feel free again—as long as he lives. Whatever he chooses to do, or not do. And all because of a single irreversible decision.'

'Why! if he's innocent!'

'Did I say he was innocent? You declaimed something about knowledge. Today, Mr Smith, knowledge may be synonymous with guilt. In certain circumstances a man or woman may know too much. Now that kind of knowledge is perfectly harmless so long as it's contained by admittedly imperfect Acts of Parliament or whatever. Rather like enriched uranium you see, fine, while it's controlled by those graphite rod things . . . but once let it escape, go beserk, run out of control—trouble. Trouble either way; because when it's spent—what do you do with the waste? You bury and monitor it in one instance . . . monitor and bury it in the other . . . I would hate that to be Mr Constance's fate.'

'I remain perfectly indifferent.'

'As Mr Smith, yes of course. But I think *he's* in rather a cleft stick as they say.'

'If I'm Smith, I'll be under observation; if I'm not, you'll still keep an eye on me, is that what you mean?'

'Not quite . . . you've cut off all ties on your own admission. That makes you vulnerable. Simply as an hypothesis, it could be shown, don't y'know, that Mr Constance had shed his allegiance sufficiently to rendez-vous with a foreign agent in some obscure part of the country, where he was about to part with information to which he had access—before defecting.'

'. . . to where?'

'Oh, I don't mean in the physical sense of crossing borders and all that Boy's Own carry-on. I mean the mental defection of one who finds his immediate world repugnant—prehistoric.'

I glanced at the word more than at the man who had the grace to smile a confession of guilt.

'Society, Mr Smith,' he continued, 'is too delicately poised to allow such—lush sentiments to prevail and gain currency.'

'Society,' I replied, 'like the megalasaurus, is doomed anyway.'

I had had enough but, cats or men, curiosity undoes us all. 'And if you find this man?'

He shrugged and closed his eyes. 'I suppose we'll want him to account for a missing document, top classification, something to do with the E74 system—' he opened his eyes wide as innocence. 'It's missing y'know. From his place of work.'

Perhaps I changed countenance, and if I did, it was surely excusable. It happens to others—but to oneself? Why should a freeborn Englishman even consider the possibility? The answer was inescapable. Hadn't I reminded myself this was 1984? Hadn't I sneered at Orwell's prevision and written of other ways?

Well, here was one of them, smirking enough to provoke a surge of sheer loathing for a human veneer covering nothing very much. He didn't bother to hold all the cards against his chest.

'The proof,' I said, with care, 'would be hard to come by.'

'Not too hard, Mr Smith,' softly, as not to disturb sleeping spectres.

I watched him get to his feet. The kind of man who performs every action with a negligent grace—the hallmark of those with money—or power.

'You'll be off now?' he supposed.

'I shall rest first.'

'Good idea. I'll be in the vicinity if you've an after thought you want to share on your way out.'

He took up his raincoat and walked to the door, turning at the last moment. 'By the way, Mr Smith, do you consider yourself to be an important person?'

The question most favoured by gauche psychiatrists.

'In the society I live in I'm as important as you are.'

I saw, from his expression, I'd offered the only possible insult to which he was entitled. Willingly I had signed my death warrant.

He left the door wide open and I could afford to smile like Tantalus after his first failure.

I thought for a long time, how best to steer my course, and then I wrote till I reached precisely this point.

Of no return.

And I write now.

I, James Edward Constance, state that, had I been permitted, I should have depended on Nature to take the necessary steps by which I might have faded out of this inexplicable world with the least fuss and bother.

I committed no offence against this country, the polity or any individual therein. At most, I abandoned a deadly situation I could no longer live with. As I value my soul I dared not face the long, the endless night that must follow the daily study of the many effective means of destruction. Looking about me I saw how far advanced was the latter day plague in destroying what most matters in our individual totality—the pandemic of materialism corroding—soul-destroying.

It is no longer possible to walk safely, mind, body and soul, anywhere in this world.

I might have turned my energies to protest, but where? Greenham Common? What is the value to mankind of a sectarian crusade against annihilation without absolution?

Increasingly, I came to a conviction that there's no room in this world for any but those who reluctantly, anxiously, avidly, religiously, patriotically, contemptuously, excitedly, intellectually court destruction and their share of the death wish. To be ruled by ghouls and fools is to partake of crumbs from the rich cannibal's table, to worship their doctrines is to celebrate mass blacker than their nights' work.

To opt out, permanently, seemed the only way. I took it, only to be reminded that I no longer belonged to myself, if I ever had.

My crime, failure to be committed.

And what does that mean as today's trinity?

Committed, to one side or the other.

If not, then committed to one institution or another.

Again, if not, committed for trial—in some sort of camera.

1984 . . .

Leviathan. No, Mr Hobbes. A prehistoric world filled with carefully programmed monsters. Their disguise is perfect.

This account is closed . . . only, I'll mention a consoling and inescapable truth. No matter who, and I myself am one of them, the evil men do is visited on their heads a thousandfold—not loss of life—but death of the soul . . .

I shall close the door and see the true face of Janus, the one I vilified. This time I am on his side, as he is on mine.

Here is as good as there. Sooner is better than later.

It's only a matter of time . . .

# CADENZA

'Long live Dezhni Gorcan, over-running President of Poldavia; but may he live longer in retirement.'

That was the gloomy greeting heard not too long since in all the liberal cafés, cliques and cabalistic circles of Prem-Lusz, capital extraordinary of a mortifying land. 'This accursed region is plagued by wolves and mountains and the weather was never worse in Caledonia,' as Agricola complained in his unpublished military memoirs.

Classical criticism is seldom forgotten, and the Roman grumble kept and enhanced its validity very nearly to the present day: no one wanted Poldavia. From the well-documented mutiny of Hannibal's elephants to the day Field Marshal Goldstein took his panzers around instead of across the treacherous Buggebirgers en route for the Russian campaign, none, man or beast, had found a good word to say in Poldavia's favour.

The very natives couldn't stand it. Contented Poldavians are happily settled all over the world. The rest, some three millions, languish in the motherland, and most of those huddle in the capital or its environs, having gravitated despairingly from the country districts to the one spot that could be called flat, wind-free and congenial, or nearly so.

A hardy race, and infinitely adaptable, it had created a vast industrial complex serviced by a majority of the 1,800,000 inhabitants. No one disputed their claim to live in the most concentrated, overcrowded, historic and dynamic city in all Europe. Mainly because it's not yet agreed that Poldavia *is* in Europe.

Necessity rules, of course, where there's no more than subsistence farming in two thousand square miles of bleak and rugged terrain that can't trap an accidental coach-load of tourists in the best summer months.

All of which, and to some extent, explains the pervading gloominess of the Poldavian character. Geopsychologists probably have it about right when they conclude that a high percentage of the natives are ashamed of their country . . . proud of it in public or under torture, quite otherwise in private.

An interesting recording was once made—in neo-Wendish—of a typical pot-house exchange in Mesbrani village somewhere along the Prem-Lusz/Logelei road to the north.

'This firkin country.'*

'Misery.'

'God passed us by.'

'He pissed on us first, sir reverence, likely on his way to America.'

'And on his way back . . . misery.'

A snatch of the local rhetoric bandied over a glass of the national beverage which itself does nothing to raise the spirits; but explanatory enough to put this dreary land into perspective.

The capital, Prem-Lusz, like many principal cities, hides, if it doesn't palliate, the broken heart of its hinterland. An air of artificial gaiety, common to huge industrial areas, beguiles the stranger into a false analysis of the national temperament, if his stay is brief enough. Feverish gloom might easily be mistaken for sober animation in clubs, beer-halls, Kneipes, Schattkammers and cafés, conveying little more about the collective personality other than that it's split. How could things be otherwise in an utterly ambiguous nation?

For Poldavia is, in State Department jargon, pivotal, standing as it does so exactly between East and West; neither Slav nor good pickled-herring European it's no wonder personality is divided. (The double-headed Poldavian wolfhound on the old and abolished national flat explained much.)

A leading psychiatrist once asked, 'What is our nation? All city, no country, industry rules, agriculture languishes, the city prospers, the outback is feudal poor, the West holds its nose and woos, the East looks down its nose and indifferently strengthens its influence simply to counter the capitalist threat.'

On reflection, one must accept a grain of salt. He *was* in pyjamas, screaming those words from the top of a stationary tram in Euclid's Square, and had to be coaxed down, tenderly removed, and is now well taken care of.

The unfortunate professor does exemplify the problem however.

---

* Firkin: used as a diminutive of a unit of measurement, hence: small.

He lives in a city dominated by political tensions inevitable where a country falls so neatly between ideologies. This way? or that way? are enormous questions to a maddened donkey caught between two carrots dangling from sticks, frontiers apart.

And the Vexling citadel dominates Prem-Lusz's being as politics dominates its thinking. On a craggy eminence, 700 feet above the plateau level, stands as imposing a fortress as the sickliest romantic could desire. A thing of accretions it faithfully reflects every period of Poldavia's chronically untroubled history. But, to the practised eye of a Vitruvius, each addition merely mirrors the *impressions* of Romanesque, Gothic, Renaissance or whatever, carried home by Poldavian dilettanti from their travels, studies or embassies abroad.

Each century, from about the eleventh, had its share in the hotch-potch, just as the city descended the hill in outwardly identifiable strata, like a fossil guilty of publicly exposing itself, till it spread over the roundabout plain in all the unplanned, riotous ugliness of nineteenth and twentieth century industrial burgeon.

Leading citizens, top ballerinas and the intelligentsia live prestigiously in old, magnificent and mouldering houses under the Vexling ramparts, the descending orders live in roughly concentric rings all the way to the proletarian twelfth circle at the city confines.

The arrangement made for good order whichever party held power. But some may ask, if the country was so negligible in the designing eyes of warning powers, why did it take pains to create a massive stronghold of such monumental futility? Stuck up there, it couldn't possibly defend the people clustered about its foundations, leave alone the entire principality.

At second glance the answer is simple. *No* country cares to feel that it isn't worthy of being under threat. Defence, armaments, a bit of an army, is as necessary to national self-esteem as an efficient rail or airline service. Poldavia, therefore, laboured long under the deliciously spine-chilling illusion that it offered as much strategic value to aggressors as did any other state.

Geography needs have nothing to do with ideology. If would-be aggressors considered the matter at all, they'd calculate there were easier ways of going in either direction than to traverse a God-forsaken tract that even the Poldavians couldn't stomach.

But Vexling assumed a domestic importance it could never have achieved, *aes triplex*, on the larger scene. Central to the lives of the citizens, it housed in its ample dimensions more and more of the institutions needed to control their destinies. The palace and all its offices were followed by the courts of justice, the university, the unique house of correction and, as bureaucracy increased and multiplied, room was easily found for Ministries, the Police Secretariat, the Polderacshûs or parliament, and much else besides. Everything touching the nation's progress and well-being had its roots in as centralised a system of government as any to be found in or out of Europe.

We are not concerned with Vexling as some variant of Kafka's psychogenic creation. His castle hints at possibilities of sinister intent. The Poldavians would laugh to scorn suggestions that Vexling hinted at any such things. 'It *is* sinister, but it's also necessary to the proper functioning of the country.'

Hate it as an instrument of repression, tolerate it for its paternalism, worship it as a shrine of despotism, friend or foe, inimical or not, there was no national survival without it.

If this account so far suggests a Michelin guide to some quaint excrescence on the broad back of Europe—not that Michelin deigns to mention it—that's because there is no comprehending the extraordinary event that rocked Poldavia and the world in March 1984 while the snows still covered its uncongenial surface, without some knowledge of a country that, to a majority outside Europe's chancelleries, Washington's State Department and Moscow's Kremlin, scarcely finds a place on the map or merits an item in most newspapers.

Snow. Like icing softening the severity of that great, rambling confection above 'Prem' as the ratepayers affectionately abbreviate their city's name. A hive of activity those bustling courtyards, the endless byways, mere mazes for the unwary. Apart from the hordes of bundles of headscarved women sweeping the snow from eight principal squares and innumerable lesser ones, busy officials, students, lawyers, doctors and clerks scurry everywhere, stumbling over snowpiles, showered with snow by the vigorous broomsweeps of the *vochni* who return the victim's curses with better than they get in good gutter Wendish. Limousine sleds glide with a slashing note over paths leading from one acre to another. No cars are permitted to any but the President and his entourage above 500 feet.

Spring, it's rumoured, is in the air across the border, but the

Vexling citadel looks as wintry as it did in October last, and the rare trees up above in the Palace grounds won't bother to parade their greenwares till April.

Overhanging this lively scene is the vivid impression that everybody hates each other's guts, the language is so forceful and unrestrained. That too is part of Poldavia's meaning. The people *are* animated, *can* laugh, *can* joke; can do all in short, that other nations do in the way of oiling life's grinding wheel, but the national physiognomy seems to deride those facts. Almost every Poldavian appears to wear an expression of mourning, to sport a sorrowful air as if a loved one had gone missing even when one is telling a filthy joke to a drinking companion in a low Schattkammer. The listener will hear it out to the end in gloomy silence then burst into sudden bitter laughter, or a smile will wreathe his sombre features such as to make the wreath meaningful.

Some who know the country well believe little else but that this national trait has kept the invading hordes, troop or tourist, beyond Poldavia's borders. It's depressing to move about in a pervasive atmosphere of feverish mourning. If someone isn't dead, they ought to be. Travellers, unavoidably delayed by circumstances, have been known to attempt suicide after three days, driven to it by the dichotomous behaviour of people who laugh but look as if they wish they, or you, or someone, anyone, had passed away.

Thus far, we know something of Poldavia's geography and its cloven character, but little of its politics: easily summarised.

Naturally, government is hybrid, partaking of socialism and capitalism in a five to one ratio. The left permanent majority has, over the years, devised a system of controlled tolerance to private enterprise. In effect, it said: we'll take care of the means of production and domestic distribution, *you* go ahead with marketing our surplus manufacture to the rest of the world, East or West.

Fallen between alien systems, this seemed an eminently sensible solution to a difficult problem and the exporters, entrepreneurs and assorted shysters, happily took their cut and more than their cut of profits; but, as a former prime minister slyly pointed out to his 32 outraged colleagues in the 40-seat Polderacshûs: this way, who needs a stock exchange?

Patience! The crux of the affair is round the next corner.

As more trading contracts were made with the West, the interests represented by the eight permanent members of the

Symbiotic Democratic Party grew increasingly restive. They, the exporting factors, were making greater profits year on year; their sales initiative and aggressive marketing techniques had gone far to create a favourable trade balance with both sides of the great divide. It followed: their power should carry more weight in management of the country's affairs. Therefore, the voting blocs should be recast, to give parity between the parties.

The government ignored the threat. What was worse, it gave no orders to monitor the warning signs at large though it commanded every possible facility for internal surveillance through its small but highly efficient security forces.

In January the Russian ambassador mildly commented on an influx of sharp-dressing business executives 'shooting from the lip'.

Prime Minister Kremp assured him business was booming. Merely a trade delegation.

Then why, Borislav wondered, were posters appearing all over the city soon after their departure, demanding more democracy?

'Our people are grown prosperous,' was the reply, 'they're looking for something new to spend their money on.'

Borislav was no more convinced than the rest of the diplomatic community. Ominous signs suggested a gathering of the storm; the miserable burghers of Prem were muttering, the police were short of morale, and some of the thousand-strong army were newly daring to argue with their political lecturers. Students demanded the right to strike and actually threw a snowball at the Vice-Chancellor 'to symbolise their grievances'.

A minor rash of self-imported media-men providentially found a whole series of events worth reporting and, suddenly, Poldavia figured on the 22-inch map of the world.

The snowball affair was teletaped, beefed up with a lurid commentary.

A demonstration at the dynamo factory: teletaped. The workers, complete with banners, were actually clamouring for better films in the factory cinema, but everything was written or spoken in neo-Wendish, so the world never knew that—and nobody explained.

A queue at Lischmann's the baker's: teletaped. A tearful woman telling the camera that three members of the Lischmann family were down with Poldavian mumps and only one idiot to serve hundreds; but Wendish is a diabolical tongue so the world didn't know that either. Food shortages, obviously.

A gas explosion in the eighth circle: teletaped. A street casualty in the Glintza Prad, surrounded by police waiting for an ambulance: teletaped. Hours later the world shuddered at plain evidence—of what?

Brilliant mediatrics! Daily the unvarying messages: how terrible this total repression of the human spirit in poor Poldavia. *We* know, don't we, what *they're* capable of—and here are the pics to prove it. Just look at those faces.

The authorities woke up to discover they'd tolerated, in good faith, a murky PR exercise conducted by seedy aliens with doubled loyalties. The foreign 'correspondents' were thrown out, of course, but it was too late. The feedback gave ample notice of unrest: sporadic riots broke out, unknown since the repressive days of the last Archduke's regime. Stormy sessions in the Parliament House served little purpose. Emergency decrees for tighter security merely inflamed the situation.

'We are free men!' Duschnik, the leading shop steward at the Polda Sewing Machine works, stepped forward and shouted at the Prime Minister making a tour of inspection.

'Then you've nothing to complain about,' retorted Kremp and the teletape of the 'confrontation' was scrapped. Duschnik had bungled it, his controller admitted, spitting his disgust.

The Presidential palace consisted in an extensive suite of rooms in the Courcy tower dominating the great complex of Vexling citadel. Its colossal proportions fairly copied the better known French stronghold admired by some Poldavian crusader eight centuries ago.

An impressive ground-floor audience chamber was surmounted by an equally fine banqueting hall. The private apartments were on the next floor. The Hammer and Chisel, national flag of unity, flapped over all, to be lowered only when His Excellency went to bed. As Poldavian protocol has it: a man of consequence must be awake to be effective.

Dezhni Gorcan's family life need not detain us. After all, he scarcely behaved as if it concerned *him*. His wife, younger, well-built, but oddly prim about the mouth, played little more than a background supporting rôle in her husband's life. She seldom spoke in public or private, was known affectionately by the rabble as the Smile. In fact it was the kind of grimace that badly needed analysing. Taken with that downturn of the mouth and the severely straight steel-grey hair the soubriquet suggested heavy irony.

As a loving parent Gorcan could claim a daughter at an expensive Swedish finishing school and a son who ran the soap monopoly, given him by the fond father as a coming-of-age present. The rabble promptly nicknamed the lad, Bubbles.

Of Gorcan what can one say? Surely, the mass of contradictions stuffed into that great frame fitted him for leadership? Brilliant and stupid, reserved and expansive, industrious and bone idle this silver-haired, pot-bellied master of political cunning wished, he said, for no better title than 'Father of my Country'. He got it.

Being known affectionately by the rabble as 'Dad'—and with good reason.

Popular, certainly, until the advent of those sharp-dressing executives. Then, a liberal organ, *Maniskra*, published an opinion poll which proved by numerological prestidigitation that Dad's popularity had slumped.

He was, apparently, the father of only 27 per cent of the population.

No one likes to be on the wrong side of the popularity rating— that's why they're so effective. Gorcan, rightly sensitive to criticism, decided the time had come for drastic measures. He sent for Lawzlau Kremp and, at this moment, the two men are conferring in Gorcan's study.

Lavishly appointed, with a dominant, highly ornate Bohemian desk placed right-angled to the renaissance chimney-piece, in the depths of which great logs are burning brightly. On the desk bookends hold a finely bound definitive history of Poldavia, in one slim volume. On the walls, between high towering library cases, faded tapestries illustrate the glorious events of Poldavia's past though, to speak truth, no one has yet managed to make head or tail of them.

Above the chimney-piece depends a solid gold, high relief map of the fatherland, dully reflecting the soft glow of a converted 'chain' chandelier. Massive curtains, cloth of gold, are undrawn and, clearly visible through the high window, is the furthermost circle of lights from Prem-Lusz's distant suburbs.

As for the room's occupants, they're crestfallen from facing unpalatable truths. Prime Minister Kremp, a fussy little gentleman, balding, eyes diminished rather than dignified by gold-rimmed spectacles, a manquéd pedagogue, compulsively fingers the report he has just conveyed on that day's parliamentary business.

He glances nervously at the President, almost imploringly, unwilling to break the long silence. Gorcan stirs uneasily, a leviathan waking and breaking from bad dreams about Hobbes and such like.

'Twenty-seven per cent . . . this country has known peace and prosperity for thirty years. For thirty years I have been President. Explain, Lawzlau.'

Kremp walked, as the Poldavians say, all round the invitation before he responded. 'It's simple. Then, it was quite another situation, less complicated by today's technologically based struggle.' Kremp's thin, metallic delivery impressed far less than his actual grasp of the realities. 'Now they begin, openly, to poach each on the other's hemisphere of influence. Woe betide us, if it is, as I surmise, a final jockeying for the most favoured position before the day of Countdown.'

'You were always a pessimist.'

'Of course. The art of politics is to disguise the deepest pessimism under the highest optimism. And I venture to remind you, I warned they were planning disruption, were suborning by financing the opposition. To our certain knowledge the top SDP people have numbered accounts in Switzerland.'

'Scoundrels!'

'Victims of conflicting loyalties. My country or my currency.'

'And so, this tirade by Deputy Mardian today?'

'He's grown rich on kickbacks from his own constituents and seeks opportunities to invest in—foreign securities.'

Gorcan chuckled grimly at Kremp's choice of words. *His* indictment would have been more pithy. 'This attack is aimed at me, not the Party, or even at you. "Long live the ever-running President *but* . . ." That's some consolation for you and the party members at any rate.'

'Not at all, Excellency. Strike off the head and the limbs can be lopped at leisure.'

That, too, was worth a grim smile. 'I think our friends in the East would move fast to aid a paraplegic.'

'Occupation? I'm not sure. They've both tried it and—what's the Washington term? Counterproductive. No—occupation through ideas, subtle, insidious, infinitely more destructive of the national will.'

'Ours,' thoughtfully, 'was an occupation through ideas.'

'Was! We got there first from choice and popular concurrence. There's no better way.'

'Fine. How do we stay there?'

'I have no idea.'

Gorcan audited the statement for a note of insolence. Decided it *was* a plain statement of fact. 'You are a great comfort, Lawzlau. As the chaplain to a condemned.'

'I said *I* had no idea. You'll observe I set a third chair at the end of your desk when I came in.'

A presidential shrug. 'One of your colleagues to join us later, I suppose. Minister of the Interior?'

'What interior? Poldavia has none.'

Irresistible that national pastime: running down the country no one loved.

'Perhaps,' with a smile, 'I was thinking of the mind.'

Kremp nodded sombrely. 'Perhaps I too.'

'Who then?'

Before Kremp could reply, Gorcan's PPS appeared discreetly at the door to announce 'The Security Commissioner, Excellency.'

One flowing movement from the door's opening to Yaroslavl Saachik's flamboyant entrance, perchanced a fanciful hint of three dimensional poesy. From this point, the merest suspicion of melodrama entered into a critical state of affairs and would remain to the final curtain.

The dapper secretary softly closed the door leaving the two statesmen, heads turned at right angles, to regard the newcomer and his colourfulness with amusement and a touch of envy. Such style, such a bearing, so much damned self-assurance!

Saachik projected youthfulness beyond his 47 years, was taller than the national mean, had more pronounced Slavic features, had come as a child refugee with his mother from the Ukraine. The Nazis had shot his father.

From his university days Saachik had been dominated by two concepts: justice and the imagination—imagination *per se*. He endured with complete equanimity the banter of friends who knew mutual irreconcilables when they saw them.

After completing law studies he practised in the lower metropolitan court for a year; but satisfaction eluded the junior counsellor and, to his colleagues' surprise, he forsook the profession to enrol

as a police cadet. He qualified and patrolled for five years, was
promoted sergeant, gave exemplary service and graduated to
detective status, investigating with such success and flair that he
became captain and finally, senior commandant in the force by his
forty-second year. Whereupon, he transferred to the smaller, but
infinitely more powerful Bureau of Internal Security with a muster
of less than 200 including clerks and cleaners. Four years later he
became, by process of natural selection, the country's third powerful member of a triumvirate: Commissioner Yaroslavl Saachik.

Methodically, and by taking pains, he'd found a way to reconcile
the imperatives of justice with the mercurial power of
imagination—as he understood those things.

He prized good manners, but flouted conventions believing they
had no place in a socialist state. He accepted with contempt the
necessity for power's panoply, the huge desk, tapestries, golden
maps and the rest; only the array of telephones on a table under the
window merited his glancing respect. As for Saachik's personal
appearance: no concession to the Head of State.

From the jaunty fur cap, to the embroidered shirt, to the baggy
trousers, tucked into short, black top-boots, the white bearskin
jacket flung Dolman fashion over a shoulder, the totality was
undeniably striking. Alone and unarmed, he went about the city,
thus making no secret of his vocation as most heads of Intelligence
prefer. But then, he *was* an intelligent fellow; happily married, and
with three bright children.

Took in at a glance the crisis atmosphere and modified his
cavalier expression by just enough to fit the occasion; bowed briefly
to Gorcan and took the offered place broadside of the desk to face
the fireglow.

'Kremp enjoys springing surprises, Saachik. He promised a
treat. I had no idea he meant you.' Morosely. 'Things must be bad.'

Saachik nodded agreeably. 'Do you wish for a verbal report?'

'I imagine that's why Kremp wanted you here.'

'No,' glass and gold rims flashed in the firelight. 'I requested his
presence to discuss solutions; the problems we know about.'

Gorcan cast a speculative eye over the two men wondering how
well they got on together. Coups and talk of conspiracies: these
days one could never be sure. In fact, they were very nearly on
terms of warm friendship.

'With your permission, Excellency, I think we have a

solution—or rather—I'm groping towards a resolution which could be more—aesthetically satisfying.'

The President's grimace suggested disgust. 'You have the semantic advantage of me Saachik.'

'I hope your Excellency isn't anti-semantic,' from Kremp. Everyone knew of the PM's harmless little vice, knew he preferred puns before butter; it wasn't as bad as publicly breaking wind, but they ignored it just the same. So nobody laughed. They all studied the play of flames in the hearth instead. The room was stiflingly hot—a real Poldavian summer. Saachik discreetly loosened his shirt collar.

'If I may summarise the situation and relate it to the resolution I have in mind?'

Gorcan nodded mechanically, without the enthusiasm attending genuine hope. Kremp composed himself to listen making a Gothic arch of his hands: Perpendicular.

'We are,' Saachik began, 'what the English call "pig in the middle". If you prefer, the super-powers are playing soccer with Europe as the ball, trying to force their opponents to kick an own goal.'

'The balls are flying in all directions,' Gorcan, another kind of referee, grumbled with some feeling.

'One,' Saachik argued. 'The size of it is what counts, how much of Europe, Scandinavia, the Balkans, is to be listed as derelict in the event of a nuclear strike. Hence the determined attempt to detach loyalties.'

'That much I conveyed to His Excellency,' Kremp observed impatiently. Saachik appeared not to hear.

'For whatever geopolitical reasons, they aim at us. They raise their sights, aim high, and so, they aim at you. If you tumble, we all fall down and the minority, under western influence, becomes the majority. In their book a right wing minority is the equivalent of a left wing majority. So much is clear.

'At first sight, there seems to be no logical answer to the dilemma. Move swiftly to repress the SDP, deny the rights of malcontents to plot, word and deed, the overthrow of our regime, *they* will weep triumphantly—we told you so! Watch out in the West—save us from these brutes who trample on our fundamental freedom to plot, scheme—and overthrow *their* regime. See, on TV, what our oppressors are doing to us.'

'You are saying we dare not make martyrs?' The President began to show more interest.

'We dare not make anything else.'

At which the audience sat up. Gorcan especially. 'I don't understand you,' with care.

'Are you suggesting violence?' Kremp, no less carefully.

'Yes.'

'To make martyrs—which you agree—'

'*One* martyr only, Excellency.' A play of eyes as between two men.

'—who?'

'—you.'

Somewhere, in a neighbouring room, a stately clock chimed the hours, muffled sounds timing the drama unfolding on the next-door stage, but no one bothered to count those hours.

The President, grown pale, otherwise dissembled uneasiness, kept remarkably calm despite the evidence . . . after all, some kind of palace revolution, complicity between these two? Unwelcome thoughts had him flicking wary glances from one to the other. In the top right-hand drawer, a Mettlinger .34; by his left foot, a small plunger needing the slightest pressure to bring effective help—from two of Saachik's men . . . loyalties.

Not that he was imperturbable, but curiosity still reigned and he felt partially reassured by Kremp's expression of unfeigned horror.

'May I enquire,' steadily, 'if the victim is to be willing—or coerced?'

'N'no victim can be said to be willing,' the P.M. stuttered.

'I apologise for the shock words can inflict by their plain meaning, your Excellency. If I may continue . . .'

Gorcan, though bewildered, welcomed his apparent reprieve, gladly invited clarification.

'To describe desperate measures in everyday parlance creates confusion, because the limitations of language . . . words, Excellency, how to find terms equal to the hidden intention.' Saachik paused, to be sure of the presidential eye.

'You will recall what happened to Kennedy?'

Again the audience tensed. Unmistakably, the theme stank of assassination.

'Well?'

'The death of a good man? Perhaps. But lessons were learned from Dallas, conclusions were drawn—and acted on.'

'Again, I don't follow you,' curtly. Gorcan sensed he was being forced to bite on an unpalatable bullet.

'Can anyone fail to notice the number of world leaders who have *survived* "assassination" attempts in the last few years? None of them loved except by the fanatics, one or two mediocrities chasing the popularity ratings. And it works, of course.'

A musical voice, slowly selling an idea to circumspect but fascinated buyers, anxious to be held, as it were, in the very bowl of Saachik's hand.

'Go on,' urged the President.

The golden map of Poldavia made a perfect focus for concentrated thought. Saachik took time, picking his way forward across the bounds of their credulity.

'Shakespeare, Excellency, was a wise man. He could assert with less evidence than we possess, "all the world's a stage". So it still is—but down to the dimensions of a mannikin's toilet, a breeding ground for posturing, imposters, cantebanks and mountebanks. Very well. Why should it escape the notice of powerful interests that this theatre of the absurd might further those interests? A captive audience. Why not *engineer* situations best calculated to establish leadership more securely in the popular—'

'Affection?' Gorcan supplied.

'No, Excellency. In the popular debt. Almost to die is to sober the generality, creating a peculiar sense of obligation; the national sentiment will accept the necessity for a little more restriction of freedom so that such dreadful sacrilege will not, must not, happen again.'

'Sacrilege is a strong term,' Kremp ventured.

'Why? Votes, parties, democracy, power, sacred or profane, the divine right to rule is common to leadership. It's the very root of my theory.' How, he wondered, could they not see that: the *failed* attempt creates a living, unassailable monument of righteousness even in the worst of tyrants. Almost religiously significant the survival of such a man who can rule at will with an accusing finger.

Gorcan pondered this for seconds . . . 'good. I see that. But is one to survive with the notion that a happy escape *can* only happen to the unpopular man?'

'Death solves nothing. However virtuous the victim, his reputation has no political validity. He provides fodder for the historians and little more. But if the real or supposed scoundrel lives, he's a survivor; a survivor is heroic because heroes are, by definition, contemptuous of death. Popularity restored, even grudging admiration from your enemies, because you faced death—and won.'

'I thought death was heroic,' wistfully said, as if, after all, one might be missing out on something.

Saachik concealed his amusement. 'There are stupid heroes, and wise heroes—the wise ones survive.'

'Then you leave me no choice. I will survive.'

'But the means, Yaroslavl,' Kremp's enthusiasm was hardly statesmanlike, had that squeaky quality of a schoolboy plotting in the dorm.

A fact not lost on Saachik who stood and walked to the window, gazed at the concentric circles of street lighting ebbing away as far as the eye could see. Pinpoints of traffic headlights crawled in endless convoys, larger blobs of illumination marked the passage of tram-cars on their unique progress round and round the city from the first circle below Vexling to the twelfth. All this he comprehended while his imagination toyed with Dante's grotesqueries and the plan—the plan untainted by petty men's enthusiasms.

Below, to his left, he could see the pepper-pot towers of a minor château in the Frantichek Square—the Academia Hospital. To the right, just within his ken, the Poldavian State Television HQ and, immediately below, the loomy bulk of Poldavia's sole prison.

Ingredients?

Another, stranger thought crossed Saachik's mind as he turned, impressive, every inch the artificer of destinies, to the two latest members of an endangered species: holders of high office.

These petty men.

*That* was in his mind until he'd regained his place at the desk.

'A few moments' rehearsal will suffice. Mainly, it concerns a fragile plastic sac of genuine blood sealed to your hand—the one with which you do *not* wave to the crowd.'

Gorcan paused in the act of doodling or note-taking. 'Crowd?'

'On Wednesday you address the Annual Trades Union Congress at the Matrinenhalle. They'll put on the usual show of loyalty as you arrive.'

'The orchestrated welcome,' Gorcan snorted.

'The castrated ovation,' Poldavia's prime minister could *not* leave words alone; but satisfaction was short-lived, soon died under the President's scowl.

'As the assassin raises his pistol—you'll know exactly where he stands—you turn to the crowd and make a final flourish—you see the gun levelled, the trigger pulled. In that instant you raise your left hand—clapping it violently to your chest—blood will flow, will be *seen* to flow by the OB camera trained on the proceedings.'

Gorcan, writing rapidly, looked up with an approving smile. 'Good.'

'Poldavia sees at once what the world sees next day—impact, immediacy.'

'And then?'

'The assassin—'

'The would-be assassin,' Kremp corrected, primly.

'Will be shown scuffling with the police, while security officers screen you from further attack.'

'And observation,' Gorcan, portrait of a man now entering wholeheartedly into the spirit of make-believe.

'You will appear to be driven to the hospital before disappearing briefly from public view.'

'Is that all?'

'By no means. Let's give the ghouls and fools what they crave. We'll go steps further than the pathetic charades they foist on *their* credulous apes.'

'Go on.'

'In that most dramatic of all theatres, in the camera's eye and before an audience of millions, you will undergo surgery—a delicate procedure to remove the bullet.'

Blank, the President's expression. Kremp reacted with a nervous giggle. 'Oh, come now!'

'I checked with Glawitz. Tomorrow, a patient of his is due for lung resection, same age, same build—that's good enough. Glawitz is amenable.'

'He's a good party man,' Gorcan conceded.

Saachik explained that he would use the Bureau's own TV team, formed by him when he took the job. If TV is the staple diet of a nation . . . make it serve.

'No patent objection there?'

The Security chief regarded Kremp a shade superciliously. 'I don't see it.'

'Identity.'

'The viewing public will see as much as surgeon Glawitz is concerned with, the operational area, so to speak.'

'Very good. Most authentic,' the 'victim' nodded his approval.

'For continuity we'll need a running shot of you as they take you into the theatre—an introduction to the saga of the fight for your life.'

'Saachik, do as you please. It's not often one fights for anything at such trifling cost.' But the flippancy gave him pause. 'Foolproof?'

A play of humour about the eyes. 'Failsafe. The actors cannot forget their lines because there is no script.'

A few details to settle, drinks offered and declined—Saachik regretted—still much to do. A pat on the back from the President, an approving smile from Kremp and he was gone leaving them to reflect, as the chandelier to the lustrous map, on brilliance.

Saachik went his ways with the nonchalance of a man who knows success in advance, because he has worked and schemed for it to the very last contingency.

He strolled through the grounds savouring the beauty of those rare and ancient trees, snow laden, conscious of desultory flakes cooling his face still flushed with hearthfire, waved familiarly to the armed security men at the main gate, stopped for a word with the dog-handler just setting out on patrol, a pat for the pinscher at his side.

Once out of the grounds his buoyant mood climbed, went counter to his descent, past those old, decaying picturesques so favoured by the intelligentsia, through winding alleys where houses yearned towards each other, only prevented from falling into each other's arms by great baulks of timber spanning the upper regions. There were lights in most of the windows, an old Poldavian custom, to guide the footfalls' way. At which he nodded with inexplicable satisfaction. 'That's right,' he muttered. 'That's right.'

To follow Saachik's footprints in the fresh fallen snow is to reach a minor court surrounded by high, richly façaded residences in which some of the country's bureaucracy functioned. He thought of the clerks hunching and punching out vital facts and figures for storage in the data banks installed in damp and musty cellars, while they warmed themselves by traditional 'timber stoves', above. That too, gave him satisfaction.

'Dichotomy—the world—not just Poldavia, split . . .' Aloud! to no one! He chuckled, paused by the tiny frozen fountain, squinted up at the pale shimmers of office windows, and wondered at himself. Philosophising *en clair* . . . exaltation or exultation; had the plan or its approbation from the moulders of the fragmentary future, affected him! No. The plan alone—triumph of the imaginative process . . . He laughed aloud and leaped trepak-style, to land beneath the pinnacle he'd piled for himself, higher than the standard on the tower of the Vexling citadel, just visible, floodlit, above the chimnied buildings to his left.

Sobriety returned. Self-mockingly he adjusted his expression, felt for the Mettlinger in his pocket, then struck off to the right through a long covert, or passage-way debouching on to another, larger courtyard reached by a dozen stone steps which brought him level with the Second Ramparts. He bowed facetiously to the statues of old Poldavian dignitaries lining his route, until there, barring his way, was a wall so deep it held small lock-ups, shuttered shops that once had been the quarters of bored leathercoats, tired of standing watch against an enemy that never, ever appeared.

A turn to the right brought him parallel to the wall which he followed for a hundred yards or so as far as the 'great obstacle to freedom', the Prem Panopticon. Redundant for defence from the day of completion this massive bastille had found employment at last as a prison, a circular gaol on six floors with cells on each. In the centre a great circular void had been capped for mercy's sake to keep the wretched inmates from winter's bitterness.

Poldavia was proud of its prison, sneered at the Englishman's effort to create a poor replica in London. Wasn't a bit surprised when they pulled it down. No one would dream of turning the Panopticon into an art gallery.

As in fairy tales, all doors opened to Saachik. No, he did not wish for coffee. No, he did not wish the prisoner to be brought to the more comfortable annexe. Nor did he need the lift, preferred to climb the hewn steps of the old stairway to the third level, only accepting the key of the door leading to it.

The cells themselves had no doors; there was no privacy anyway, however much one ignored the revolving closed circuit TV screens centred on a shaft running from top to bottom of the edifice. By convention, one did not gaze idly into any but the cell to be visited. Prisoners were free to wander into each other's quarters.

Votschinski could never pass for a Poldavian. He had the barren, brutal cast of feature common to his ethnic breed. Flat, grey as endless rainswept plains. The slim-line lips and a shifty eye justified his boast. Out of forty years, ten inside and ten on the run.

He just about noticed Saachik's entrance; returned with studied insolence to his book which the Commissioner snatched and tossed on the bed before straddling a chair at the small deal table between them. Votschinski lounged back, full length, and regarded the ceiling.

'I know all about you,' Saachik confided.

The villain couldn't take his eyes off that bit of ceiling, it was really interesting.

'Fifteen years: armed robbery: no remission.'

And no reaction.

'It's five years since you came in as a political refugee—that's another name for scum. People who can't do it all over their fatherland, they go and try someone else's, eh?'

The ceiling fascinated still.

'Good thing you didn't kill that night-ward. At your trial you said you didn't need to—could have if you'd wanted. I checked on that. Military service and the regimental trophy—for marksmanship. Vanity never lies, eh?'

Perhaps the ceiling wasn't all that attractive.

'Twelve more years to go, Votschinski. How d'you feel about it?'

The gunman lowered his gaze and Saachik noted green eyes—like sour grapes. 'You know I can't handle your crappy language.'

'How about German?'

'Why not? A good, manly tongue.'

'I was saying: twelve years to go. But you'd rather stay—take your punishment, eh?'

'Scheiss!'

'Oh . . . I'm wrong? Apologies, Votschinski.'

'Just state your business. I'm a busy man.'

'It's about watching you walk out of here a free crook, with an exit permit and dollars; not sufficient to fund America's deficit, but enough.'

Votschinski slewed a cautious eye in this genie's direction. Maybe he should rub it up the right way— 'There's gotta to be a catch,' the diplomatic language of scoundrels.

'You're perceptive.'

'Knowing a bit more wouldn't spoil my appetite.'

Saachik spread both hands, all fair and square. What's to hide? 'But first I need to know your mettle; cowards can be a problem. Y'know?'

Votschinski never fell, but he slipped a little under Saachik's charm. Most people did. Not that he was all things to all men but toilsomely he'd acquired that knackish art, talking their language, nuances thrown in, and talking it a little more effectively. So Votschinski smiled, evilly enough to make gorillas flinch.

'Try me,' he invited.

Saachik didn't rush things, gazed steadily at personified villainy for long seconds, weighing it up to a scruple before slowly drawing the Mettlinger from a capacious pocket.

'Double or quits—the gamble that ends all, or begins everything.' He spun the chamber out of Votschinski's ken. 'Your choice.'

The man licked his upper lip, glanced at the revolver, at the sudden prospect of fortune snatched from misfortune, then caught sight of the endlessly circulating camera snooping as it went, not twenty feet away—and nodded.

'Go ahead. The book was boring me anyhow.'

Saachik smiled understandingly, brought the long-barrelled gun—one of the world's most accurate—to the level of Votschinski's forehead. Again, he released the catch, spun the chamber, slapped it back into position, cocked the trigger—re-steadied his aim. Votschinski's eye never blinked. A second away from perdition, he watched that finger gently easing back the trigger.

The report rang echoing round the prison; startled silence gave place to a sustained hubbub through which two men sat in mutual contemplation.

'You missed,' softly, with no tremor.

'Blanks. Six of them,' as softly. 'I couldn't afford to lose you.'

'I know—but blanks was clever. It surprised me.'

'You'll be released tomorrow and brought to my office.'

'And then.'

'Recruitment.'

'For how long?'

'Ten seconds.'

Saachik dismounted abruptly, considered his protégé with pursed lips, then glanced away, reached for the book scattered on the bed and noted the title, *Kickback*. He smiled and deliberately placed it in front of Votschinski who'd scarcely moved throughout.

'As you were,' cryptically. And he was gone.

The 'day' dawned fine and crisp, sky an icy blue heralding snow showers forecast for the evening. A persistent breeze from the northern uplands broke on the rugged citadel and careered down the hill, across the squares, vaulting over the ramparts and on through the narrow bye-ways whipping the shovelled snow-piles into a whirl of dervishes at every corner, harrying the housewives' steps, tearing at their shopping bags and carriers, scurrying the long-coated, fur-hatted government clerks to the shelter of their stuffy offices, scourging the *vochni* into prodigies of sweeping and shovelling. Weather to keep the city on its toes.

Wherever friends and acquaintances met, in steamy coffee-houses, cafés or Schattkammers, the rhetorical question followed hard on the greetings. Rhetorical because, by now, everybody in 'Prem' had heard of 'the posters' if they hadn't seen them. Brief and to the point, they spoke volumes in portent.

'Long live the over-running President!'

The curtailed quote from an opposition deputy's speech two days old was placarded everywhere. Black on white, it said all too clearly: here's the writing on the wall.

What more open challenge to the State by those in sympathy with the Opposition? And in practical terms how much responsibility belonged to the Opposition itself? Partisan or not, anger and fear tempered everyone's thinking. Who could have been so stupid as to compromise the forces of reaction or freedom so thoroughly?

Strangely enough those forces never once suspected Saachik. Why should they?

How could they know a sober-suited business-man went brief-cased the previous evening, to a hostel for the unemployed, recruited fifty men to plaster self-stick 'coupons' in every part of the city between two and four that very morning?

No questions asked when the pay's good.

'But was it wise, Yaroslavl?' Kremp always sounded querulous on the phone. Why-was-I-not-consulted inflections suggested nervous grievance, the politician's occupational disease.

Saachik's faint smile implied all: every man is calibrated by the size and imminence of crunches and crises. But he explained equably enough. 'They committed themselves; they are further committed. Tonight, they may be fortunate not to be committed—for trial—conspiracy to cut off the Head of State.'

Which left the Prime Minister with little to add.

Meantime, one of Saachik's men, skilled in the art of make-up, had given Gorcan the pallor of a dying man in a small, unused room somewhere in the rambling Hospital Academia. The TV team took him to a specially cleared corridor. Lying on a trolley, and draped with a blanket they wheeled him at speed, attended by an orderly supporting a plasma drip, towards a theatre.

Three attempts gave a very professional running shot, panning up to the legend 'Theatre 2' as the assemblage swept through rubberised doors into the pre-op area. The clock above registered 5.14.

Elsewhere Votschinski was being briefed on his part in the affair, learning with undisguised disbelief that it was a 'dry job', no one would get hurt, and he had the gun and the cartridges to prove it.

'I don't understand, but I'm glad,' he seemed very relieved.

'Why?'

'Because if I was really set to kill that guy, how would I live to tell the truth?'

Privately Saachik wondered what difference it could make. A killer indulging in niceties! But he smiled copiously, like a village idiot, as if the point had never occurred to him. Which it hadn't.

Otherwise, he spent the day studying the reports flooding in from his agents as to the signs of disaffection abscessing throughout the city. All he read persuaded him he had the answer.

Butterflies in the stomach! He shrugged off the uncustomary sensation cursing himself for a momentary lapse; now, of all times, to behave like a player! But then, he excused himself, what was the situation but a piece of stagecraft, a one-off performance with a first and last night? And he, one of the actors who struts and frets upon . . .

Why no! He clapped the fur cap jauntily over untidy iron grey hair, scanning the mirror for his true reflection: puppet master extraordinary. Marionettes programmed to perfection; he had only to watch at leisure as they jerked their way through the scenario, be ready to untangle strings at any critical moment.

Just after 4.40 he checked on the President's departure from the Residence. A sleek black Mercedes purrs at the front door. The chauffeur, one of Saachik's men, reports to him by radiophone. Satisfied, he fires last minute instructions at subordinates and leaves the main building to find his car ready to go.

He drove, with his senior agents to where the severely classical Matrinenhalle stood in the third sector midway between the third and fourth circle, a matter of ten minutes as the wheel turns.

Saachik drove. The short journey would be silent. He preferred to drive in silence. The three officers knew what was coming, of course. They were nervous, but dared not show it. Diverted themselves with studying his eccentric approach by an indirect route adding five minutes to the trip, but which brought him, suddenly, behind the presidential cavalcade.

4.55. An exquisite piece of timing.

Night and darkness above; ahead of them the Matrinenhalle, bathed in floodlight, at the end of the link road, one of many 'spokes' intersecting the twelve wheels of Prem-Lusz.

A build of traffic: rush hour thrombosis. The union delegates would have missed the nightly odyssey of a city going home. Sirens and the bright orange threat of the outriders' flashing helmets carved an easeful passage for the man due to die and the one who makes it possible.

Not a bad turn out on a freezing night, after a day's work, but the average Poldavian thinks nothing of taking to the streets for a show: film stars, foreign dignitaries, union men, even the President. No fry too small to attract a few thousands whatever the climate. 'The more hateful the weather, the more lovable the fireside,' proverbially explains much about the divided Poldavian character.

They won't stay long; a rousing cheer for Mr Bigwig and then homeward for the most part. They'll stand, meantime, in patient expectation, blowing on their fingers, thumping their chests, stamping their feet or leaping violently into the air to encourage circulation. Vendors of hot coffee appear as if by magic and do a steaming trade.

But there's somewhat else about this turn-out. Saachik shoulders his way prospectively through the crowd with his aides, makes for a certain lamp standard, one of four ornate beacons fronting the shallow steps rising to the Matrinenhalle. He senses an alien mood among the knots of men and women about him:

conspirators planning a cool reception, mooting a serious demonstration? Nothing violent, of course. The very idea!

Still, something in the air apart from the first drift of nocturnal snowfall. He checks his watch. A minute to go. The President's car approaches the main entrance. Saachik, his eyes on the car, inclines his head leftwards. The agent watching him glances that way and marks Votschinski conspicuously alone by the second bronze standard, as if the bystanders had divined his brand of leprosy and drawn away . . . the agent detaches himself and slides roundabout to Votschinski's rear. Saachik smiles grimly at sight of two men, right hands in their pockets.

Playful or whimsical, in this fraught element, he contemplates the four glass bowls in which the brilliant filaments seem to float in captivity, and muses on all that's confined in something, fish or men, mankind and the greatest globe of all . . . then lowers his gaze to where a small knot of worthies vie to open the big black door and welcome His Excellency. Light from the stroboscopic helmets of the nearest outriders splashes into their eyes, bounces off the Mercedes' high polished blackness, offending the sight of everyone within range.

Saachik squints, an eye to the President, the other on Votschinski. The President alights, the car door slams and the car glides away. Hands are shaken, a thin, ragged cheer struggles into being and grows apace as Gorcan climbs the cascade of steps; applause already, because it moves? Irony or affection?

The sober suited union men follow and, as he reaches the top step they hurry to each side of him, melt into the background leaving him solitary in the limelight to face the clamour of the crowd.

He turns and, explosively, Saachik has a vision of a petrifact trapped in one of those glassy gewgaws which, shaken, pretend animation, snowfall, amusement imprisoned. Frozen, the moment of turning as Gorcan raises his left arm in a clenching salute, and two arms are raised elsewhere; two shots ring out, and two men fall, one in the pose of dying, the other in the throes of death. Five o'clock plus one.

The TV crew sited to the right of the steps catches all. A video-packman ranges over the crowd and gets the proof Saachik needs.

Poldavia first, and then the rest of the world; an electronic drama played out in seconds.

There's the agent, gun in hand, already straddling the splayed out, played out leftovers of Votschinski, the would-be assassin. Alive—what a tale he'd have had to tell!

And the would-be victim? He too is seen to fall by the crowd and the box-watchers, who accept with less than Saachik's critical eye the manner of his going. The puppet-master finds time to wince at the disjointed performance of a very wooden actor.

It isn't Gorcan's fault. He was never shot before, so he goes through a pack of motions; claps his hand mightily to his chest, produces a satisfying spurt of blood, but the damned fool takes his hand away, *still standing*, as if to show crowd and camera what a hole it made! And he staggers, yes, staggers, in a small circle to start with, then backwards, facing the camera, ever backwards, an expression of intense agony increasingly distorting his features to the point of absurdity. The shot, tired of waiting, seems to zoom in to finish him off, showed clearly, in close-up, his eye roving about to see who means to break his fall as two or three of the shocked unionists rush to his aid. One of Saachik's men gets there first, almost pushing him to the ground, but inexplicably collapsing under all fifteen stone of the 'stricken president'. Saachik curses and giggles at the deadly earnestness of farce as he bounds up the steps to mask the feast from a ravenous camera.

'Shut your eyes!' he hisses at the dying man.

'Did I do well?' A new Roscius! Caring more for tomorrow's drama reviews than for playing a false note in history's partita.

Cutting into the scene Saachik had the videoman take a close-up of the President before he was carried down to the waiting car. A commentator droned a lurid account of all that the audience could see for itself.

'The chief of security, Yaroslavl Saachik, flings himself into the driving seat, a monument of calm in the total confusion, he wipes blood from his hand as the stricken President reclines between two officials in the rear seat, and the car gathers speed, racing against time, drives out of this spectacular moment in Poldavian history.'

Some of the crowd dispersed to cafés or Schattkammers to mourn or celebrate what looked like the careless loss of their president. The rest hurried home to look for themselves on the replay.

The Trades Unions delegates opened their Congress in the Matrinenhalle bar and dared not leave it till they'd fully discussed this uncalled-for interruption in their affairs.

On TV, between the action, well briefed anchormen floated possibilities that certain opposition party members had maybe washed their hands in the sink of iniquity . . .

While Gorcan, listening complacently to the radio reports of his 'critical condition', goes by a roundabout route to the rear of his palace stronghold, an identical car, with four identically dressed 'shadows', screeches to a halt before the hospital's portico, not three hundred yards away. Doctors and orderlies are on hand to take 'all that remains of our cherished leader, Gorcan' post-haste to surgery.

No close film work here—just a medium shot of some body being tenderly lifted on to what the Yankees call the 'crashcart'.

Impeccable timing! But hadn't Saachik himself written the small print of a brilliant scenario?

Thirty seconds later agog viewers *saw* their president momentarily filling the screen, deathly pale, hurtling towards the theatre. Well, that had to be veritable did it not? There were the words above the door: Theatre 2. The clock above registered 5.12 . . .

Yesterday . . . today. More or less.

The camera crew had time for cigarettes before trooping in to record an operation.

Historical histrionics. Never before, on TV, have so many seen so little of the Head of State, draped, as he is, in greenery, a mere square foot of his chest visible *after* retraction. Before that, the tensed viewers saw only masks, eyes, slapping of instruments into rubberised hands, the hiss of suction apparatus, the fine tuning of anaesthetic paraphernalia and all the rest.

At which time, in the comfortable atmosphere of a below stairs ante-room in the presidential palace, Saachik and Kremp are celebrating success in bumpers of the national beverage.

'Brilliant, Saachik, superb!' Kremp is in a rare state of ecstasy, inflamed by the colourless 'firespit' only Poldavians dare to drink.

The Security chief lounged before a TV console, glass in hand, searching for the corniest cliché available. His sense of humour was too strong to allow him any but a contemptuous view of the situation.

'We are not yet out of the wood, my friend,' plangent as a tocsin.

'Eh? What d'you mean?' Kremp's nervous system depended on oiled wheels and built-in majorities.

Saachik waves his empty glass at the screen. 'The patient could die on the operating table.'

The startled reaction gave way to a sickly smile. 'Your little joke. For a moment I believed His Excellency was on that table.'

'No, Lawzlau. He is presently on television. What an artist is Glawitz. Such dexterity.'

'And you are a master-builder, Yaroslavl.'

Saachik shrugged, not shifting his attention from the coloured square. 'Of what, after all, but a house of cards?'

'To save the constitution is something more,' the PM had no doubts.

'Perhaps. You do not watch?'

'Operations make me feel uncomfortable. I have the irrational conviction they do not have room to do such things within the confines of an orange crate.'

Saachik smiled. 'But where would we be without this play-pen, this hucksters' Schattkammer, this two foot theatre of the ludicrous?'

'Not to be underestimated.'

A finger stabbed at the screen. 'QED! There's no better anaesthetic.'

'Local.'

'Of course. It leaves one free to do everything but think? Long may it never end.'

'You know,' the Prime Minister had found a more congenial point of focus in the rare Ambrosiano on the wall before him, 'I see this developing into a long-running saga, like the English "Fornication Street".'

'Coronation Street,' Saachik corrected. 'Let's hope not. I have heard it is full of people who die or go peculiar.'

'Ah—Coronation Street. I had some idea that was a video nasty.'

'No—it is not video.'

'Even so. Could we not develop the humanitarian theme? A glimpse of our recovered President, in his would-be assassin's cell, pronouncing forgiveness?'

'His would-be assassin is dead,' dryly.

'It could be anyone, seen from behind,' the PM argued.

'That's ... true.' Even as he watched, Saachik's agile mind paltered with the possibility.

Kremp refilled his glass and wandered away to a resumed

contemplation of the Ambrosiano. It felt good to be warm, even to be slightly drunk enough to feel free for a while from cares of State. He let his thoughts sink into the folds of that rich blue robe . . .

Minutes later he was startled from reverie by six resounding shots, by Saachik clapping his hands.

'Bravo! What sleight of hand! Glawitz has "extracted" the bullet.'

Kremp was in time to see an assistant holding the bloodied piece of metal for the camera's inspection.

'Ware wolf!' with feeling he breathed aloud the national motto; official declaration of defiance and triumph against the odds.

More time passed, more rapt contemplation of The Lady on the Rocks, before Glawitz pronounced to the world:

'Poldavia may breathe again.'

An affecting moment. Almost audible, the collective sough of relief; whatever dissensions existed now had nowhere to go but down—underground. Poldavia had found unity in a beautifully orchestrated moment of crisis.

Audible almost as another, distant sound hardly denting the room's essential silence. Kremp registered the possibility, then dismissed it.

But, minutes later, a palace servant hammered at the door and burst in so violently as to bring the two to their feet.

'Prime Minister! His Excellency has been shot!'

An excitable young man. Such a sensitive face. Kremp was about to reassure him but Saachik snapped: 'Of course, idiot! You saw it on television.'

'I don't know what I saw on the television. All I know is, the President's dead!'

'Yes. Quite right. You're upset, that's very natural and loyal,' as a Cabinet man Kremp knew how to soothe wounded sensibilities. 'But the President will live—the bullet is *kafuch*. No more bullet, eh?'

And he actually winked at the astonished flunkey who gaped with excruciating vulgarity from one to the other.

'I—I don't understand. I—I followed a long trail of blood on the corridor carpet and—and at the end of it was the President.'

'The President is alive and out of danger, nitwitissimus! Now go about your business.'

'But all that blood on the carpet! How can he be—?'

'Furg off!'

Whatever the circumstances, no self-respecting Poldavian would remain in the same room with such an obscenity. Urgently as he felt the need to argue, the servant caught Saachik's glare full frontal, bethought himself of discretion, valour and such-like, and went.

Two minutes of ambiguous silence followed. Kremp, a prey to ill-defined misgivings, ventured a few words. 'I suppose His Excellency heeded your instructions not to let himself be seen up there?'

'He gave most of the staff tickets for the Prem-Lusz/Sheffield Wednesday European Cupwinners Milk Mug first leg qualifying football match.'

'But that's tomorrow!'

Saachik closed his eyes, searching the darkness for patience. 'Then he most likely gave them this evening off too.'

Another minute, another misgiving.

'Yaroslavl, why should there be blood on the carpet?'

'I don't *know*! And it's time I was off.'

'I can't stop thinking about what I heard a little while ago.'

Saachik's fit of exasperation brought him face to face with his companion. He put a forefinger to Kremp's cheek and gently pulled the flesh downward.

'As I thought, friend. Your cornea is steeped in alcohol. Go home and sleep. Poldavia will be safe for the night . . .' his mocking smile faded as he gazed into the PM's eyes, misliking what he saw. 'Blood . . . on the carpet?'

Kremp nodded. 'The President—at one end.' Hoarsely.

No more words, only doubts and action enough to dispel them. Saachik was out of the room before Kremp could rouse himself sufficiently to scurry after. He glimpsed the tall striding figure at the end of a long, curving corridor, reached it breathlessly to catch sight of the last of him taking a narrow flight of communicating stairs by storm, panted on and up, hearing Saachik's resounding threats and flung commands: 'Everybody under arrest! Stay where you are! No one to leave the citadel!'

Struggling for air, drowning in dismay, Kremp rounded the stair-landing to come on another long and impressive panelled gallery. He checked from sheer exhaustion and shocked disbelief.

Sprawled by a small, overturned table was the unmistakable body of Dezhni Gorcan, sometime President of Poldavia. Saachik nearby, seemed to be thrusting a servant through the wall. The wretched man scarcely had breath to babble incoherently.

As in a dream the Prime Minister took his first decisive step on the down fall.

'What happened?' he whispered, then louder, to quell an uprise of hysteria. 'What happened!'

Saachik unpinned, as it were, the poor devil held in his hand, watched him sag under a weight of terror before turning to Kremp with a chilling expression of baffled fury. 'The house of cards!' he bellowed. 'You forgot the joker!'

Again Kremp stared down at the recumbency, patiently, as if waiting for it to get up. After all, it had done so once before . . . at the same time he wondered vaguely who could be murmuring in feminine-sounding tones:

'True, Saachik. But it doesn't pay to forget the Queen of Spades either.'

Bizarre, the conversation that followed. They watched, utterly confounded, as the Smile, tainted by that strange configuration of the lips, advanced towards them, the gun curiously held in her hand, while she waved dismissal with the other to the snivelling menial. At close quarters Saachik saw the Smile for what it was: menacing repugnance. The eyes were dead.

Saachik, casting around for possibilities, eyed the Mettlinger and weighed its potential—in her hands. He doubted Kremp saw the extent of their predicament. For his part, he had imagination enough to relish some of the unforeseen situation, however regrettable.

'You said nothing about aces, Madam.'

'I hold them.' Could such smiling simplicity be natural? The voice was hollow enough, dank as a dungeon, and he realised he'd not heard her utter so many words before this rencounter. Perhaps she divined his thoughts.

'Thirty years, Saachik, ever since you were a scruffy adolescent. Thirty years as the shadow of—what?' she stared with evident curiosity at whatever lay at her feet. 'The youngest Leader in our history—well no, there *was* the Cardinal Archduke centuries ago—a mere infant—another creation.

'The obituaries will be kind, no doubt. A devoted Servant of the State for all his faults. We know the recipe. As our proverb goes:

the higher the meat, the more piquant the sauce. But there's no relish could satisfy me, because, you see, I know the man. Shadows go everywhere and observe all. Infidelity? That's nothing. But to be relegated, regarded as a mere appendage unfitted to hold the least opinion in matters that concerned *me* as much as the lowest drab . . .

'So I listened, and I learned, I held my tongue, and I smiled. I lived up to his low expectations and suffered you all to tolerate my insipid presence, you never suspecting *I* was the one who suffered at your endless functions, occasions, congresses and what not else. Sheer, undiluted, deadly boredom.

'But—I listened, and I learned, I prayed like a mantis . . . and I waited. Until tonight, when that fool returned and laughed outright at his cleverness, which was your cleverness, Saachik, I never doubted that. Then I knew my time had come.'

'*When* did he tell you?'

'Ah!' she considered him briefly, speculatively, like a Black Widow spider troubled by pangs of hunger. 'You recognise how crucial timing can be in the print-out of destinies. Yes, he told me after I learned from the television that my husband was at death's door.

'What, gentlemen, do *you* imagine I saw striding into my sitting-room an hour or so ago? What was I to think of a man who considers his lifetime's partner so negligible that he breathes no word of his impending death? *Which* was my husband? The square of carefully butchered flesh on a TV screen, or this hearty stranger who, I'd been persuaded to believe, couldn't conceivably be the man I'd lived so unobtrusively for.

'I listened, as he chuckled and boasted of the part he'd played, until I could listen no more. I wanted no part of the phantom returned from the dead, no part of the actor playing my husband's role to my face—and playing it badly. So I shot them both—'

'Do you—do you have any idea, any *idea* what you have done!'

Saachik winced visibly at Kremp's singular lack of control. The situation was fraught, agreed, but to be fraught oneself—neither elegant as to bearing, nor forgivable as to a lapse of good breeding. And his training reminded him: one learns more by keeping silence.

Madam Gorcan considered the outburst. 'What's done isn't as important as finishing what's begun. We have a new situation,

gentlemen, which inevitably means redundancies. I have tele-
phoned the security guards at the main gates. Surrender?'

She handed the revolver held oddly by the barrel in the crook of
her thumb and forefinger, to the nonplussed Prime Minister.
Saachik caught his breath sharply, involuntarily. At which she
smiled, even more enigmatically, if that were possible. Kremp
stared stupidly at the weapon in his hand, trying hard to comprehend a fait accompli.

'It's perfectly clear, Kremp.'

Certainly to Saachik, perfectly, crystal clear. He watched two of
his best agents move into view, guns in hands, professionalism in
their features.

'Prime Minister Kremp, I accuse you of the wilful murder of
Dezhi Gorcan, of complicity in an evidential plot to establish
Yaroslavl Saachik as President of Poldavia . . . or words to that
effect. Please take these men away, and have that removed as soon
as possible.'

'What do you propose to—But this is preposterous! The
evidence—'

'Is in your hand, Kremp—is at your feet, Saachik . . . had it been
televised of course, things might have been more difficult.'

'And you, Madam Gorcan?' Cool as ever, curious as ever, the
former Security Commissioner could still wonder mightily at the
denouement.

'Dead men tell no tales,' ominously. 'This one lied—but what
he tells Poldavia from now till the obsequies, is the truth.
Goodnight, gentlemen.'

A brusque jerk of the head from one of his most trusted
henchmen prompted Saachik's wryest smile, as he turned to go.
Crystal, pistol clear the denouement.

'Farewell, Your Excellency.'

And that, dear reader, is how Poldavia acquired the first lady
President in its long and uneventful history. Her opponents are
beaten for the day, but not despairing for the morrow. She is no
more than fifty-three and may yet do a great deal of the kind of
damage that only men can *un*do. So they tap their thumbnails in
unison with the popular acclamations and whisper the new refrain
as they drive over the gratings covering Prem's excellent sewage
system:

'Long live Her Excellency, the saviour of Poldavia, but—'

# A WESTERN

'Oh Mary Lou, I never knoo,
How much to fall in lerv with yoo,
Till th'day ah found you layin' in mah arms
Then I knoo ah had it comin' to me.'

TAKE IT EASY, folks, the singer and the song both is pure
colouration, though likewise it behoves me tell you plain out, if
you ain't rodeo, wagon-wheel, sapodilla, sage-brush-minded, this
here yarn ain't for you.

Now there go I misnomerin'! Ain't no yarn; leastways, it's like
I'm tellin' you gospel true, not as to Mary Lou up above—that's
good old, brand new Country 'n'Western to kinda specificate the
flavah—

It's no earthly use; I simply don't flair to that kind of junk jargon.

To begin purely, my informant said: I know you'll be fascinated.
This is a true story—might have some ephemeral interest like
Romeo and Juliet or—or Bonnie and Clyde or—

If we're into ephemera, how about Pelleas and Melisande, or
Waring and Gillow? I wondered. My irony chastened but did not
suppress enthusiasm. Volatile, this friend who firmly believes I
need a constant stock of 'ideas' for my magazine stories, most of
which are published in other lands. Once more he'd saddled me
with an outline, seriously self-persuaded I could bracket a fragment
of twentieth-century love lore with the greats—as if the stars need
tinsel for company.

He almost persuaded me but, as usual, and after I'd made it clear
our prosaic times pitch no higher than Frankie and Johnny level, I
did condescend to show some interest in what little he had to tell.

Impressed against my will, but not overly so, I promised to think
about it, and, in time, I checked on the essentials, to find that my
wildly imaginative informant had, for once, spoken truth. Frankie,
for so I shall represent him in due course, and Belle, for so I shall
recall her, really did exist. They all did . . .

And the more I learned—but that's to anticipate the nub and the story; so I gladly begin afresh, leaving the sad vernacular where it belongs: with those gentle pathetics of the Bar J ranch who seemed uncannily to know how best to handle it.

Desmond Mongan lived on a council estate at the raggedest edge of a northern town that had lost its character after a passionate affair with the Industrial Revolution. The plain wanton of the past had degenerated to the present drab bristling with TV aerials, like sluts' curlers, in its outdoor hair. I don't pretend to know what that would mean to a lot of people who'd prefer to avert their eyes when motoring or blundering on foot and by chance through a council housing estate cobbled together in the Sans Souci Sixties; but I have a fair idea how 32 Silverside Avenue affected Mongan who was born there, grew up there, schooled from there till fifth grade and seldom left the environs except for a package of Costa Brava with his folks. He was certainly there till not so long ago.

I'm not sure I enjoy describing the lad as he appeared to the world at large. Strange, how illiterate people become when one begs for a third party thumbnail sketch: 'oh well, y'know, he was kind of . . .' with an effort one somehow gathers enough impressions to fill the passport page. Height, five nine, brown hair, birth mark, left cheek, prominent. Eyes, grey. An exciting sea colour in some, hardening wet cement in others. Weeds straggle in poor soil, but let's say Mongan is slightly built; facially he had the kind of features studiously ignored by the better class of adjectives, excepting that perpetual slide about the eyes and the tongue forever oiling the mean line above an economy-sized nether lip. His is not the stuff of which characters are built.

They say he hated football at school, but remembered how compulsively he kicked stones or litter along the dismal streets of his neighbourhood. Coped with school itself by practising the difficult art of immaterialisation. Somehow, even when a frustrated maths teacher flung chalk at him, he was never there. He effaced himself so habitually his parents couldn't always be sure he was home or even in the same room.

At seventeen he tried a disco, and never tried again. He joined a youth social club and resigned in sheer disgust when he found one was supposed to talk—and even discuss things.

He seldom talked. At mealtimes the Mongans had long given up trying to draw him out on the day's petty happenings, were vaguely surprised and highly flattered if he said 'thanks' or 'got any pepper?'. Father Mongan distinctly remembered him asking that once.

'What *did* he do then?'

'Not much. Watched television mostly.'

'In a world of his own,' his mother said, briefly coming out of hers.

I had taken the trouble to see these people, just long enough to grasp their life-style. They had none and I left with an impression of a carefully programmed Neanderthal married to an unshapely pile of women's magazines. There could be no scintillating exchange of words, ideas, with such a cast, in such a setting.

In a world of his own.

That came later. Until then, Mongan made do with the one he'd found to hand. It was sterile, static; contained little to fire enthusiasm or sustain even an unhealthy desire. Not so much a world, as a bubble too strong to burst, too transparent to conceal the daily panorama of a concrete crapscape littered with plastic, take-away containers.

Perhaps I do him an injustice. In a hostile world, most people take up a defensive position. Perhaps he'd cultivated a head down self-containment against pervading mediocrity but lacked intelligence not to fall into an obvious trap. Smothered his existence to become the nonentity that droops best from a standard of living.

He did, apparently, make one joke in his life and it may hint at lost opportunity or simply rate as a verdict. A schoolfellow asked if his Mum went to work. 'No,' he'd replied. 'She's on the streets.' The other boy looked shocked and delighted. 'Coronation Street, Mondays and Wednesdays,' Mongan explained. That he volunteered this without a smile adds a little more to nothing very much.

At twenty-two then, life looked set fair to pass him by. His parents, who'd never really started on their child, gave up on him and concentrated on his far livelier elder brother, presently thriving in the RAF and already a pretty senior technician. Father Mongan believed in technology. 'It jumps out at you all over their house,' a neighbour confided, half enviously, half head-tappingly. 'Mongan's always whirring away with some bloody gadget in his garage.'

So Mongan Jnr shared his spare time with the TV, an occasional

Saturday cinema and, for a while, with another spiritually underfed lad, 'Merry' Ellis. 'Merry' he'd earned for looking so downright miserable. He had the same starved-of-life look as Mongan, was shorter, more hunched, even against a bitter wind that never blew, and definitely less inclined to meet the world's eye.

They would go for walks together into the country most weekends; but they scarcely talked, just walked until one or other spat and said: 'That's ebloodynough,' and they'd return by the same route, shuffling over the Corporation rubbish tip, buying chips in the Wallsend Road takeaway to revive flagging energy. They never supported the local football team and that kept them outcast to their contemporaries.

The two young lads worked on the same premises: a double-fronted DIY shop in the lower High Street. It throve mightily, was never less than busy, with so many know-alls thinking they could better the regular builders and decorators, especially with half the council houses newly bought. A lot to buy. A lot to do. Even more to put right.

Wallinsey's only DIY was a suckers' gold-mine—the kind where they put gold back.

As a matter of course Mongan and 'Merry' would take their lunch break together: coffee or coke and a wadge at Flo's Eatery. They'd munch stolidly with heads down over the *Daily Mirror*, or just smoke and watch the queue shuffling by until Merry would mention: 'It's abloodybout time we was went.' And they'd go.

They never once, in eighteen months, so much as discussed the weather. I particularly asked Ellis about that. 'What was there to discuss? It's either bloody rainin' or it didn't and what's weather forecasts for then?'

Came the day when Ellis quite suddenly disappeared. That's to say, he went home in the evening and next morning he failed to show up for his share of the day's toil. Fat Harry, the boss, was furious. 'What's he wanna do that for?' And sacked Merry on the spot where he should have been standing.

No one bothered to enquire after the lad's health or well-being. Mongan certainly didn't raise the question and went through the day counting out screws or cutting hardboard without a thought for his friend and colleague of a year and more. Took his lunch-break alone and went expressionless through a cheese wadge as if Merry had never been.

'Merry not in today then?' Edna behind the counter called as he was leaving.

'He's dead,' Mongan explained, in a rare burst of converse, and left it at that.

A solitary is one thing, but one who goes through the motions of living is very nearly untouchable. To say that he got through the working day, helped to put the pavement 'eye-catchers' to bed for the night, left the premises without 'goodnight and sweet dreams' to Fat Harry, walked home, hands pocketed, eyes to the pavement, kicking at whatever came to foot, let himself in, sat watching TV before supper, did the same after supper, then went to bed, is not exactly to describe a day in the life of Ivan Denisovitch and may even beg the vulgar question: so what?

A sociologist might well find a clue here in Mongan as to the quality of life in this kind of town, this breed of people, at the backend of a dismally failed century. In a word, we have ridden into the badlands of apathy and indifference born of materialism carried to the extremes of self abuse.

So, Merry is dead, or he's sacked. What difference? And a Mongan, encouraged to believe in nothing that he can't see with square eyes, would not enquire for Ellis, would not seek his address, would certainly not buy a wreath or attend the funeral if he *were* dead.

He still took his Saturday walks over the rubbish tips and not too far away. Shambled home mouthing his paper of chips with vinegar-flavoured lack-lustre, no trace of enjoyment, of anything.

Three months more of this mercifully ends an episode. Memoirs of a Provincial would be racier. A Dumas, given such ingredients for a surging tale of adventure, must surely have preferred *felo de se*.

A young man for a hero who does nothing, says nothing, *is* nothing! 'Why,' to put famous last words into Dumas' mouth, 'should imagination boggle unless it has *some*thing to boggle *at*?'

Two events befell, repriefing Mongan from total oblivion, though it was breathtakingly close. They were, literature—to belabour that unhappy term—and a coincidence.

One Saturday evening, his parents chancing to be away for a wedding in which he had not the slightest interest, even though it did belong to his maternal grandmother, Mongan found himself alone in the house with a disquieting fact. For some reason the whole TV network blacked out, quite suddenly. A lightning strike, the viewing card said. If it struck that quickly, he reasoned, it could be over twice as fast. So he sat and watched with the total absorption of one who is easily satisfied. After half an hour the viewing card began to pall; he turned the thing off and studied the blank screen for a change. Eventually he switched on, presumably to see if there was anything he'd missed on the viewing card, but it did very little, if anything, for him. Switching off yet again he went into the kitchen for a coke, returned, laced it with the paternal rum, and settled back to endure the accusing silence of his own company.

A sprawling solitary in a waiting-room, shifting from buttock to buttock as the quartz clock pointed but said nothing. Another cigarette, a few more sips of the rum coke, tongue in constant motion, eyes sliding over a roomful of familiar objects but always reverting to that frightening blank screen that wouldn't say or show anything.

He was thinking of trying once more, or activating the stereo cassette for a bit of noise, when his eye chanced on the aforementioned scrap of literature.

Under his father's chair (a Swedish *Kunnigstol* with a mini-computer in the upholstery which could calculate 48 interparamatic positions, but not the near horizontal 49th on which it was presently stuck, so the chair all but filled the area before the Astro Intergalactic Space heater) was a tattered paperback with a cover bright enough to stir Mongan's satiable curiosity, and he actually got down on his knees to recover it.

A workmate had lent his father a Western, three months ago. *The Fall of the Ranch of Ussher.* Father Mongan was very nearly into the last chapter.

His son stared at the illustration: a beefy cattleman wearing what might have been deerskin pyjamas clutched a half-wrapped female in his arms. She didn't look particularly cold, perhaps because the ranch was burning merry-hellishly in the background. Young Mongan glanced at the last page, then at the middle and, for some inexplicable reason he flipped to the beginning.

He went so far as to read the first paragraphs:

'Way up on the battlement brink of the mesa Hank Ussher sat like a king enthroned on horseflesh. Steel blue eyes ranged the far horizon looking for those centaur silhouettes that could spell a whole lot of trouble, even for a Winchester man. The writ still

didn't run this way, nor the Flag. Apaches laugh at flags. Hadn't he
heard tell how they once captured Old Glory and let their squaws
make skirts and such? He shuddered at what he'd heard . . . but,
down there was Eden with a chance. He could trace the silver
ribbon of river all the way through with the green creeping away on
the low left bank to make pastures and promises. This is the land
and the land is good. Cattle country.

'Hank breathed deeply on the sage-brush scented air and
echoed the promise in his heart.

'This land is good, and this land is mine.'

School had cured Mongan of books. He'd resented being dealt a
volume and an injunction: this is marvellous, read it, then write an
essay explaining why I think it's marvellous.

But here, all suddenly, manna in the wordless wilderness. Alleg-
ory may light on the unlikeliest subject: a no-count, two-bit
creature, dressed in subcultural rags, jeans and sweatshirt, stumbling on a book dropped from the hand of boredom. Because it's
there, because there's nothing else, because he has dim recollec-
tions of words and meanings and long, long sequences, he picks it
up and begins slowly to turn into something else.

Truly, and inescapably, in the beginning is the Word: Way up on
the battlement brink of the mesa . . .

It takes time. Out in any kind of wilderness, the ignoble savage
will circle a find with suspicion. He'll go miles off and return
because he forgot to be curious. He may finger it once, abandon it
twice, and still come back to make trial, hunker down and open it
. . . back page, middle, and thence to a beginning.

So it was with Mongan. In that technological wilderness called
'home' he padded round the flimsy, cast it aside, went to the sterile
Superfit kitchen to fix supper. Ham n'eggs. Coffee and an
unfamiliar far away look in habitually non-conductive eyes. Aware
or not, he'd laid the sense of that paragraph to his heart. From first
munch to last sip the forlorn was out and away up there on the
mesa's edge.

Not that he had a clue what a mesa could be. And what kind of a
throne gets made of horseflesh? But something rare had percolated
and he sipped therefrom not recking of the grounds.

A personal dance of Destiny? High words for low fellows unless
the truth be for all! Mongan, dance, destiny? What *is* he on about?

About the back and forth of a mind accidentally stirred. And a return to that dreadful sitting-room filled with stereo, transistor, video and unplayed computer games, TV, Astro Space heater, *Kunnigstol* on the blink, paddywhack furniture—and the pulp literature laid on Mum's comfort bag, a glorified sack of beans guaranteed to take anybody's shape however grotesque.

He eyed the cover picture hopefully, but it didn't move, so he switched on the TV. Saturday night, and Dracula still on strike! It was a national disaster. He turned off the offending instrument, flopped into an armchair and, five minutes later, surprised himself still clutching the paperback. He took another look, after glancing around as if he were performing the improper. Re-read the opening paragraph twice, then ventured down off the mesa for the space of a page or two before laying, not flinging it aside with a single expletive. Crap!

Another drink—less coke, more rum—a restless wander about the house, which didn't take hours, then back to his chair and a studious disregard for the *Fall of the Ranch of Ussher*.

Time passed, but not the questions, those unbidden queries he couldn't answer. Were the Apaches far away? Did *they* burn down the ranch? And where did the girl spring from?

Curiosity. Life's mainspring.

Late that evening Mongan read a whole chapter and went thoughtlessly to bed.

So much for the literature: time for the coincidence.

Nothing appeared to have changed in the intervening week. To talk of life going on in the same old way is old fashioned dynamics. The wastelands soggy with affluence, are the marshlands—and there's no 'going on' in a bog. At best, it heaves a little, a bubble may extravagate and even burst. It's the bursting bubble from the lower depths that makes society's headlines . . .

Therefore, a Mongan quits his bed, prepares to leave the house, pours milk on his cornflakes, slouches to Fat Harry's DIY, opens up, puts out the pavement display, and waits for the mugs to arrive. Lunch-break, more till-bashing and home again. Supper. The telly.

Nothing changed?

In one enormous, tiny respect, yes.

Mongan recovers the book, palms it elaborately, unseen, which is highly likely in that dense jungle, and retires to the bathroom to read another chapter in comfort. So much defiance of a non-existent taboo.

Who would notice if he came down patting his hair and sat around in a skirt and blouse reading *Emma*?

By Saturday the book is read from cover to cover. By then he knew all the answers, by then he'd sidled into the local library, found a dictionary and located the exact meaning of mesa, Spanish and all.

There was a wise man once who skirled his sadness thus: everybody hears, right enough, no one listens; everyone looks, right enough, no one sees.

True. The Mongans might look at their boy, but that's a matter of optics. Had they been ten times less indifferent they might have remarked a change, that new-come faraway look in the eye, less evidence of a slop-cloth tongue, more of a gait, less of a slouch and little kicking of doubtful objects along the pavement.

Otherwise, a surly sameness, to parents, customers—and the girl in Flo's Eatery . . . her spectacles narked him. Girls shouldn't wear those things. Should be naked from the neck up like Nature intended.

Nobody continued to get change out of Mongan so, no apparent change.

Till Saturday.

And therein, on a cold and wintry afternoon, high on the battlement brink of the Corporation rubbish tip, a lone figure peers down the long, long ribbon of Wallinsey High Street reaching all the way to the abandoned gas-works; absorbed in a Lowry view of the world. Keen grey eyes seeking for a sign or two of the new world swimming hazily into his ken. He waited, but nobody on a mustang came war-whooping down the far slopes of Connondale, the hill sheltering the north-eastern bit of town from the mine on t'other side . . . not a saloon to be seen . . . only a mucky old character nearby turning over last week's refuse, poking his stick into bloating black plastic bags: a scavenger at bayonet practice, disembowelling foul decay for a pastime.

Mongan watched and softly cursed the ancient for a rat in man's clothing. Notable. Time was, a week ago, he'd have ignored, turned, slithered down with eyes only for his path.

Now, he came down from the mesa following the ancient Indian trail that led to the river below. Above the grey scud of clouds hides a fierce golden ball the Piegans call Ember till Darkness, for who knows if it will rekindle and return? But it no longer beats down on the solitary traveller new come to the territory of the Yumas. There's water at last to drown a long thirst; but, as he turned out of the rock stacks forming a tiny canyon, Hank Ussher . . .

As he turned the corner of Arkwright Street into the downmarket end of that endless High Street, the day-dreamer caught at an impression: familiar, that figure loping ahead, as fast as a bulky maroon hold-all would allow.

Mongan followed casually, not too concerned if he lost him in the Saturday crowd of shoppers. But he did pass the takeaway shop, too thirsty to care about chips, which meant salt and more thirst.

He caught up with Merry Ellis at the traffic lights.

'How do, Scout.'

Ellis leapt like guilt itself, turned a startled face to Mongan and then relaxed. He even smiled.

'Howdy,' he said, and they crossed the road to the tune of a hundred bleeps, which gave Mongan time to reflect how Ussher almost always greeted folks that way, but Merry never had.

'Goin' abroad then?' he nudged the hold-all.

Ellis looked furtive at that. 'Jus' goin' to Flo's for a wet,' he obliged.

'You'd need it, 'umping that lot around.'

Ellis made no reply, gave no invitation. Mongan kept company for something to do and because he did wonder vaguely what Merry was up to in general.

The girl, Edna, was off-duty. Her mother ran the place on Saturdays. Sour faced she served their coffees and otherwise ignored them, even when Merry asked: 'Edna about?'

''Aven't a clue.' Tight-lipped.

They settled in a stall for four, lit cigarettes and eased themselves around in search of maximum lounging comfort.

After a silence: 'What d'you call me "Scout" for?'

'I dunno. Manner of speakin' I s'pose.'

Another silence.

'Fat Harry's still sore about you flittin'.'

'Missin' me blue eyes I shouldn't wonder.'

'He'd poke 'em out soon as look at 'em.'

'Too bad. Couldn't work me notice out, 'ad this cush goin' for me, see?'

'What's that then?'

'Job trainin' scheme. Money for jam. I'm learnin' to be a phucking butler.'

A *long* pause. 'What's that then?'

'I commute to Manchester and pass the salver round. Home every weekend. Exes in advance—I'm feathered.'

'What's a butler?' Mongan persisted.

'Who cares a—? the gaffer says, Just remember, lads, if you're working for the filthy rich you're bound to dirty y'dickey sooner or later aren't yer? I've got that written up over me bed.'

'Goin' back there now?' Mongan nodded at the travelling bag. Again that sheepish, caught out look. A butler! With that fugitive visage!

'I told yer. Weekends off. That's somethin' different.'

*C'est* astonishing *vie*. More words presently passed between this pair than had escaped them, outside the course of DIY business, in eighteen months.

Better to string together Merry's spasms of explanation and leave out the intervals of silence or the picture dims to indefinition.

'It's my gear—for tonight like . . . I don't wear it on the streets Saturdays—you wouldn't live . . . y'change when you get to Bar J, all the guys do. Big Jake keeps a room upstairs for changin' . . . there's one in most towns if you're in the know. Very selective . . . if I do me butlin' in Manchester I'll most like join the Bar H Didsbury ranch. One o'the best . . . ridin' lessons—the lot . . .'

The effort had been too much. Merry crooned a snatch of 'Mary Lou' before lapsing into lethargy enough to give Mongan time for thought.

'Y'mean,' he ventured, 'there's places n'things where guys can play at bein' cowboys?'

Merry's sudden dignity was a peculiar thing to behold. He sat up, more or less straight and very nearly looked Mongan in the eye.

'Play! What d'you mean *play*? Listen, you don't horn in on those places for nothing. Like, I don't mean payin'. You gotta *know* things. You practically gotta pass exams. Like I mean, we take it serious. It's top button.'

'Know things . . . what kind of things?' Mongan was breathing tight, unaccountably moved, knocking furiously for entrance. 'Well go on! What kinda things!'

'Take it easy. Er—you gotta know about Injun tribes and their reservations. Scratch Gravel Mountains, Kid Curry and the Great Northern, Pompey's Pillar, the Bonanza Trail, you gotta know Oklahoma is two Choctaw words meanin' Red People, and about Derringers and—'

'And mesas?' Mongan leaped excitedly into this sudden flood of exotica.

'Mesas? Why sure, mesas and the badlands of Dakota and—'

And a whole lot more. As he pushed further West, Merry's character colourised, eased into *alter ego*, shiftiness gone, eyes keen and sunsquint as they ranged over prairies in the mind.

Mongan listened, more than half-rapt, but an eye to the lone rider poised on the tablelands somewhere up above the wheezy coffee urn . . .

'How do I—how d'you get to join?'

Ellis eyed his companion with detachable interest. Started out to say one thing, then changed his mind.

'Man, you don't join *any*thing. You look in for a jar—and the rest is up to you.'

'But how does anyone get to know?'

That seemed a fair question. 'Well, you kinda find out. I got the word about the time I quit Fat Harry's. Maybe a bit before.'

Mongan looked around him, thought about the suppurating sameness of Saturdays, and made a decision.

'You goin' there now?'

'Sure.'

'Can I—all right if I tag along?'

'Why not?'

Tagalong has a baptismal ring, initiatory if not Sitting Bull exactly but, White Man, let's say, on a Mission. Those journeys without return . . . the one Mongan took that rainswept Saturday evening.

Unforgettable, let that not appear in doubt. How could it be otherwise, walking into a world as remote from Silverside Avenue as t'other side of the moon to a horoscope? The time had come for Mongan to live nowhere else; like a discoverer of lost continents who returns but never comes back.

At first sight, just another pub. They'd turned into one of the town's older thoroughfares, ill-lit, malodorous, oblatitious. Then in through the 'public', past a few early regulars, and up a narrow flight of stairs to the meeting room at the far end of a lengthy

passage. Half way along Merry stopped at a door on the left.
Mongan heard voices and giggles; he looked a question.

'It's the changin'-room. Partitioned. Guys one side—gals the
other. Big J runs a strict outfit. I'm gonna change—go in that end
door, get yourself a wet and I'll see yer.'

The door opened suddenly and a tall gangling fellow in high
boots, Stetson, checked shirt, chaps and hip-thumping gun holsters
almost collided with them both. 'Pardon me!' a back-slapping
voice.

'Howdy Kansas! How's Dude City? You jist got back?'

'Tha's right, Laramie. Sick o' bein' homesick. Hear tell the
Doc's soapin' the box t'night.' Mongan almost looked around for
Merry Ellis who'd surely disappeared.

'Most does every night,' with a chuckle. 'Y'know the Doc'.'

The Stetsoned phenomenon dawdled long enough to enjoy
Mongan's open-mouthed admiration. The eyes were frank and
smiling.

'Buddy o' yours, Kansas?'

'Well, we ain't enemies. He's interested.'

'Dandy! Welcome to Bar J, stranger. Hope you stay. Introduce
us later, Kansas.'

Mongan, trance-like, watched and listened and then listened
again as the spurs tringled along the passage-way. He heard the
opening door release a hum of happy talk and moseying music
before it reclosed leaving him desirous of nothing but to follow and
become part of whatever lay beyond.

'He sounded—you both sounded—' he licked both lips, agonising for the right word '—the real McCoy.'

'Yeah. Not bad for an undertaker—not that I should've—'

'Undertaker!'

'Why not? We got a Liberal councillor, Boots the Chemist's
manager, a schoolteacher, all sorts.'

Mongan stared in disbelief. 'For Chrissakes, that's out o'my
class.'

'It'd be out o'mine when I'm a phuckin' butler; but there's none
o' that class distinction crap at Bar J. We're one big happy family
and what's wrong wi' that?

'Look, you go on in and I'll see yuh.'

Is all. The mere opening of a door for the experience of one's
life.

From the moment he stepped into the Bar J Ranch Mongan knew he belonged, and if that smacks of pulp fiction, so be it. A grave is the last niche of all for all; the niche that comes before is variable. To heighten the tone, briefly, Mongan had found his.

A barn-like room over and back of the pub, had once some pretensions to be the town's assembly rooms, but realities killed the pretence. The money ran out and left a drill-hall container starved of panelled walls, Turkey carpets and a fine plaster ceiling.

What Mongan saw was not so much a transformation as a splendidly garish cover-up, and none the less impressive for that. Thirty feet of bar, brass-nailed and cuspidored, ran almost half the length of the room to replicate a 'Wild West' saloon. Authentically, most of the liquor was under the counter—in a shoot-out bottles were often the first casualties.

An incredibly long mirror patterned with old scrolled and gold-embellished advertisements reflected a colourful scene enhanced by the cherry-red wall hangings, the gimbal mounted oil-lamps (converted) and a hundred nailed-up relics of the West as once it was: yellowing Wells-Fargo timesheets, a stark WANTED poster, black on white, Indian blankets, wampum and other artefacts, a 'Breech's Bible' and, for a centre-piece, an enlarged reproduction of William Harnett's 'The Faithful Colt' hung high to spread its nostalgia over all.

Opposing the bar, a pot-bellied stove gave out genuine heat in winter, and sometimes there'd be a gathering of guitars and songsters rehearsing old pioneer favourites and bunk-house bawdy.

Dominant the dense blue smoke of stogies, cheap black cheroots and hand-rolled 'Virginias'.

A way of life, in short, that followed through from wall to wall, and nothing existent beyond, nothing of importance.

Mongan's comatose sensibilities awakened and reeled. No personal experience, no TV spectacular had tested them this far. Unprepared, they were bound to succumb to an intoxicant unforeseen, unheard of. Not surprisingly his courage failed him. Though few of those thronging the bar or lounging at rough deal tables gave him much thought he shrank willy-nilly to the dimensions of an interloper, a tenderfoot out of his element.

Sidled, like an unwanted man, to the far end of the room and a vacant table. Not company, not refreshment, but time he needed to absorb this megakaleidoscopic display slow whirling in a time capsule. Remembrance of old Western films and a snatch of drugstore literature was no preparation for the—reality.

Otherwheres the dream world, but not here. Mongan touched, with a neophyte's conviction, the meaning of life through a kind of faith. The very sawdust at his feet promised its fulfilment.

Mongan had fallen in love.

He gazed around with an old echo translating through his blurry consciousness: this place is good. And this place is mine.

Gazed at the three girls with pompadour hairstyles and dresses to match, laughing behind the bar, at the waiter with black-oiled locks and a white ankle-length apron. Cowpunchers, ranch hands, Confederate troops, teamsters and a rustler or two, lounging contentedly over rye whiskies, beers or just plain cokes, the smell of leather gear, the clink of spurs, Single-six guns lazing in low-slung holsters, converse Western-style, and girls in flounce and furbelow; nearby a poker-game with four high-spenders, seegar-chewing, eyes slit to their cards, raising the ante in a wondrous orgy of make-believe for real.

And threading through the dream span, the melancholy strains of an old new billet-doux:

> Oh Mary Lou, I never knoo,
> How much to fall in lerv with yoo,
> Till the day ah found yoo layin' in mah arms.

There came a mist in Mongan's eyes, nothing so brutal as the fog seldom lifting from them out there . . . out there, he learned in time, meant Injun country.

Such intelligence as he had lacked the philosophic content to question what he saw. Why? Because it had to be—and so, it was.

A character sitting alone at a distant table struck the first and only false note. Too new to this earnest game of serious charades Mongan failed to appreciate the authentic cherry topping an elaborate confection. The man in black, frayed city clothes of the Eighties and a black wideawake hat, conjured half visions of river boats, Mississippi gamblers and a pearl-handled Colt to settle debts. From black string tie to blinding white shirt linen, the dandyman lived his part, predatory, sardonic, arrogantly tilted back with his chair, an eye to all that went on around him.

Somehow, he annoyed Mongan, as one might resent the fly in Gilead balm.

Did Adam thus, one wonders, in some far flung paradise, gaze on his seven days' marvel with an eye to the serpent downstage sinister, stretching bide-the-time lazily? Allow Mongan's unspoken question as to where that languidly uncoiled darkness fitted in with this new den of Eden?

An hour passed without loss; only enrichment and, tentatively, a sense of belonging somewhere at last. Idyll was happening to Mongan, unconscious of the passing wonder in this hour's sloughing of a useless, ill-fitting skin.

Unseen, except perhaps by the black and white anomaly tilted back to the wall, watching for heels—Achilles style.

Bar J was rapidly filling up to Saturday night's high-water mark. The music a little louder, the guys and gals a shade more exuberant, the pastiche a degree less obvious. Nothing got out of hand. The almost self-conscious pattern of behaviour was good and good-humoured.

Mongan, surfeited with impressions, received another.

Merry, waylaid by an acquaintance, came in at last, the living demonstration of a metamorphosis. Not just the suit of frayed deerhide, but the wide brimmed Boone hat, the slung holster and a sheathed bowie knife, conspired to make another man not known to Mongan.

This frontiersman with a twinkle in his eye approached with the half-smile of one who'd learned to mock at an impoverished personality left in the changing room. But could this keen-eyed, upstanding young fellow with a trail-blazer's lope, be the grudge-mouthed Ellis of the DIY, the 'Merry' of those forays to the Corporation rubbish park?

'What's it gonna be?' he called.

'I—I'll leave it to you,' Mongan was too confused to think of a drink fitting the occasion.

Merry, who is now Kansas, returned with a couple of ryes and sat straight-backed, and smiling.

'Welcome to the club,' he said. A voice full of assurance.

'I'll drink to that,' Mongan responded with feeling.

They talked for quite a while. At least, Mongan, anxious to know every last relevance, gladly let Kansas do the talking. Fluently Kansas put his companion plumb in the picture, as *they* say.

'First, don't go thinking we're bit part players out of Okla or Annie Get Your Gun. As I said, you don't have to *join*, but if you wanna belong, you've gotta be dedicated serious. Once you *do* start, you'll maybe feel stupid, awkward, like you're playing some game or acting up. Some of the magic's in what you wear—it makes you become someone, maybe what you really are and never knew it. By itself it's not enough: you have to kinda practise, and most of all you have to learn. Like, once every month a guy comes from London or somewheres, and he talks about maybe Conestoga wagons and the pioneers, or some little known bandits, or the scouts who showed the army this or everywhichway. Now that was a talk I heard when I first came here so I knew right away what my part was. I got fascinated, so now I could lead you blindfold along the Osage Trail or Pike's Route to Pawnee Village.'

'How about guns?' Mongan wondered.

Not Ellis, but Kansas was too polite to laugh aloud at a naive question, though he did smile faintly. 'They figure, but they don't rate. We know just enough to know. Like that picture up there—a gun hangin' on a nail. Ignore the Hollywood buffs; guns isn't lifestyle which is what really interests. Now take old Doc Willis: he ain't here yet but he comes along with his little medicine bag, and what he doesn't know about medical practice and quacks out West and a whole lot of other things you could write on a dollar bill.'

'And all this Western talk?'

'Y'mean how do folks come by it? Well . . . I guess you slip into it. Like Doc Willis says, it's not a language, more a lingo, basically English, but if you wanna dig deeper that's up to you.'

'Deeper . . . how d'you mean?'

'Well, there's more to it than "Howdy pardner". You gotta remember—every nation under the sun went that way, and every one chipped in a word here a phrase there—the Indians too. Fine you don't get the full lingo in John Ford specials because the customers wouldn't understand. Listen to some of the boys round that stove just chawin' the rag and you wouldn't understand it either.'

Mongan nodded, headsore at this astonishing flow of—words. Ellis! Of all people! Jabbering fit to bust.

'Who runs the outfit?'

'Big Jake. Who else?'

'Is that the guy in black holdin' up the wall?'

Kansas screwed round to be sure exactly whom Mongan had in mind. 'Nope. Big Jake is really Andy Williams, the pub landlord.

He started the whole thing two, three years ago, just to give the unemployed lads something to do. It grew from there till now you've got all kinds.'

'A way of selling more booze.'

'Wrong. He sells coke all round at cost price, right? Anyone out of a job, no more than three pints a night, right? And if you *are* in work, no more than three shorts, right? So don't tell me he's not in it for the fun because *I* know he's more respected than the Mayor.'

That was nice; reassuring too. No trouble. No exploitation. But something niggled back of Mongan's mind. Scanning the room, as if in search of the catch, his eye chanced on the black-garbed figure everlastingly toying with its drink. Mongan swallowed his and didn't try too hard to banish a troublesome thought.

'The feller in a funeral suit.'

'What about him?'

'He's got a funny little shiny black bag by his side. What's he supposed to be?'

'Fox Mullins? Nothing special. We leave him be.'

'Why?'

'I guess he prefers it that way.' Kansas examined his empty glass with unusual interest, then looked up suddenly and all but fiercely. 'Quit staring at him!'

Mongan was taken aback. 'Just lookin'.'

'Don't. Is all.'

'But—'

'I know what you're gonna say. But Mullins fits because he doesn't fit, like Doc Willis says.'

'Like . . . you mean, people avoid him?'

Kansas shrugged. 'He's a loner—and he'll stay that way most evenings—because he fits. Drinks are on me tonight. If you drop by again it's your shot.'

Later Kansas introduced him to Big Jake who spent most of his time overseeing the business below but came up whenever he could, to be where his heart was—with his creation. A paunchy man—avuncular in parlour parlance—middling in years, and a widening smile under the ten gallon hat he slapped on so soon as he stepped through the door. An outsize 'howdedo' and a free beer was Mongan's initiation and enrolment in one.

'If you take to us, we'll take to you, Frankie, no sweat,' and there was no disguising the northern nasal twang.

Mongan smiled and said, fine by him, only his name wasn't Frankie.

'T'is now, son. Outside of here we're anybody or nobody and we don't enquire. In here, I look at you and I say to myself, straight off, that's Frankie.'

'Big J's baptism,' a bystanding cowpoke chuckled.

'That's right. That's how I got my big happy family,' and somehow, the grin spread wider. He was, Frankie could see, very likeable.

'How did you look at Fox Mullins?'

The big smile disappeared, snuffed as a candle. Expressionless eyes went from Frankie to Kansas. Not a chill factor in the air exactly but—

'Amigo, tell Frankie the place in Manchester for the gear he needs? If he still wants.'

'Sure, Jake.'

'And explain how there has to be an unwritten rule for any well run outfit.'

Kansas reverted to type for a brevity, but recovered enough to nod, and that was all to it till they were seated again and Kansas *cum* Merry could collect his thoughts peaceably.

'Frankie . . . don't ever do that—'

'I only asked—'

'That's it! Don't ask. Not about anyone. In here is what we are. Questions like that is about—about outside. If you skewered your grannie out there we wouldn't wanna know. That's Mongan doin' his lousy thing in Injun country . . . so what! Frankie wouldn't act like that anymore than Kansas flogged screws and emulsion at the DIY. Okay?'

Chastened, Mongan said right. But he couldn't back away from the niggle he was hard pushed to define. Didn't *any* of them feel curious about each other within or without the bounds of this strictly enclosed order?

The contretemps was forgotten. Big Jake smiled affably as ever when once he happened to catch Frankie's eye. That was about when Doc Willis came bustling in, Sears Roebuck suited, balding, diminutive and puckish; there was an immediate air of expectancy in the smokey-blue air and almost everyone smiled and looked glad to see him.

In a way, as I had it from Ellis, Doc Willis was Bar J's

anchorman; full of a doctor's gravitas, but serious also in his search for verisimilitude. Close to retirement, a schoolteacher by profession, an historian by choice, it was reckoned he knew more of 'Western' lore from Jefferson's to Tiffany's day, than any man this side of the Atlantic.

Veritably, a medicine man, charming the circle within which they encamped for a few weekly hours, giving it a cohesiveness, a genuine sense of belonging to a past he bullied into life, when they might have been, so easily and without him, clumsy gatecrashers in fancy dress.

Doc Willis made himself responsible for their finesse.

That evening, apparently, he enthralled them for a whole hour telling of the massacre of the Cheyennes and Arapahoes at Sand Creek, Colorado, described in detail things never seen in Soldier Blue; as if he'd been there, that mild little schoolmaster, and seen the barbarities of the day.

Held them in the palm of his hand to the conclusion:

'I could tell you of many more; but it's all history repeating itself and too much of history is bloodstained. What's important is putting *any* period through the mangle to squeeze out low down ideals, and windy rhetoric to keep the flag flying no matter what the cost. Relive any "golden" age and you'll find the tarnish with the varnish and the guilt with the gilt; don't ever ignore the one because you're infatuated with the other. Look both ways: we talk of Injun country, the Indians talked of the White Man's Land.

'So take it all in all, good and bad, discover a coin has two sides, and you'll truly relive the past—*any* past, no matter how many years ago it belonged to others.'

Applause Doc Willis would not tolerate. People nowadays, he said, are clap-happy; but he wasn't averse to any drinks that might be offered. So, most Saturday nights he left Bar J a little the worse for wear, the only man Big J allowed to quit the place in that condition, and someone always drove him home.

One other thing happened that memorable evening.

A girl joined them at their table after what Doc called his 'little impromptu'. Of her, Mongan had caught snatch glimpses now and then, as of spilled quicksilver.

She seemed to be touring the tables, chatting to friends and acquaintances here and there, then getting swallowed up in the standing crowd to reappear somewhere else at last. Vivid the impression of a small figure in white buckskin breeches and checkshirt, some kind of straw hat hiding most of her auburn hair and some of the face. Most of all he looked for the smile and the liveliness—that was the spilled quicksilver.

He tried to 'place' her as she approached, and could only think of a prosperous rancher's daughter, such as Hank Ussher had married after he settled.

'Hi, Kansas,' she dropped into a chair between them, not deigning to look at Mongan. 'Who's your friend?''

'This is Frankie. New addition.' Kansas nodded sideways. 'Belle.'

Mongan coloured for any or no reason. Attractive young women and DIYs seldom see much of each other. 'Bell. What kind of a name is that?'

A certain way girls have: rounding their eyes in coquettish surprise. 'What's funny about a name meaning beautiful?'

'He got bitten by a quiz-master,' Kansas explained.

For the moment Mongan felt out of it. He couldn't avoid asking questions and he couldn't rise to their level of dialogue. 'I'm sorry . . . Big Jake never gets it wrong.'

Mollified smiles. 'Well if you condescend using it don't forget it ends with an e.'

Which surprised Mongan. 'Bell—e?'

No malice in their laughter.

'Okay, forget the e or my reputation's lost and that's no good to a minister whatever it does for his daughter. You promised me a drink when you tracked down the rainbow's end, Kansas.'

Kansas made a long, suffering face. 'It's my night for sweatin' liquid assets.' He went all the same. Belle was everyone's girl.

Mongan's shyness kept him staring after Kansas, much as he wanted to look at her.

'He's changed.'

'What d'you mean?' sharp enough to merit a glance, before he explained.

'I knew him when he couldn't put two words together.'

'Could you?'

Proving what could be done with two words, Belle taught him the lesson Kansas and Big J hadn't quite got over. He found himself at the receiving end of a profound and not too pleasant question. She saved him the trouble of replying, leaned a little

towards him and there could be no avoiding the fact, she *was*—
pretty.

'There are two ways of living or surviving these days. Either you
ask questions and survive the answers. Or you don't ask, and just
live. Okay?' she smiled to soften the impact of words. No girl likes
to be didactic.

He didn't answer at once, was too busy liking what he saw, smile
and all. He liked her voice, not an affected drawl but just enough
soft Yankee flavouring to fall easy on the ear.

'It's my first time here,' a defensive apology.

'Fine. Second time you'll know better.'

For sure there would be a second time. Mongan had no doubts
about that.

Strange, crowded garden of Eden where all the main gardeners
had somehow drifted into a vacant plot.

We jump Mongan's period of apprenticeship. To watch a bridge
being thrown across river from one bank of time to another can
strain the best of attentions.

He made remarkable progress in his newfound Western world;
right from the first week during which he took time off to visit the
Lone Pine Creek Emporium in the big city. Could afford the four
hundred needed to bedizen a brand new personality, shiny as a
deputy's badge. Scarcely spent a penny of his wage till now. What
had there been worth buying?

There isn't time either, to describe the rare sense of exultation,
of unwrapping, possessing, handling and donning, and at last,
*becoming* Frankie, one delicious evening in that featureless Silverside Avenue bedroom.

Or to chronicle his pride and pleasure when Big Jake, Kansas,
Belle and many others pulled out the 'swell' stop for a wow of
genuine admiration at his first 'showing'. Even Doc Willis had a
word for him.

'Like your outfit, son. Credit to the Big House.'

He'd flushed with delight.

Nothing marred burgeoning well-being except changing-time at
the end of a session. He came to dread aftermath, the down-pulling
undertow of a drab personality reminding him of what he really was
outside those snatched hours of seem-to-be.

Humping his gear Mongan would walk homewards with Ellis,

neither saying a word about today, just now, or even tomorrow. Two strangers in company, silent as travellers over a Corporation rubbish tip, till their ways parted for the duration of Reality.

Mongan or Michelangelo, heart and soul is fine-sounding but, allow the lad may have an inkling of its meaning however tawdry the concept. He listened and learned, read everything he could lay hands on having the remotest bearing on his obsession. Every night, Monday to Saturday, found him at the Bar J absorbing and growing imperceptibly into stature of a kind.

He gained confidence, grew clear-sighted, developed a thrustier jawline; purpose built, one might say, to try a fall with destiny. In gait and posture he never looked back to that first broken evening, had studied how to handle the lingo, was become an old-timer with months of concentrated acquirement under his gun-belt.

And a part-timer too. Not to be forgotten, that Mongan and the rest reverted to type so soon as they breathed the outside air of the world. What Big Jake saw in Mongan resembled nothing of Fat Harry's recollection. Retiring sort of lad. Not much to say for himself, polite to the customers. Did his job passably and what more could I ask?

It came as a shock to Mr and Mrs Mongan when they learned their youngest was 'a secret cowboy' . . . four square eyes on the blink are not a pretty sight.

Segregated personalities; but, it appears that, outwardly, a schoolteacher fussing over a maths project could still live calmly in his more significant world, be it only a stage coach run to Denver for a medical congress; an apprentice butler might be learning how to mind the Ps and Qs of the Us while working out a feasible trouble-free journey to the Algonquin for the census-takers; a salesman explaining to some ignoramus why new wood needs a primer, could be close-handling a jail-breaker through the chaparral because that's what a deputy-marshal is paid to do.

Day dreamers; individual worth, negligible. Only coalescence, the meeting of like minds at Bar J could give them a sense of belonging—somewhere.

One other factor jarred, alloying Mongan's happiness.

Fox Mullins, of course.

Not to begin with. Frankie found enough to occupy the mind to give Mullins much active thought in those blissful days; lounging, listening and learning. A book, or a hand of cards, and much talk to cover the silence of years. Long pow-wows with Hank Fulbert, Dutch Meeson, O'Rarity and Silence Svensson who waxed garrulous, mainly about the Swedish colony in Nebraska, ending every long-winded solo by assuring everybody he talked too much. *Ja visst!*

Most of them were specialists, the girls as much as the men. Belle could tell of the Bible country because it happened she took her fictional father's ministry seriously.

But through it all, the talk, the laughter and the melancholy moan of 'Mary Lou' there sat Fox Mullins, on two legs of a chair, black wideawake tipped high, and eyes ranging mean enough to cower coyotes, as O'Rarity once opined.

'Takes in everythin', gives out nothin',' Hank Fulbert summed up before scratching his conscience. 'He don't mean no harm.'

And they'd have missed him if he hadn't been there. From Big Jake to the latest newcomer it was known without much understanding that Fox Mullins was axiomatic; the tiny grit without which no oyster gets promotion to pearldom. So long as he stayed more or less chairbound, content to finger his whiskey glass and enjoy the scenery, no one was likely to swoon.

But, Mongan asked himself, what would happen if, someday, Fox Mullins moved, made a tour of their little world . . . would that be a different matter?

The ball began to roll that way one Saturday evening about six months after Mongan's introduction to the Bar J.

He was sitting at his favourite end-of-room table with Belle and Kansas, idly listening to the Western music droning through the hubbub. A drink was half way to his lips, and there it stayed as glance met sardonic gaze. Not for the first time Mullins was eyeing Frankie in such a way as to give him extra pause. Plainly he did *not* like what he saw.

'What's wrong?' Merry Ellis never had Kansas' perception.

'That Mullins is wrong. Bugs me stupid.' Pure northern tones; nothing of his acquired unhurried drawl.

'Take it easy, Frankie,' Belle cautioned, eyes to the table. 'He doesn't mean any harm.'

'This place should have a bloody parrot. We could teach him to say Fox Mullins doesn't mean—!'

'And he doesn't do any,' Kansas cut in, sharply.

Frankie looked hard at his companions, unable or unwilling to

believe either. He tried to match their fool tolerance—live and let
live he could go along with but it takes two to square that little circle
and . . . and Mullins actually smiled, full at him, as if he was
enjoying some joke about other peoples' dilemmas.

Belle's restraining hand on his arm told how much he needed to
stave off ugly, unfamiliar sensations. How could anyone stomach
that arrogant darkness indolently rubbing its spine against the
chairback?

Angrily he turned away to find himself trapped between two
islands of concern, and that troubled him no less, convinced him
they knew more about *bêtes noires* than they cared to tell. Belle and
Kansas had reasons written all over their faces for protecting him
from himself. Or Mullins.

He never dreamed they might be looking at things differently.

Mongan took the problem home with him. Obsessions never end
up in lost property offices. He thought about it through the working
day, puzzled over it in the sleeping hours, knowing the while he
could do nothing about a fellow who simply stared at him.

Myths begin with what's known of the unknown. Mullins
existed, and in such a way that a man's imagination could run riot
over a single ineradicable impression of the black-suited figure.
Not about what he affected to be at Big J's; all Mongan's
conjecturing ran the other, forbidden way.

What *was* he outside the charmed circle?

Mongan lacked the means to conjure up anything like the reality
he knew existed beneath the façade. His efforts were crude and
childish, but curiosity grows by what it feeds on.

From thereon the situation tended a little further when Fox
Mullins first appeared to act out of character. Early one Saturday
evening Mongan, now going strong with Belle, was listening to
Kansas' enthusiastic account of *Copper Camp*, a lively book about
the mining town of Butte, 'they had a judge out there called "Long
Distance Mike" on account of his tough sentences', when Mullins
materialised abruptly at their table.

Not disconcerted but curious at first, Mongan's reaction to this
near view. What was there to worry about in those nothing much
features, the grubby discontent about the pallid eyes, the physique
of a weakling, a whiff of cheap after-shave? The shabby suit held no
terrors, the whiteness of linen was suspect . . . distance lent what
proximity had never heard of.

He hovered long enough to accept an invitation to join them, but it never came. Studiously, he ignored the males. 'Hi, Belle,' soft, non-fibrous tones.

'. . . hi, Fox.' Nervously, with a glance at Mongan.

'Six months a'more since you dropped by ma table for a drink. How come?' There was mockery in his regret.

She smiled and made a show of matching his banter. 'Only call when I'm invited.'

'Let's say I'm invitin' you now.'

Easier to accept, to keep the peace. But she paused and he pounced on her constraint.

'That is,' bitterly, 'if your friends ain't particular.'

Note the dialogue, steeped in tawdry. But no one present saw things in that light and nobody said there had to be intellectual content in the quest for any way of life . . .

'I'm partic'lar on my personal account,' Kansas grinned, amiably enough. 'Belle's her own problem.'

Mullins shrugged and 'gave his consideration' as western folk say, to Frankie who preferred to study the table's top.

'Maybe the deputy could raise an objection.' No response. 'Lone star law n'order, huh? My, I should be scared.'

There was no ignoring a deliberate provocation, more than half expected; and no advantage in rising to it. By now he was far gone in admiration of Belle, owed it to her if not to his unwilling self to prove he could play by the rules of the game.

'Now law n'order is one thing you don't need worry about, Mullins. Didn't I hear tell you run the biggest morgue for longhorns in Dodge City?' He sat back satisfied and gazed at the ceiling as having more to interest.

'Jayhawk, tell your friend I don't run morgues, but I frequently visit, in case I meet up with someone I used to know. Comin' Belle?'

'She's happy where she is!'

'Please, Frankie.' Again the reassuring touch, and Mongan let it pass, but watched her following Fox to his table.

'Why does she have to—he doesn't own her!'

Gravity in Kansas' long regard. 'Belle isn't doin' anythin' she didn't do before you showed up. She has reasons—'

'What reasons?'

'No questions. No questions mean no trouble. No trouble of any

kind. If Mullins is a mean streak, you'll find one in any chunk of
society, right?'

'Since when was it necessary?'

'Since anytime. Like Big Jake says, there's aggro anywhere you
care to go in the big wide world. Our style is to put up or shut up and
with luck it gets tired, gets up and gets out to try someplace else.'

Mongan listened and thought hard, long after Kansas had
finished. Mistakenly, he concluded they were all tenterhook scared,
not of Mullins as such, but of what he seemed to represent: the
destructive force that could burst the bubble of their corny, reach-
me-down Utopia, and that he could understand. So it was cheaper to
smile and nod.

'Okay. I'm sold . . . but why did he call you Jayhawk?'

'Well don't that prove he's as much a part of Big J as anyone? The
Jayhawk's a bigger joke to Kansans than the pier is to Wigan.'

'So?'

'So he's very informative, which means he takes the whole thing
seriously.'

'The better to break it up.'

Kansas shook his head, positively. 'I know different.'

Frankie couldn't argue with that, and didn't intend to; because
Mongan, not Frankie, was working at the problem in his own way,
beyond the confines of Big J.

Nothing more untoward happened that evening.

It's possible, if Frankie had known a little more, things might not
have turned so—lethal. It's possible, if Mullins had changed into a
fool's parti-coloured suit complete with cap and bells, and aimed his
smile in some other direction, maybe Mongan could have favoured
Kansas' live-and-let-live point of view.

But, protagonists never learn. Mullins wouldn't change and
Frankie couldn't, fated as it seemed, to experience one of those
fascinating psychological switchbacks of personality making nonsense of the universal pretension to live consistently on one level
only.

Recall, Frankie had acclimatised to a deputy marshal's character
with Big J's approval and a wry comment as to what else could he be
with all those questions? Search and enquire motivated Western
lawmen, and they'd cross state boundaries or hell's frontiers to bring
in a malefactor.

Frankie, the deputy, convinced himself of Mullins' deeper mystery—outside of Bar J—therefore he posed a kind of threat to the community—inside the Bar J. Possessed of a badge, he had the self-given right to investigate. But to satisfy his curiosity, Frankie had to cross the state border disguised as Mongan. That, in turn, meant breaking the code.

Some days after the 'confrontation' he found the resolution and the pretext ... to act the lawman tailing a villain in the name of justice ... which is nowhere the same as Mongan seeking revenge in the name of Frankie.

He'd wandered in at his usual hour to find Belle waiting for him at their customary table. By now everyone knew they were going steady, just as far as the Bar J entrance door and no further. So there was a double joy in these evening excursions, and anyone could see he had eyes only for her.

There weren't too many people about at that time, but one of them was, inevitably, Mullins.

Frankie approached and, as if by chance, Mullins changed position, uncannily sure of which side of a split second to shoot out the leg that trips unwary passers-by.

Mongan, or Frankie, stumbled, recovered quickly and turned white-faced to find himself staring into the barrel of his own pearl-handled colt, an elegant piece of reproductive futility.

Mullins was sighting it straight between the eyes with solemn intensity while Frankie stood incredulous, transfixed by an enormity.

'Bang!' said Fox Mullins. Then he smiled, twirled the toy dexterously and presented the butt to its owner.

A voice calling his name saved the situation, cleared the red hot mist clouding his vision and he took the gun delicately, replacing it where it belonged, never taking his eyes from Mullins who wasn't smiling now.

Mongan left him with an unspoken promise and, sick with humiliation, made his way to Belle.

Strangely enough, no one but Belle had seen the incident, it happened that quickly.

Feverish words welled like sweat, trickling from the mouth, hands shaking, an almost physical retching at the thought of being worsted by nothing better than Mullins. 'I could've—I dunno what I couldn't have done! If you hadn't called—you and Big J—that stopped me—he'd throw us both out—I told you he was no good. That's it—I'll fix him my way.'

'Frankie.'

'He's an outsider! And you and Kansas and Big J are too damn stupid to see it!'

'He's pulled that kind of trick before—believe me it's nothing personal.'

'You're wasting your breath. I dunno what's in him, jealousy, plain meanness or—'

'Fox didn't do anything out of character, I promise you, Frankie.'

She was pleading a lost cause, lost forever on Mongan. Frankie calmed down, came round to her side of the question, talked and joked his way through the rest of that evening, but his thoughts were gone another way; they had to do with waiting on the clock.

At about 10.30 he finished his drink and noted that Mullins was into a two-handed game of pinochle with one of the people who bothered with him. For once, Mullins seemed unaware of his existence.

'Hey!' Frankie reminded himself aloud. 'I promised to meet my young cousin off the train. She's stayin' with us.'

Belle looked faintly surprised. 'You never said—'

'She's only fifteen, young enough to be worried if no one's there to meet her. See you, Belle.'

And he rushed, like any man in a hurry, with not a glance in Mullins' direction.

She looked a little hurt. Fox wondered if they'd had a row. If it concerned Belle, he missed very little, and he missed her most of all.

In ten minutes Mongan had discarded Frankie and stowed his gear in the dressing-room cupboard. Once out of the pub he turned left and went some 40 paces along the alley to where a smaller thoroughfare, an ill-lit lane, outflanked the bulk of the inn and the smaller building nearby. He rounded the corner and waited hands in pockets, neither patient nor impatient, and not much in the way of thought passing through his mind. A steady drizzle fell with a just perceptible patter, ran rivulets down his leather jacket, flattened his hair, found its way along the natural gullies of hard set features.

Had the skies opened up and shed torrents, he'd have noticed nothing but his purpose. The other half of an hour passed before he tensed into a furtive pose. A creature of habit, Mullins regularly left at eleven.

A darkened figure, middling height, detached from the pub's entrance and went right, to where the lane debouched on Wallinsey's ridiculously long High Street. He carried a hold-all and that prissy little black bag, walked at a clarity gait, clipping the pavement with the black leather shoes belonging to his outfit.

Mongan's style of moccasins made little noise, though he need go sure-footed on the greasy pavements. Keeping 50 or so paces behind his quarry Mongan could easily make out the blackness of tight cords and a black tailored reefer jacket. Nothing noteworthy in this view of a young man homeward bound, hunched against the rain and a rising wind, a bag in each hand.

No problem. He never once looked back, ploughed on steadily, crossing the High Street, turning off to the left and traversing a long straggle of pre-war nondescript semis, skirted the iron palings of Oldcorn Park till he reached Locksley Avenue, a double row of villas leading to the railway station; the other side of town, far from Silverside.

The shadow hovered long enough to give Mullins time to reach the gate. At a glance he knew those trim lower middle-class dwellings exactly fitted what he suspected of Mullins' private character. At a glance it hints at Mongan's inverted snobbery.

Three quarters of the way along the Avenue Mullins turned into a neat little front garden, its grass plot surrounded by brown hydrangeas, clanged the folksy wrought-iron gate behind him, entered and quietly closed the door of a house already gone to bed.

Mongan made tracks enough to bring him on target as a hall light flashed on. He smiled, semi-enigmatically at the little pine signboard with its unimportant message, Dun Romin. He'd sold dozens of those at the DIY.

Sixty-four Locksley Avenue. He walked on at a slower pace as far as the station across from and 50 yards past Mullins' place. That might do—unless he was a commuter. Crossing to the almost deserted frontage where a forlorn town taxi waited hopefully for the last train, Mongan found he had the perfect, unobtrusive view of Number 64.

Nothing gained by loitering. The wind swept unchecked across that open space driving the rain spit-hard into the eyes. Mongan took a short cut home by way of the canal bridge, found his parents were already abed, took a bath, reset his digital alarm and finished the day.

He was out of the house by seven, back at the railway station before half past. Oblivious of the newspaper seller, ignoring the trickle of Manchester bound commuters, he kept his intent on the house with its wooden message and a garden full of brown-paper flowers. After twenty minutes or so, a man of middling years appeared at the front door, closed it with a houseowner's care, got into his car and drove off.

It was nearly another hour before Mongan's patience got its reward. Mullins himself opened and closed the door calling something into the inner regions as he did so. He turned left at the gate, heading away from the station. Mongan jerked his head, a gesture of satisfaction, and kept a distance between them, making a long shadow as the Indians say, knowing Mullins had a job and that he worked locally.

In the High Street . . .

In a spacious carpet emporium, filled with rolls of Axminster, Kosset and every kind of floor covering. Sales posters in the abundance of glazing shrieked of enormous reductions . . . and there was Mullins, no more than creep high, letting himself into the still deserted premises! If seraphs laugh in hell, then Mongan's smile might pass for seraphic.

He loitered in the area till more signs of business as usual enlivened the place, then strolled casually to the window, to stand gazing into the interior of a high-class establishment elegantly identified as Wall t'Wall. Content to wait as long as it took for Mullins to reappear, it had just occurred he maybe worked as a clerk in the back premises when again he had his reward. A big, fat one.

Mullins hove into view fumbling with buttons, head down, so that, for an instant he could have been anybody. Mongan checked, peered harder and luxuriated in a prospect that had to do with humiliation; shame that knows no redress.

He had only to wait, to hold his ground, watching this —thing—under glass; scientifically observing. Until the figure, pathetic in a warehouseman's brown coat, idling the time till customers materialised, became aware of a lone window-shopper . . . but different, unmoving and inexorable, no slewing of the head that goes with bargain hunters . . . just staring . . . staring at *him*!

He too needed time for recognition and, when it came, the change was frightful. Because there was no change. Expression nil, leaving an uncanny impression of a sudden cardboard cut-out, or an enlarged Instamatic of one caught in the act of doing nothing. Two dimensional.

Ostensibly, a couple of youths regarding each other through a glazier's divide, but more, much more, to that static exchange. As when, one of them whips out a smile; a flash of teeth, white as a Bowie knife stealing sunglare. The sweetness of revenge.

Mongan need go no further but, lacking finesse, the intelligence, the delicacy of brute beasts, he had to go on, to twist the knife and listen for screams.

Had to enter the shop, approach the little man in a brown coat, trapped, rat-cornered between Mongan and the smart-suited manager cleaning his finger-nails in the background.

Mongan looked all over that well remembered face, as one might examine the effect of turning a stone in some foul backwater.

'I'm needin' a piece of rug to pull out from under an old friend.' Softly. 'A sample piece would do just fine.'

It took time for the victim to articulate: 'Over there.'

Casually, Mongan strolled to a pile of samples, picked up the first piece to hand, returned with and paid for it, watched Mullins roll and wrap it with unruly fingers and received it with a polite 'thank you'.

He left the place with not another word or a backward glance at the brown coat.

Saturday night at the Bar J is *the* night—maybe 150 young and not so young *aficionados* gather in fellowship; drink, gamble a little, talk a lot and laugh even more. And why should this Saturday session be any different?

Belle and Kansas are there—the usual table—waiting for Frankie to show up. Even Mullins is present, hides his suffering under the swart suit, but the keen eye might opine that something is lacking. He seems unable to comport himself as of recently. 'Fox looks like he's drawn a pair of jokers in a poker game,' Dutch Meeson observed to no one in particular, and then forgot about him.

One thing never varies; not once does he take his dolorous gaze from Belle who smiles once or twice in his direction but follows through with the slightest of frowns. Friends drop by as usual, a word and a laugh with her and Kansas, for they're both popular and she's mighty vivacious, and there's a touch of sad pride in Mullins' regard, that this should be so.

Kansas too, sensed the small cloud over Bar J's horizon. Stole glances over his shoulder every so often prospecting the familiar yet not so familiar view of a Mullins ill-at-ease, hand fumbling pointlessly with the shiny little black bag at his side. He recalled long after how he'd seriously wondered, for the first time, just what Mullins toted around that could be so all-fired precious. Guns? Drugs? Poker chips? With Mullins could one ever be sure? In Bar J of course.

But something, he silently insisted, and with a tracker's instinct, was wrong.

Well of course it was. Everybody could see that from the moment Frankie—or could it be Mongan?—appeared at the door and pistol-shot slammed it behind him, turning all heads, hushing the babble, leaving only Tex Ginnis murmuring on about that everlasting Mary Lou.

We're in the drablands of the timeworn hills of Hollywood at last . . . or maybe we never left them.

Scene 4—take your time. Still shot, then pan left to right. Mullins staring left, apprehensive, fear newborn in the eye, faces, more faces, puzzlement, tension, lowered tumblers, Doc Willis quizzical, Mongan himself meaner eyed than Mullins could ever manage, pan length of bar to the right, outward facing fellers, elbows on the counter, the gals knowing drama when they see it, excitement, apprehension, the barman caught in the pause with a head-high tray of beers.

Mongan ruled the lull, walked forward like a slow bullet, spurs jingling as they should do in the saloon silence. In his left grip he had an odd-looking bag of some kind.

Extras, bit part players, principals, all, set the scene to perfection. This was high noon under cover and a few hours late.

Mongan—not Frankie, surely—stopped by Mullins' table, slapped down what appeared to be a bag roughly cobbled from carpet material? With rope handles?

'Present for ya, Fox. You'll recognise a *carpet* bag when y'see one? You'll know what a *carpet* bagger is, I reckon. A guy who carries his *all* in jus' such a portable . . .'

He walked on, reached the far table and sat, uncaring that all eyes were on him and his iniquity. Belle's, horrified; Kansas indefinably agitated, switching his gaze from one man to the other. Then, reaction, attention reluctantly turning to the man they all loved to hate; but not anymore. Fascinated, one might suggest, they watched the slow death-throes of a personality, the disappearance of a city-slicker, name of Mullins, dropped by a slow bullet; they, not knowing details, but sensing for sure the magnitude of a man's defeat.

Had it coming to him? Well, no. They had too much old-fashioned compassion to look that hard for justice. But they couldn't be sure *why* he suffered so far down and, for decency's sake they turned elsewhere until, slowly, the evening's hubbub resurged to a near normal pitch.

Only two people knew why he'd turned into nothing in a dandy black suit. Not Mongan and Kansas, but Kansas and Belle sat incredulous, impotent with shock.

'I should go to him,' Belle half-whispered.

'Better not,' Kansas gently dissuaded her. 'It'd make things worse for him.'

'He's looking at me . . . oh my God, he's looking—'

'Let it be, Belle. For his sake.'

Not much, just a snatch of flimsy. Dialogue that held not a shred of meaning for Mongan who might not have existed, close as he sat in their company.

Few tried to be aware when Mullins stood abruptly, eyes tragic as those of a vivisected dog, but fixed on Belle so that she had to look away, and, when she could raise her head at last, he was gone. The shoddy 'carpet bag' remained on the table.

She started to rise once more, but Kansas knew better.

'He needs time, Belle. Not you.'

She stared for a long time at him before words came, '. . . I'm goin' 'ome,' she said. Flat northern tones; deader than a Southern belle.

Long time too, once they were alone, before Kansas could bring himself to speak.

'What the *hell* got into you! You didn't have to do that.'

'I had to teach the creep a lesson.'

'Because he played a kid's trick on you? He's played it on every guy in the place. No one bothers.'

'Why not?'

'Because he *belongs*—and you don't.'

'You saw how he treated Belle!'

'Why not. She didn't shed tears. And he never broke the code. *You* broke it!'

'How would you know?'

'How would I—? Okay ass-hole, I'll break it good and proper this once. I knew Belle when she was married to Mullins, better than eighteen months ago. And I knew it didn't work out—no one's fault. It just didn't work out. They split the blanket—separated. I brought her here because I knew she was sad and lonely with only that bitch of a mother saying it was *all* her fault. He followed her one night, started coming here himself just to sit and look at her because the poor sap still worshipped her. He just sat there, no harm, growing a new character, learnin' like the rest of us, another same man, and Belle another same woman—so everybody's happy. What the *hell* did you have to pull that carpet-bag stuff for! What's a carpet salesman got to do with Fox Mullins! You . . . you brought the lousy stinkin' world right in here where it never should be . . . Injun country . . . piss off, Mongan, you're Fat Harry's deadspit and he made me feel sick.'

And that, friends, is about all there is to it. Subsequent details are sparse and not too edifying.

Next day, the body of Herbert Oldcastle was fished from the Wallinsey canal a mile or so out of town. According to the local paper it was dressed in a fancy suit of clothes 'of antique cut' and a white shirt to match. A wide brimmed hat was found on the canal path and a black, patent leather bag in his left hand contained a white wedding dress and two sprigs of artificial orange blossom.

The deceased was about twenty-three years of age and was known to be incurably deaf, though a highly proficient lip-reader. Occupation, carpet salesman and fitter.

Inquest material. Sombre enough to change life for a lot of people. And, after all, that Western world was just too fragile to prevail against the harsh realities of a curious, callously indifferent can of worms that long since lost its Maker's label.

Evidence shows, not surprisingly, Bar J was never the same again.

Once in a while Merry Ellis drops in at Flo's Eatery for old acquaintance' sake, though he scarcely swaps a dozen words with Edna, the bespectacled girl, who serves coffee and such. And to look at them, one would be hard put to recognise Kansas, the finest scout in the whole Great Territory, or Belle, the once beautiful daughter of a Methody minister in some town south of the Rock Island Railroad.

Heard tell Mongan lit out of town long ago.

# THE IMMORTAL COIL

ADAM SPENSER'S BEHAVIOUR on the southern thoroughfares of London that momentous day in April, not two years since, was quite atrocious. To blunder through two sets of red lights and otherwise fail to signal one's intentions as to left or right turns is to wander straight into the arms of trouble. And rightly so, he would readily concede in less pensive mood.

Pensive! to bump into and very nearly dent the kindly patrol car hauled in at the roadside to bar his wayward progress suggested the antics of a reckless man to its unsmiling occupants. Before they'd reached him Spenser had shaken off enough preoccupation to appreciate the meaning of plight.

'Are you all right, sir?'

Right enough to gaze with whimsical interest at the polished boots or shoes surrounding him, as it seemed. He thought of Gulliver and mused how very Lilliputian prostration could sometimes be. All a matter of falling off. Fascinating too the reflected light from passing cars, sliding over the nearest footwear like clarified butter.

As he failed to answer, the two slightly bothered officers hefted him effortlessly to his feet. 'We've got a right one here, Len.'

The one who wasn't called 'Len' repeated the question originally asked by the one who was.

'Yes, yes, perfectly fit, officer. My own silly er—'

The unfinished admission put them firmly back on the line of duty.

'Very glad to hear it,' crisply. 'Doubtless you're aware you've broken every rule in the Highway Code relative to your—vehicle?'

Spenser looked genuinely horrified, an impressive reaction from a man with patently honest grey eyes. He had however a milk-white mien that made some amends for an otherwise ugliness aggravated by uncombworthy wispy yellowish hair. Spenser never looked less than a mess.

Ugliness. But plainly not an ugly customer. The law guardians glanced comprehensively at him, his transport and each other; and tacitly agreed to go softly.

'Do you know where you are, sir?' Len wondered.

'Oh yes. Camberwell New Road. I live across the Green—near the parish church.'

'We really ought to breathalyse,' Len again, mock seriously.

'I er—seldom—only at Xmas. If I remember.'

'You don't say so? And here it is April. Can't have a weaker head for the old demon than that, Charles.'

'Too true,' said the other.

Spenser seemed interested in a total irrelevance. 'Is your name—er—Charles?'

The officer thus interrogated stiffened. 'And why not?'

Len smiled. 'He's dead against Charlie—on account of right Charlies and comics and that.'

'Nightwatchmen used to be called Charlies.' He waved a hand south towards the Green. 'On the right—used to be an old style police station—you know, with a stable door. The public stood outside to make their complaints.'

'Live and learn,' then, more officially, Len enquired if 'that' was his bicycle?

'Er—yes it is.'

The officer proceeded to tweak the tyres, test the brakes and even condescended to flick the bell, listening intently the while. 'Very nice. D minor,' he confided.

'Is it?' Spenser looked surprised and even made an effort to appear delighted.

'He's a bell-ringer off-duty,' Charles explained.

'Really? How very—' he tailed off hopelessly. Almost always the small change of conversation failed him at the very last word.

Len helped him over the gap. 'Take it as a friendly caution. You're vulnerable enough on that thing without flushing the rule book.'

'I'm—much obliged to you,' gratefully. 'Had a difficult day and I suppose I was riding home a bit too—' he made a prodigious effort, 'too reflectively.'

'Uh-huh. Bad day at the office, eh? Now I'd take bets you work in a big office, thirty-floor job.'

The delinquent started to say one thing—and settled for another. 'Yes.'

A few more words of kindly caution before they drifted away leaving a dishevelled figure looking after them with an expression of such transcending bitterness that, had they known, they might have made a few further enquiries.

Rain began to fall heavily. Traffic swept along the Camberwell road like chariots in drenched armour, wheels hissing on its greasy surface. Spenser heard with dull indifference but translated automatically the sounds each car made in passing; the swish of a sultanic scimitar, each stroke a severance. And he stood yet, pondering the pitfalls of cloying alliteration, not knowing his recent mentors sat impassive watching him by way of the rear mirrors.

'Queer guy,' Charles muttered.

'Thick on the ground these days. But villains don't normally ride bicycles.'

Nevertheless they waited till Spenser remounted and passed them without recognition, pedalling with better circumspection towards Camberwell Green, Vicarage Grove and home. He never knew they followed, passing him precisely at the moment he pushed open the gate and wheeled his bicycle up the trim little path to the prim little villa that once had been the pride and joy of a never so prim music-hall queen of last century's Eighties.

He paused at the front door long enough to savour the moment. It was ritual, this brief surrender to all the impressions of the day, good or bad, and it had to do with a vocational imperative.

In Adam Spenser's ponderous existence almost every event had a significance to which he clung like a bulldog—if that breed really is notable for tenacity. Not only remembrance of things just past but, opening the door, shutting the back door, watching clouds, observing a constable's boots, making coffee, all the minutiae of everyday living, mechanical to most, were to Spenser indispensable grist to the mill of his workaday world and thus, to his subsistence. His livelihood, in short, depended on a clever manipulation of the commonplace.

Poor fellow, he was a novelist, fairly established, moderately successful, relatively unknown, comparatively competent in his craft and so, as a literary wit once observed: 'of all parts of speech, t'is adverbs most undo us all.'

For whatever aesthetic or anaesthetic purpose, a Spenser can't stand indefinitely in a deluge contemplating his front door. Sooner or later the man in a brown coma must open it, enter, and wheel his

bicycle into the sitting room where Hilda, his wife, sits glued to a
turgid TV spectacular designed to appeal to the kiddy in most of
them . . .

'*What* do you think you're doing?' she lost interest in *Access Man*
at sight of one seemingly pledged for life to his transport. No hint
of emotion in her arid query, only the slightest stress on 'what'.

Adam badly feigned a startled air. Irritating, that suggestion of
Socrates bumping into the world, Simon toppling into the thick of
it from his stylites. Knowing him too well Hilda bothered not at all
to curl a lip as he backed out with a muttered, unfinished apology.

He returned wearing a smile and no raincoat. Shorter than H.G.
Wells, hair spiky, a face no less baggy than his trousers, Spenser
hardly cut a dashing figure. The eyes redeemed but that smile
would always be an error of judgment cut, as it was, on the bias.

'You look a mess,' some kind of comparison, perhaps, with *Access
Man*.

He explained his mishap with the bicycle, slumped into an
opposite chair by the gas-log fire. Cold, hungry, miserable, he tried
with a desperate cheerfulness to show none of those things.

'Did you—?' he began.

'No, since you ask. I've had a lousy day,' she said, flatly. A run
down patient, mouthing symptoms.

He relied on silence. After five years he knew by heart the
pattern of the senior floor manager's life in a three-star depart-
mental store. Even knew what must come next.

'Four shop lifters.' He'd long since avoided sight of a gleam in
her eye. Vitiated triumph. Surely that little virtue belonged to the
past—with the Romans? Albeit he looked faintly surprised, having
bet on a tally of five.

'And the rationalising campaign doesn't help. Parker's resigning
next month. Sauerkraut omelette tonight. I don't feel up to much
cooking. Cutting staff is lunacy . . .'

He nodded agreement, felt genuinely sorry for her problem,
endured in a world he knew little about, but wishing she cared
enough to worry about his. Contrition came quickly as he realised
he was being unfair. She couldn't know of a problem still cooling
on *his* plate.

*Access Man* had almost died its episodic death. She started to
leave the room. Adam tried to be 'accommodating', wished she'd
stay, badly needed to talk.

'Don't you want to finish that—that—?'

'Crap you were going to say. I know the ending. Mitzi Collier gets contracted out in a car crash.'

'How do you—?'

'It was leaked to the Press last month.'

She went. He bounded to the Box and switched the thing off. Returned to his badly worn Parker-Knoll and lay back extended to his limits, taking in the sudden, unelectronic peace. With it came reflections ranging from the spent years to the present momentous day.

Habit. He could seldom prevent his thoughts forming into a summary such as he endlessly composed for his yarns. Off the cuff memoranda spanning lives, expanding incidents, inventing situations, likely or not, but always a quest for the perfect composition, fact or fiction, friend or foe, wife or—self. Thus:

Adam Spenser, of no fixed disposition, born well north of the Watford Gap, but not well born. Too early divided between divided parents he pronounced a plague on both houses filled with two fathers and as many mothers, vacillated through fifth year and then went it alone—to London. Too young at sixteen, but work was easy to come by in those days. No job suited his restless, not unintelligent spirit, but always a critical eye to the multifariousness of that bustling capital of the self conscious Sixties.

More and evermore absorbed by his day time surroundings he took any night job he could get, learned to live on four hours' sleep and random snacks so he could attend the Commons debates, the Law Court wrangles, the Bow Street parades, bear-baiting at the Stock Exchange, museums, meetings, tournaments, demonstrations; climbed every possible vantage point adorning or disfiguring the great metropolis, sharpening his powers of observation to a viewpoint, took to making notes, fashioning a short-handled style that would later be held against him, opprobiously, 'rather idiosyncratic'. Those adverbs again.

Having, in his twenty-eighth year, completed a survey of all the sects and denominations London had to offer, one of his fathers—he could never remember which—died leaving him £500. Still seething over some piece of social injustice studied in the morning paper, he read the solicitor's letter almost as an afterthought. Almost.

One of those flashes of inspirational lightning avoided by wise men struck Adam Spenser all, so to say, of a heap. Violently off-loading vague thoughts of becoming a dissenting minister—impossible to say whether he meant religion or politics—he threw up his position as a night switchboard operator, took a room at the wrong end of Ebury Street and wrote a novel. After which he concluded he wanted no other than to be a writer. Whereupon, and very sensibly, he tore up his first opus, and rapidly penned another. Which was accepted, published and even welcomed, with only a smattering of adverbs to qualify the reviewers' good opinions.

After ten years Spenser could name eight novels to his credit, a reasonable publisher, a small readership, Hilda, a new bicycle and the villa in Camberwell.

Hilda, with a room in the same Ebury Street house, came early into his modest collection of chattels. He would read to her his daily output almost before she'd recovered from a gruelling day behind the department-store counter—handbags—almost before she could finish preparing an evening meal for both of them. He was outlining the plot of his third story as they walked to the registry office. They were reading the proofs of his fourth novel the night she asked, quite calmly, to be taxied to the hospital.

Cot deaths are damnable affairs, too often leaving the parents, mothers especially, with a feeling of guilt. By the time he could bring himself to master his fifth story Hilda had returned to her old job. Worked so feverishly management misinterpreted it as zealousness, promoting her for her loyalty.

But, something had come into and gone out of their lives. Not imperceptibly, but quite suddenly, the Damocles sword lowered itself to repose in uncompromising nakedness between the occupants of a once conjugal Slumberland.

Spencer was the first to theorise that Hilda could never again face the fact that sexual love could kill.

Hilda was the only one to divine it.

To do him credit, he'd respected her notion, however misconceived, and never dreamed of buying a scabbard for the sword.

The cards are dealt. Life must go on. The childless couple gave to work what could nevermore be given to the cradle. Hilda prospered and shared in the affluent years, found in the new god of Materialism something imperishable—unlike flesh and blood. Spenser, half-supported by her earnings, wrote, tore up and wrote again.

He was published, it's true, by a House noted for its tolerance; but increasingly it sensed a missing ingredient, or rather, suspected too much was showing. Tendencies to radicalise every issue Spenser touched on, suggested a firebrand incendiary enough to reduce all to ashes. So far, kept in bounds he could command a limited interest. With his sixth novel he threatened to bore. Gentle hints at this point had little effect; broad accusation of 'extravagant suppositions' by the waning band of reviewers worried Spenser not at all. The crusader was never born who cared how deeply rust bit into his once shining armour.

But when sales fall and royalties dwindle, even complacency must look askance at the writing on the balance sheet.

'It isn't as if you can't write, Adam. Consensus has it that you're still good and could be better if only—'

If only . . .

Spenser, more comfortably ensconced at home, but tacked, in spirit, to the edge of an uncompromising chair in Threlfall's office, painfully recalled every word of that interview not a stone's throw from another thorny subject: the Elgin Marbles. One of his few impressive accomplishments, that total recall; quite uncannily so.

They ate, as always, in a small, homely kitchen: bentwood chairs painted white edged a rough deal table, washing on the airer and cereal packets on an open shelf, that kind of familiar setting. Spenser idly watched Hilda opening a can of peaches but, it might have shocked people under no edict as baneful as his, to know he saw little more than an idea, hardly an embodiment of someone he accepted as Hilda, as he accepted the can of peaches; but where was actual proof of the essential contents till they were liberated, displayed?

Briefly, and in typically spasmodic fashion, he'd regaled Hilda and the half neglected omelette with all that had passed in Threlfall's office. Very nearly all.

Half aware of half concealed anguish she shook out peaches into bowls and brought them to the table.

'Evaporated?' she offered the can in a flat tone of voice still echoing the doctor's explanation, 'Cot-death?' Yet Spenser knew, in sadness, how spry she could sound with customers and colleagues. He shook his head and concentrated on chasing goldfish with a spoon.

At times she found grace enough to admit how—disappointing

—life had become, and would make a special effort. He was too sensitive not to recognise amends, so her belated show of interest brought no immediate reaction.

'Was that all he said?' she repeated.

'I'd have thought it—' he paused to find a simple, meaningful word, '—enough.'

Almost genuinely bewildered in spite of herself. 'But if they published your last—'

Spenser scooped a goldfish and let it escape. 'That's just it. Very nearly my last as far as Threlfall's concerned. A hint's as good as a wink.' Not only completing sentences but delivery thickened by a Lancashire twinge never too far below the surface.

Hilda grew decisive, peaches, shop-lifters and much else forgotten for *some* of the duration. She saw clearly he was badly affected by the day's events and needed a bit of—of stimulus, encouragement—or something. 'People haven't stopped reading you. What more do they want?'

'Profitability,' abruptly, 'they want big bangs, best-sellers and Nobel Literature prize packets—to be fair to them, they also want me to share in my . . . prosperity.'

Spenser's unprepossessing features could have done without the disfiguring taint of bitterness. All suddenly he seemed to mirror the world as he'd portrayed it in two or three thousand pages. For sure the eyes remained true to his real self and even they . . . as if he'd applied tincture of wormwood with an eye-dropper.

'You must go on as you always have.'

With a change of tone as he couldn't remember since the three of them were last alive. He looked up and at *her* almost for the first time since homecoming, but with anguish and hopeless enquiry such that tears must have come from any but a woman so determinedly bereft.

'I appreciate that, Hilda, I really do. But it won't wash with Threlfall. If only because of what he—'

'What! What did he say?' Not solicitude, resentment rather, charged her outburst; that he should so deliberately keep her in the dark with some unpleasant, still unrelated fact.

Undeniable. But only because the poor scribbler couldn't bring himself to report aloud what, like a dubious incantation, had haunted him all the way from Bloomsbury, across the river, through the redness of traffic lights, at the feet of nonplussed police officers, along the garden path and into the light of home, happiness, *Access Man*, canned peaches and overcooked sauerkraut omelette.

Yet, it had to be said, if only to convince the one person who'd cared in once-upon-time days that Threlfall had advised lightly, but not in jest. He roused himself and addressed the kitchen clock way above her head.

'He said, "why don't you put more sex into your tales. It's a sure-fire way of raising sales these days, and you can still make the points that seem so dear to you".'

Whereupon Spenser repaired to the bathroom and privately wept while Hilda washed the dishes.

Time is the dash between Tragi and Comedy. In Spenser's case the necessary interval lasted for weeks turning to months during which he strove to agree terms with a barely palatable truth.

Tragic or comic, crisis in any man's life begs a review of all he thought he'd lived for. Spenser, in that process, tracked down the nexus between his days marital and professional. Yet, paradoxically, he saw how unwittingly he'd laboured to keep the two apart; had, by so doing, banished all significant emotional content from his work because very little existed in the one formal and forlorn relationship he'd ever aspired to.

Review, for him, meant reappraisal of all his work, published and otherwise. Apart from a superficial boy and girl encounter in that first novel, there occurred hardly a playful peck let alone a sexual situation, express or implied, in all else.

*Amour propre* dug him in the ribs with a wicked leer: could the world possibly think him ignorant of the ins and outs of—things?

Nothing more said to Hilda. She had too little interest in his work to act the confidante and he somehow felt it would be 'coarse' to discuss the larger question anyway. Which led him to wonder if, after all, he'd slipped unwarily on a Puritan streak.

Squarely facing the three F's: fumes, fizz and fornication, he could deny smoking, seldom drank and couldn't remember looking at women in that way at any time of life except briefly, he supposed, in those halcyon days with Hilda.

Then how the hell, he more than once demanded of *alter ego, did* he enjoy himself? A shame-facing question to most of manhood but the truth appeared to be that Spenser lagged far behind his fellow men in pursuit of the pleasure principle. To be precise, he had not that cast of mind paraphrased as egg-timer mentality by the renowned behavioural psychologist, C. P. E. Smellt. Let him speak for himself: 'Three minutes for a cigarette, fifteen for a cigar, approximately seventy for a shot of Bourbon and two minutes in top gear for a lay if you're undisciplined spermodynamically. No wonder the human race keeps on coming. For survival on blissful terms it *has* to try everything once and that's the meaning and genesis of habit because nobody believes in once.'

If Spenser hadn't read Smellt's *Pleasure gets you Nowhere— Somehow* he could still have managed because frankly he enjoyed almost everything. Not with an open-armed, lips parted, panting after kind of pleasure, but quietly, almost shyly, he cared so much about life in its commonplace details that he came perilously near to being a man in love with mere existence; a rare and suspect breed these days.

In other words, to itemise Spenser's share of the pleasure principle would fill a phone directory with a stream of consciousness and be as fascinating as names and numbers galore.

Being thorough in research Spenser read much else besides Smellt on the subject, from ponderous pseudo-tomes to women's mags. It bored him.

He bethought himself of the friend who came around once a week while Hilda was elsewhere, visiting her widowed mother in Penge. Hilda couldn't stand him. 'Uncouth' and 'coarse-grained' were the more charitable of her epithets. But it was that honest fundamentalism, that veritable rawness of character that our man of fastidious temperament best liked in Tom Dollison.

One of Spenser's books had taken Tom's especial fancy. He'd written, without diffidence, to the author and the author, gratified by no-nonsense appreciation, had replied. Somehow, after a tentative meeting, friendship had ripened undeclared, slowly over a year or two, till now, three months after Threlfall's advice to the bewildered author, he could venture to air his quandary, share his dilemma hopefully seeking a solution which seemed to recede with every hour spent in sifting the matter.

Tom, by the way, sold flowers from a stall close to the Green. Eyes twinkled in a weather beaten face not ill-favoured or disfigured by the hard knocks of five and forty years; otherwise, solemn-seeming in face of a world grown more and more guilty of taking itself seriously. Until the eyes betrayed him . . . but not this time, not after listening, seated in a favoured armchair in Spenser's tiny back-room study, to his companion's halting recital of the facts.

'Now that's what I call queer, Mr Spenser. Such as I never heard before and I've heard much.' Phlegmish tones but an oddly dated albeit respectful command of the English tongue seldom heard even among his intellectual betters these days. No salt, pepper and vinegar of 'in' jargon spoiled his delivery.

'Queer it is, Tom. Yet *there* it is. If I don't hew to the line, my credit dries up and it's Quink down the sink.'

Tom had no doubts, thumped his knees for emphasis. 'Find another publisher then. One who says "write what you like and be damned".'

Spenser smiled but shook his head firmly, poured more strong tea for his friend before he explained. 'Not that simple. Threlfall doesn't say, "don't write what you care about", only, "give it more human interest and then we'll all be happy".'

'You quoted him differently.'

Adam looked surprised. 'Did I?'

'He mentioned sex, now you're talking of human interest. There's a difference.'

The practitioner in words conceded willingly but not condescendingly. Tom was no ordinary flower-seller.

'Now why,' he pursued, 'did you talk of human interest? For reason enough, because that's what informs your stories. Remember what Plautus said: being myself a human being, I can't be indifferent to what concerns the rest of us—or was it Terence?'

'Even so—'

'Even so, I could name you ten writers who never stop dropping their trousers in public and you could match me as many women who never stop stepping out of their step-ins in print—agreed?'

Spenser smiled and said he supposed so.

'You *know* so!'

'I know that sex is reckoned to be a guiding fundamental principle, nowadays at least.'

'And I know it's no such thing. Love yes, sex no. It's the theatre of the absurd degenerating into the theatre of cruelty. Like Wren said—look around you.'

The writer said it couldn't be dismissed, half-persuaded as he was that Threlfall and the rest had a point.

'The point is *conscious*, Mr Spenser, and that puts it right out of court. Look, God never said let there be libido or Shakespeare would've turned William Charlatan and re-written *Romeo and Juliet*.'

'Meaning?'

'Integrity. Till those precious psychologues popped up every man Jack and Jill was an *integrated* personality. Treat *that* with X-ray diffraction and that's what you'll get, fractions, fractious personalities, and integrity's a dirty word.'

No ordinary flower-seller was Tom. Spenser pushed the plate of buttered buns towards him, a petty gesture of admiration. But:

'Is that quite the same thing as—?'

'I know what you're a-going to say. Yes, it *is* in the same breath as "integrated".'

'And the evidence?'

'Is on my side. Sure enough, when there was good and bad the worst criminal had a conscience, could feel remorse, scaffold or not. He was integrated enough to recall a rough kind of integrity and none the less for lacking polish. Now, a candidate for Holy Orders can strangle his mother and forgive himself ... that's diffraction, different parts of the same feller going different ways.'

He could have clarified destinies for a living if flowers hadn't got there first. But still Adam Spenser's regard for Tom just came second to a doubt that challenges to preserve his integrity would quite serve.

'Do you *want* to make money?' Tom wondered after a longish pause.

'I'm happy to make enough.'

'Well, there you are,' Tom's triumphant gesture was hardly spoiled by a handful of buttered tea-cake.

'Yes but I'm *not* making enough. That's the point.'

'. . . have you talked to the Missus about this?'

'No more than the plain facts,' Spenser was looking elsewhere.

'Ah,' and so was Tom. 'Not an easy subject.'

The meaning escaped his companion, unaware of Tom's sense of delicacy and command of tactful non sequiturs. On the scantiest evidence he probably knew more about Adam and Hilda than both of them knew of each other.

He regarded the man fidgeting with a teaspoon till the thought he'd been looking for took a likely shape. Leaning forward:

'Tell me, friend, is it advice you're wanting, or straight encouragement to go on a voyage clean contrary to your prevailing wind?'

Adam considered carefully before glancing up, no other movement but that of his eyes. 'Would either serve?'

Tom's turn then, to look unsure, if raised eyebrows meant anything. 'Not,' he agreed carefully, 'if it served better for you to work round to your own perspective on the matter.'

Perfect accord, friendship's acme! Spenser smiled his admiration. 'You're a cunning seller of flowers, Tom.'

At which Tom Dollison beamed, waved away more tea, brought out his pipe, lit the thing and contentedly nursed it to volcanic intensity before inviting Spenser to fire away.

'Well . . . the trouble is, I brought myself up to believe all things are possible. You'd disagree?'

A decided shake of the head. 'No—saving the gravitational theory.'

'And the thought was deep down uppermost as I rode home that night. I knew Threlfall was right, knew I could do it if I wanted to.'

'Any fool can pander to the masses.'

'No—that's not quite what I mean . . . simply a question of standing outside a self-imposed frame of reference. To do what you enjoy doing, doing it well, and doing it repeatedly is like saying "I prefer taking the line of least resistance because it's more comfortable".'

'I can guess if I don't know, the effort writing books must cost. I sweat freely writing a post-card.'

Objection easily overruled. '"Laboured" is the preferred term among reviewers. And a case can be made out d'you see, for a touch of masochism in our line.'

'No, I don't see. Longinus never mentioned it and Dostoevsky never practised it.'

'I'd argue Dostoevsky.'

'Argue then. Masochism is self-imposed nonsense, his was inner anguish because of outward conditions. He did it in Russian but that don't alter the fact it was necessary.'

'Necessary?'

'Greatness is suffering—beyond the last ditch.'

'Oh, come now, I'm talking about me. More tea?'

'No more tea, and I'm also talking about you.'

'A third rate novelist, "tinkering" as one sympathetic reviewer pin-pointed, "with the social mechanism to find the one tick that matters."'

'I'm ignorant. Interpret for me.'

'In a word—"obsessive".'

'So if you wrote fifty romantic novels, no one'd mention obsession,' Tom supposed.

'Of course not. Romance isn't sex.'

'And marzipan doesn't grow on wedding cakes. But where does that leave you on your first point?'

Adam looked blank. Tom had to remind him. 'You're the one who believes all things are possible.'

Momentary dejection, the shadow of it passed visibly over Adam Spenser as he looked out at the window. A small, well-tended garden showed signs of Spring's none too sober influence, but the writer saw not a bit further than his theory.

'I'm glad you reminded me. True enough, a question of whether I can persuade myself that proving a point isn't another name for giving in?'

A long, reflexive silence. With much to digest there has to be a break in transmission. Tom was first back on the air.

'Give it a try. Astonish us. Prove you can and then say you won't—ever again.'

'Difficult.'

'Easier than you think. Love's difficult, but that's not what he asked for. Is it?'

A wealth of understanding was shared by two seemingly dissimilar men on that particular Saturday afternoon.

We know the sequel in essence. With the grimmest of smiles Adam Spenser sat down at his desk immediately after Tom's departure and, except for the distraction of basic daily needs, he scarcely stopped writing for six or seven weeks. Nor did he bate that humourless smile a jot. He chatted commonplaces with Hilda, discussed the developing story with Tom not at all, and his dynamic self soared above an uncustomary languor born of those barren, doubting months.

Typed and corrected *The Immortal Coil* landed in time and with an enormous thud, on Threlfall's desk.

Threlfall, in publishing terms, seldom made an error of judgment. He possessed to a remarkable degree, a quality of perception that went to the very frontiers and beyond. His staff admired and almost feared him. Remoteness they could understand and allow for; but his uncanny approach to the business went far beyond their reckoning.

Every manuscript submitted to Threlfall and Lardiner went straight to the former—Lardiner was close to retirement. A long table held the day's offerings. His secretary had them laid out for inspection by nine o'clock, at which time he would enter, glance through the remaining mail, cross to the table and select one, possibly two of the exhibits—occasionally none—whereupon he would summon his secretary and have her distribute the jetsam to his editors.

Mark! Simply by looking at the object, without reference to its content, title or category, he would hand pick, as it were, precisely the material most likely to show the best sales figures of all the works—accepted.

Presumably Waterloos are made for Napoleons. How it happened that particular morning no one knew, but it is a fact that Threlfall's hand hovered over *The Immortal Coil*—and passed on. Threlfall would explain in due course that he sensed an unsanitary aura surrounding the stack of typescript, but pique may sour the best of grapes.

By ten o'clock the novel had been delivered to Elroy Flecker—no relation to James—and though Flecker was hardly more than a three-year-old on the editorial staff he was as likely to receive Spenser's work as anybody, there being no pecking order in that sense.

A pity he got it, as it happened; a pity for Flecker's fragile peace of mind of which he had little enough to spare at any time. Pale, thin, scholarly, Flecker, at thirty, a Durham MA and a compulsive poet with two BBC broadcasts under his belt and a slim book of verse still at the cleaners, was as harassed a young intellectual as one could manage without. Everything worried him; his talent, his breath, his smoking, even his undoubted good looks.

As an editor, he proved competent, painstaking and devoid of flair, worshipping the sweeping phrase but agonising over a comma that ought, or not, to attend it. His personality was unwieldy and since no one else could wield it for him he remained an innocent, unworldly, untouched by experience which he took on board as insensibly as a container ship stows a cargo of books.

As a consequence, there are those who say that Elroy should never have received *The Immortal Coil* without a doctor's prescription for Librium, but that's to be wise after the event.

The fact remains: he got it. Started desultorily to skip through the first few pages; and couldn't put it down. All that morning, through cancelled appointments, coffee break, lunch hour and beyond, Elroy Flecker was inaccessible to any but his shared secretary who peeped round the door as often as she dared, with discreet enquiries about his health.

The bulging eyes didn't bother her, they tended appealingly that way anyhow; but the man was so obviously perspiring—freely—by half-past two, she felt loyally bound to be alarmed.

Never before, she confided to a colleague, had she seen Mr Flecker wriggle in his seat.

At five o'clock he took *The Immortal Coil* with him, read it again, drank black coffee, smoked endlessly, braved a cold shower and went to bed. Four nightmares later he woke up with 'beeswax' on his lips in a small bachelor flat hard by Clifford's Inn. One might have thought dawn was breaking his heart, the hour was so early.

From his office, later that morning, he rang Spenser and made a firm four o'clock appointment, but went through the day with a shrunken air, as if thunderbolts were in the offing. At frequent intervals his glazed eye would stray to the typescript, an act of slumbering provocation in a coy coloured folder not far from his elbow . . . pink.

At three o'clock Jane looked in to see if he wanted tea. She found him staring at the door behind her as if it hadn't opened, as though she interposed her shapely self between it and his line of vision.

'Tea, Mr Flecker?' she repeated.

He managed to force his attention on her with an effort of will, his face puckered with depthless perplexity.

'But why a *galvanised* bucket?'

No girl is attractive when the jaw sags that far. 'Bucket?'

'Yes . . . please Jane.'

'You—want it in a bucket?'

'In a—' Exasperated he brought a fist down on the desk. 'It's no joking matter! For God's sake fetch me a cup of tea. Lots of sugar.'

She went.

An hour later she removed his cup—cautiously—mentioned Mr Spenser's presence in the outer office. 'I can put him off if you wish.'

'Put him off?' irritably. 'I've waited all day to see that man. Show him up at once, Jane.'

Spenser's sea change was from customary doldrums to a billowy nor'wester. Life-style unvaried maybe but here, to a seeing eye, was a super-imposed brashness that never should have been. Wasn't he noted for his diffidence, for gentle deprecation, even of his best work? No better apologist needed and, in a sense, publishing people found him almost too accommodating, lacking that cantankerous spark invariably marking the superior talent from the many.

'He writes with the conviction that he writes from conviction,' thus Threlfall had long since dismissed Spenser.

Who normally displayed a real anxiety to be quit of the premises in the shortest possible time. To whomever he had to deal with he'd apologise for taking up so much of it. Two minutes into a discussion on editorial matters would have him muttering about editors having more important things to do. People said it was shyness; unkind spirits suggested personal inadequacy. Consensus decided on a mixture of both.

Wrong, this time, as to shyness. Spenser swaggered into Flecker's office armed with a boldness biblically associated with harlots. A different man? Certainly, if a face-lift can rejuvenate septuagenarians. A mask is reality enough, but so is what it conceals.

Flecker could be excused for not apprehending that importance. He'd twice read the work of the man before him. Man and work appeared to be in tandem. The style so eminently fitted the present Spenser he quite forgot the other one.

'So you've read it, eh?' not a lechery leer exactly, but an inflection unpleasant enough to suggest the elbow nudge of a strip-club 'pouncer'.

Flecker groped for words: a man in the dark searching desperately for a match and a dictionary.

'I've read it—with care,' he temporised, intent on sorting impressions, coming to terms with this blatant handstand of personality.

'And you'll publish, of course.'

The editor swallowed hard, peering in disbelief at so much—

blatancy. Spenser, of all people, asserting his self, his work and something more which Flecker simply could not identify. He determined to make the one uppermost point before the situation quite swept him away.

'This,' he tapped the pink folder gingerly, 'is the filthiest book I've ever read.'

'You're privileged to be the first. It's good, eh?'

'Good!'

Spenser came smartly back on his feet, eyes blazing, teeth bared, yes, bared, not for a fatuous ingratiatory grin but, plainly, for a snarl.

'Yes! Good! Mr Word Dabbler. Let's call a spade exactly that. Good! Now have the nerve to deny the choice of word before I go further and pronounce it *damned* good.'

So many exclamation marks of violence. They couldn't miss at that range. Flecker parried with stunned silence, still trying to reconcile a new missile with an old mediocrity. He put his trust in appeasement.

'It's extremely well written, I won't deny that. The story line is ingenious—er—yes, ingenious . . . but—'

'But what?'

Flecker realised a perspiring brow as a lurid scene came untimely to mind. It had to do with a jar of—he checked, then burst out: 'It's filthy—sheer pornography!'

Spenser's snarl turned to a predatory smile. 'Sexy?'

'Well yes—but—'

'But—but—but! Come now, Elroy, I've known you hew my last work into your image to my face with as effortless a flow of words as anyone could desire. Now I'm regaled with more buts than I'd find in an SDP manifesto. Kindly be more explicit.'

Flecker quailed at the mere idea, formed as he had been in a poetic mould. Not to employ the blandest, most urbane of phraseology to clothe naked thoughts seemed worse than blundering on his favourite Muse engaged in the toilet. No, this sudden stranger was too crude for words.

He tried.

'You—you mentioned on the phone, you were advised to write something more—with more of that sort of thing in it—words to that effect. In this—novel there's nothing else.'

'Sex? Explicit? Plain and unvarnished?'

Flecker checked at the flung questions. Good Lord! The fellow was right—or nearly so. 'Well not exactly.'

'What exactly?'

The editor's expression grew fugitive. 'The hero,' he blurted, 'John Thomas—'

'Thomas John.'

'Very well!' nettled. 'Does it matter?'

'Only to the carelessly tuned mind. Go on.'

'His—his *modus operandi* so to say.' Flecker's hunted look grew ambiguous. 'A portable computer complete with software, a jar of pickles, a pound of beeswax and a bucket . . .'

'Galvanised iron—not plastic. Well?'

'It's utterly filthy!' a blurt magnificent.

'Why?'

'Why?' Flecker's ruby red countenance was death to his customary pale cast of thought. 'But what does he *do* with them?'

'Doesn't it tell you in the narrative?'

'Not—not in so many words.'

'Implicit. Then I've done it.' Spenser nodded to himself, briefly pent in depthless satisfaction, triumph. Brooding calm, not lasting long enough for Flecker's battered peace of mind, startled as he was by Spenser's sudden rounding of the desk to dominate its proprietor nose very nearly to nose.

'Now *you* listen to *me*. You'll publish. I don't give a damn one way or the other, but you'll catch the train of events and you'll publish. Threlfall's no fool. He'll take some of your line but unlike you, he'll know he's got a winner. Tropic of Capricorn! *This* is the Tropics! Steam heat—miles and miles of shanty sauna town along the Costa Brava—video-vice in a million semi-detached brothels—I've taken stick from him, dirt from you. Now you'll take both from me and find your consolation in the sales charts. "This is filth" say you. *I* say John Thomas is Thomas John, so wash your mind first, then publish and be damned to you.'

'This is—!'

'Intolerable. What else to a liberal with an L so small it wouldn't show up in a midget's rectum.'

'You're being gratuitously offensive!' Flecker hauled himself up from a losing posture to look over the edge of some abyss of Spenser's own creating.

'Offensive!' Spenser pushed him down again. 'You make me

sick. Sick of contemplating years of creating situations, characters, free of the slime you didn't want but felt the public ought to have. You bemoan sex but welcome the necessary evil, just as old Mrs Grundy gets a double kick from drooling over TV toss-ups before throwing up her sweaty hands for righteousness' sake. Contempt! because I *implied* sex was a lousy, exploitable fraud leading up to the ins and outs, not worth the mentioning when there's more to life than bits of lacy flimsy and a jangle of bedsprings.'

'There's more to it than that!' Flecker found he was engaged in spite of himself.

'Look for an item in last January's *Telegraph* then tell me so again. More? Romance? True love? That's for living—nevermore for story books, Flecker. Every beatitude has to be grounded in values ... what's bent, what's kinky, what's quirky is your measure—only let it be literary. Right! I take a friend's advice, I heed Threlfall's injunction, and I sit down to write an odorous bestseller. But find me a word to make a nun blush. A bucket? Pickles? Beeswax? I'm really surprised at you, Flecker. It's all in that great universal, unwashed ... I thought you were clean.'

Not another word. Quite suddenly the cloudburst ended and the hapless Flecker found himself alone searching about, like an armchair beachcomber, for stray fragments of self-possession.

Spenser's confidence was nothing displaced. Indecent haste seemed appropriate for the speed with which *The Immortal Coil* reached the bookshelf. Compulsive from the beginning, through the bemused Threlfall, the St Vitus' staff dance, the tremulous printers, the dazed reviewers, till it landed at last in multifarious hands; begged, borrowed, stolen or sold, it created a sensation best described as a puzzled frown of ecstasy on the fevered brow of a public that was to spread from here to there and everywhere.

But why? The marvelling House of Threlfall and Lardiner asked itself as orders poured in for more copies, more editions, translation rights. Ever and again its inmates had to remind themselves and each other, not a word of obscenity, not a situation of pornographic intent appeared on a single page.

What, they wondered, had two million readers found in the narrative powerful enough to create a shortage of pails, a rise in the price of pickles, a dearth of beeswax and buoyant sales of portable computers with software? One harassed secretary had spent a morning with violent hysterics after opening a letter which simply read: 'Dear Sir, Mr Spenser is bang to rights. Plastic buckets are no effing use at all. Yours disgusted.'

The reviewers did nothing to clarify the precipitate phenomenon. To no avail Threlfall's studied and re-studied Dorothea Clutt's influential rave in *the* paper.

'I aver unhesitatingly that England will be turned inside out by this significant addition to our already rich bibliography. Mr Spenser has revealed to us, in lambent literary fashion, our collective id. I go further, and assert that no man or woman acquainted with this masterpiece will ever again walk abroad without flourishing his or her id with pride, flaunty as a carnationed button-hole or an idly swinging handbag.

'Nevermore need we be ashamed of our personal buckets, those grails of newfound meaningfulness. Freud, Jung and Schlumuky pale and tremble before triumphant John Thomas who strides through the pages trampling our willing hearts and minds under the winged boots of a fairy Colossus, knowing *exactly* where and when to plumb our each and every hidden depth. What an Odyssey! All the way from Baron's Court to Cockfosters sustained by a small miracle of science and a lump of beeswax. "What," as his eager victim, Angela, the thirty-fourth cries out in delicious anguish, "are you *not* capable of?" What indeed!

'*The Immortal Coil* is a *venite mecum*, a "must" to the thirsty body, the parched soul forever wandering through the aridity of our frayed and flaccid sexual mores. When John Thomas reflectively kicks the bucket—and how delicately, with what wealth of meaning does the author describe those gentle taps—are we not coerced to echo Edwina the forty-seventh's frissoning cry: "This is definitive"? One knows—as the left ventricle "knows" the purpose of the right auricle, exactly what she means.

'Let criticism burn for sacrilege, unless the teeniest pittance permits me to wonder at the precise meaning of the pickles; but then one must, like so many, bow to the melancholy fact that the universal John Thomas dangles, unreachable in some respects, on a higher, ever more remote plane.'

Yes, but what did it all *mean*? On the whole, Threlfall's were not taken in; while yet being borne along and aloft on the unprecedented rush, the sheer stampede of inexplicable enthusiasm, their query simply disappeared into the vortex.

Spenser refused to revoke their bewilderment or satisfy their humbly expressed enquiries. His response never varied: 'It's what you wanted. You've got it.'

He became, if anything, more retiring than before. In obscurity he'd receded; with new found fame he recessed almost entirely. In outward appearance he seemed unchanged. But only to Tom Dollison did Spenser reveal the depths of his now gold-plated anguish, a depression of spirits not even the flower-seller could lift at first.

'You're well-heeled enough to write what you like now, Mr Spenser.'

'It doesn't work like that, Tom. "Give me back my legions" is the age-old cry.'

'"Give it time" is another. And remember, you've made a lot of people smile. Sit back awhile, enjoy the commotion made by the ones who take it seriously. Let 'em make *you* smile.'

Sensibly, Spenser heeded a wise man's advice, read and listened with growing amusement to the unending plaudits, the everlasting theories, the almost daily evidence of the multitudes' total surrender —to a mere formula. Not too surprisingly his spirits ventured to soar a little with each succeeding incident of light relief. Then drooped a bit as he remembered his responsibility for so much extra folly.

Those oddities for example, who came to his Camberwell villa as to a national shrine; and the celebrities, overt and covert, seeking elucidation, enlightenment or simply to touch the mantle of this unlikely guru of the leaping libido. He played their game unashamedly, amused himself contemptuously at their expense, watched them leave with sparkling eyes, satisfied that he'd enlarged their understanding enough to claim oneupmanship among their fellows.

Excepting Mr Fukiyama perhaps. A wealthy industrialist come all the way from Hokkaido, smiling, bowing, gleaming from teeth to spectacles, immaculate to an almost religious degree.

'So pleased to meet you, Mr Spensah. Your kindness to condescend we meet most appreciated.'

Spenser assured him his pleasure, noted the powerful American accent. Offered tea and a chair, Fukiyama took the chair, refused tea.

'Curiosity brings me across time zone, Mr Spensah. Your book of course. Most successful in my country.'

The novelist murmured something about being gratified. And waited.

The industrialist cleared his throat fit to spit. 'Have discussed with many of my associates the—the mechanics of your most interesting experiments. We agree, you have mastered indispensable technique of computer know-how—harnessing hi-tech to deepest bodily pleasure. Hogh! Have recommended Fuki SK1007 being most harmonious in calculated benefit. Fuki SK1007 our improved model—much favoured.'

Spenser nodded, mildly wondering as Mr Fukiyama's comprehensive smile suddenly shattered, as it were, all over his face. His spectacles glittered like twin shards.

'But—don't understand, Mr Spensah.'

'Oh?'

'What hell Mr Thomas John get from his exquisite calculations? Women fine, except for deviationist Lola the seventeenth, with hang-up on account of pickles. Everyone else happy, but Mr Thomas John . . .'

Spenser leaned forward confidentially. The Japanese industrialist leaned in highly expectant response, features creased like a bad attack of origami.

'You forget, Mr Fukiyama. The galvanised—iron—bucket.'

Not horror-stricken exactly, the new expression, but utter failure to comprehend can look horrible.

'Bucket?'

Spenser leaned back in his armchair and gazed dreamily at the curtains behind and above his head.

'I refuse to believe the significance of the bucket can be lost on the subtle perfection of your delicate sensibilities—or those of your colleagues, Mr Fukiyama.'

The visitor flashed a smile that went in the very same flash.

'Sure, Mr Spensah. Most kind—but I—but we, get damn everything from our buckets—we try several—get nothing. So what does he get?'

'Remember the beeswax,' Spenser exhorted, a shade too solemnly, nodding the while as he gazed into a pair of thoroughly disoriented eyes.

'Beeswax . . . hogh!'

'Exactly. I see you understand perfectly.'

Those adverbs again . . . some hours later a small, immaculately dressed oriental gentleman with slightly glazed spectacles was to be observed wandering in Camberwell's environs spitting alien sounding words at regular intervals.

'Beeswax . . . hogh! Buckets . . . hogh! Pickles . . . hogh!'

Interludes merely in what proved to be a sad and irreversible decline. Happily, he reached a new, a better understanding with Hilda who'd learned to laugh again; there were moments shared with Tom and, briefly, with the narrator of this short account which, as many of you will have deduced, is to be the first published memorial to one of our most distinguished literary figures. He died happy, of a surfeit of laughter, soon after publication of an outsize tome entitled, *The Mystic Significance of Adam Spenser's Bucket.*

Poor Spenser will never be less than a paradox, because many believe he died of poetic justice, fooling the world at his peril. I incline to diagnose a broken heart, riven by the violence of laughter or, it may be, he suffered a massive haemorrhage after the too savage thrust of a well directed irony.

# THE EXHIBITION

MATRIX AND METRIX were, to use an obsolete term, devoted parents. Their off-spring had been lovingly rendered to the Greater Good of Mankind and no less carefully returned to them at the old and beautiful ceremony performed by the Elders of the community in the ancient parish hall.

They had promised Lucus, with ritual words, to watch carefully for any deviations from the code of Right Thinking, to eradicate all signs of uncleanliness (as, self-seeking, personal ambition and covetousness), always to keep his body and mind active, and to instil, gently but firmly, by precept and example, the one true Catechism into his understanding.

It entailed enormous expense, but no one dreamed of begrudging the once-in-a-lifetime luxury. Clothes to be made or mended, the life subscription to Thinktight, a monthly magazine devoted to the cult of the Reasonable. The book of Nestorius must also be purchased and, what with the entertainment one was bound to provide for the neighbours and the small presents by tradition requiting the Elders for their services, Metrix found himself left with little change from his monthly income of fifty metaloids. Yet, he reflected, the same applied to all. No one had more or less; so if everyone felt the pinch, that was to make much ado about nothing of consequence.

Son Lucus was nearing his fourteenth year and Metrix, there and then, taking pleasure in the fact, coupled it with a touch of controlled pride at thought of his thriving market garden business.

Satisfaction . . . how could that be? Satisfied! Did he not see the shabbiness of their dress oddly contrasting with his wife's new skin coat? Did it occur to him that travelling in an ancient diesel train converted to a steam system dependent on compressed rubbish blocks was scarcely elegant in this, his day and age?

Such thoughts, believe it, had perished before he was born.

Metrix knew well enough, life is not the unalloyed pleasure all those dead layers of humanity had so desperately wished it to be.

Times without number he'd read in his tattered copy of Nestorius, existence is meaningless without a degree of privation, of suffering and anxiety.

Manfully then, if not cheerfully, he could accept his problem. The boy, Lucus, worried him a little. It was bothersome that a child of his age should ask so many questions, about so many things to most of which Metrix himself had no answer.

The rule, framed as a monition by Nestorius, was clear. 'Better not to ask questions.' It applied to all, children and adults. 'Especially the children, but particularly the adults,' as Thinktight had so disarmingly summarised.

That kind of prohibition is no tyranny. The people knew Nestorius was right; knew why he was right. For a handful of millenia Man had questioned the meaning of everything from God to gaslight and, at last, had driven himself insane, locked in a mad-house realisation—there are no answers—only a fixed and irrevocable set of predetermined circumstances creating a Tantalus syndrome by the everlasting operation of cause and effect.

No, not half so much passed through Metrix's mind as he gazed fondly, apprehensively, at the boy in threadbare trousers and worn jerkin. But he remembered the Elder's advice. 'Take him to the Exhibition. That'll shift the edge off his curiosity.'

Maybe it would, but there he sat, so obviously about to ask yet another question. Something about the way he puckered his brow and rubbed his knees as though to iron wrinkles out of a crumpled idea.

'Why do they make coats out of human skins?'

Metrix glanced deprecatingly at his wife already tossing her head to show what she thought of such a question. Long and often she would talk to the boy but she never replied to any but the simplest domestic query.

Her husband was doubly discomfited because she happened to be wearing just such a coat, not smart perhaps, but serviceable and none too easy to come by. He would have to explain, knowing Lucus would give him no peace, by word of mouth, or those expressive brown eyes, until he returned a satisfactory answer.

'Because nothing's to waste, boy. More often than not, when they dig them out—the skin comes away mixed up with fibres. They're left with piles of it . . . not to be wasted. Everything has its use.'

Perhaps that would satisfy. Uneasily he watched the lad staring at the rich brown countryside so boring in its sameness, but growing more fertile with the years ... no it wouldn't satisfy. Again, that curious working of the lips.

'But why not animals and things, the way you said it used to be?'

'There're never enough—not like long ago.' Metrix felt his palms grow clammy, not because of the question, but Matrix's expression of disapproval had turned severe as though—he all but smiled at the thought—as though it was her very own skin they were discussing.

'How many times must I tell, Lucus? We never talk about the past—it's a very long way off and—'

'Then why are we going so far to see it?'

His father's frown turned to a lighter shade of astonishment. What was one to make of a child's logic?

'Because it's a specially prepared exhibition, intended to answer all the questions you ask in such a way as you need never to ask them again.' He quoted as best he could recollect a passage from last month's Thinktight.

'"The Exhibition, now in its hundredth year, is more than a part of our controlled history programme, it has become an everlasting reminder of our commitment to know and so, to discount, the past. In this year, 170 A.C. will be displayed new acquisitions to the collection, a reminder that our pioneers are working ceaselessly to unearth towns and cities that were once the pride and glory of this island before—"'

'Yes, but why "specially" prepared?'

Extraordinary! a mere word seemed to disturb the boy. Yet, Metrix understood well enough the old wives' phenomenon called growing pains. Lucus, at the threshold of comprehension and without the advantage of experience, could sense the cataclysmic without defining or even knowing the word. 'To stand, dumbly ignorant, in first awareness of the cosmos,' thus Nestorius, 'that is adolescence.'

In more prosaic fashion Metrix recognised the need to handle the boy's bewilderment with care. He must do what he could ...

'It's difficult, Lucus. What happened, you see, all those years ago—it's still with us—and it was so big, so overwhelming, so—' he paused to make sure of the one word that could do justice to the concept, 'so horrific, well, we can't, all at once, make out the meaning of a civilisation that went before, I mean—under all that—a thousand years of accumulated odds and ends, from rarities to junk, all giving the country its—I suppose you'd say, its character.'

'But we know about the rest of the world,' Lucus objected.

'We know the rest of it was the same yet different. But our world—don't forget it swept over a lot of the Continent, wiped out best part of a highly complex,' Metrix struggled with half forgotten snatches from school textbooks, 'what did they call it, industrial, social, and agricultural infrastructure.'

'It didn't happen in our part of the world,' Matrix, not only the archetypal mother, filled with the kind of complacency that makes a fool of wisdom, but a Cornish woman for good measure, made her contribution with the finality of one who has said all that could possibly be said on the subject.

Metrix, the everlasting man, dialectic to the death, seized on the superficial scrap and worried at it with grave eagerness. 'No, my dear—but that don't mean we're lucky. The muds never swept over your father's farm, but what good's a rusty skeleton of a tractor, a car chassis, a milking machine or that refrigerator thing? It's understanding 'em is difficult.'

'We know all about those,' she said contemptuously.

'We know what they are, what they were used for, but who could design and build new ones—or even put up places to make 'em in—even supposing we wanted 'em?' He turned his attention particularly to the boy. 'It created a universal madness, you see, went far beyond our bit of the world. They came from all over, looked and shuddered and never glanced over their shoulders as they went back to tell the others. A universal madness . . . all that work, striving, creating, come to nothing. It was as though—' again the father paused, trying hard to verbalise a will-o-the-wisp idea that had eluded men since the year One A.C. '—as though Man—mankind had grown too old, too tired and defeated to bother with starting all over again.' He gestured lamely towards the grimy window. 'Maybe we're too wise to try; but that's why we make do with remnants, bits and pieces of the old civilisation we've cobbled together—like the castaway in that story about a desert island . . .'

A timely gesture. They were passing through a partly submerged town; once an appendage to the great metropolis itself.

Rectangularly a strange half building with a cupola of mud stippled with vegetation seemed to be sticking rather than standing in the morass of brown soil that had choked the town to death. It was,

Metrix explained, an old office block in which people called clerks and suchlike once worked.

'What did they do?'

'Do?' Metrix shrugged his broad shoulders. 'They added things up I suppose—and took things away—something like your aunt Dynax does in the Community shop.'

Lucus studied the wallowing ruin while he could, trying hard to imagine how it must have been on that day almost two centuries ago. Well then . . . he would find a long box, stand it on end at the brown sea's edge, and watch the tide surge in and swallow it gradually—that must be something like. Except that it came from above . . .

They were passing an odd sort of pyramidal structure, not fat and well fed like the Pyramids of Egypt; this was long and skinny with scale-seeming coverings. Many had fallen away to reveal huge blackened timbers. The whole contraption stood on a square base of stone and there was a funny parapet running round so that it half resembled an old castle tower.

'A church,' his father had seen the question coming. 'I remember well, there was one in the village but we had to take it down.'

'Why?'

'They all have to come down in time—those that're left. Building materials were scarce—still are—that much wood and stone is a Godsend.'

Lucus never thought to ask more. He knew there had been religions, a sort of idol worship in great halls like the ancient tithe barn at home. Nothing he'd learned so far gave a sensible impression of what it might once have meant. The Bible readings in the parish hall had no more mystical significance than the Dickens or Conrad or Dostoevsky readings; less if any, and certainly not much relationship to the hard business of growing.

Prayers he knew about.

'Did they pray to God before it happened—like the Israelites?' he felt a boyish pride in remembering the word.

'They didn't have time.' Metrix was remembering the story as he'd read it in Thinktight—articles—scraps—written by survivors, bequeathed, submitted, published; but he spoke of it as he had done countless times in the candle-lit tavern back home. A dozen of his generation listening and recounting in turn, as though repetition only could exorcise the deep-inlaid trauma, unearth the single clue that might resolve the riddle once for all: was it disgusting Destiny, or Destiny disgusted?

'It was fantastic—any way round you look at it. A giant meteor was all they could work out at first. It took months to discover what really happened, years for the shock to wear off. Old Primus, your teaching master, reckons we haven't got over it yet . . .

'Oil and gas . . . when they did find out—it was too late. Too late for us. All because the world was chasing its own tail, using up energy to find more energy to provide energy for power stations, electric typewriters, bread-knives, cars and such.

'They found it all right—in the North Sea—but for all their superior knowledge, they didn't know that oil created an enormous insulator between the earth's surface and its interior—a gigantic volcano—as if the world had swallowed a star and it's trying to get out again through one of those chimneys or fumaroles as I've heard they're called.

'Of course, it wasn't as simple as that. Oil of itself was no danger—but one spark breaking through a crack, igniting great caverns of gas *and air*—well . . .' Metrix's voice quivered with emotion at remembrance of an unexperienced enormity—'once it started there was no stopping the earth disembowelling itself. Millions upon millions of cubic feet of gas mixing with oil and air blew up—made a crater in the whole bed of the North Sea and a lot of the Baltic . . . nothing, except for devastation; coastlines, Denmark, parts of Norway just disappeared, gigantic cracks split Poland in two and earthquakes devastated the Continent. The explosions so great, the shock waves just killed—just killed millions . . . people in Africa were deafened, the ground shook in New Zealand. And then, as if that wasn't enough, the vacuum drew up every bit of the North Sea Bed, everything, rocks, mud, sea, sand, millions upon millions of tons of it, even sucked up the plains of East Anglia—Holland, Germany—Denmark—and all that stood on 'em, towns, whole towns, ports, farms, people, trains, ships, everything . . . sucked it all up till it shut out the light of day—and threw it back again, an unending rain of death spreading wider and wider . . . the first wave was enough—the lucky ones drowned in ten feet of muck, that was the first hour—they reckon twice as much fell in the second and more in the third, and still it kept falling . . . Anyone above sixty feet who might have survived died of hunger, lack of water—or died of fright, they say.'

Lucus listened gravely, with an expression almost of piety as he fumbled back of his half attentive mind with the notion that his father had the compulsive desire of all the grown-ups he knew to go over and over the old story, just as once, so many years ago, he would worry at Matrix to tell again the dog-eared tale of Puss in Boots . . .

'The rain fell brown, for months after. Earthquakes, the tilting world gone out of orbit, as I read, not by much, but . . .' the strained expression of a man powerless to put a planet back on course, powerless to visualise disaster at its penultimate order of magnitude, but ready, with half-raised hands, to shield his eyes if he should succeed and it become unbearable.

The boy glanced at his mother and hoarded a smile. She was asleep. It meant nothing to her, he knew. Old history—in the past; what had women to do with such things? They looked to the present: you must comb your hair; troubled themselves about the future: I must get your father's supper; and that was as it should be.

He thought of all those reiterations by the Elders, wise men descended from sad generations who'd starved, suffered, survived somehow, clawing back much of the common sense long stifled under the soft continental quilt of the old Twentieth Century.

Hard times, Lucus, when you had to learn to live all over again; when gratitude for small mercies was more sublime than a Harvest festival; because you knew the bread you sweated daily for was neither sliced nor wrapped, but simply—a self-attained blessing.

Thus, a thin belt of rugged individualists, striving for the common good, had struggled out of one generation into the next, from Kent to the land of Cornwall out of which came Lucus and his parents. An even thinner line of such people existed away to the north in the wild Highlands, always sparsely populated by those familiar with life's grimmer face. They had reverted violently to primitive religion, it seemed, had become not so much God-fearing as scared stiff of his further intent.

But, as the Southerners argued, why fear him any more now they knew what he was really capable of? Anyway, wasn't there a case for being man-fearing seeing man himself was largely responsible? What he'd claimed in his arrogance before the deed, he was saddled with *ex post facto*.

No. Better to think tight, keep a curb on one's own thoughts and actions, fear the two-legged predator, shun the acquisitive and put them away when they started to talk of benefiting mankind, of progress . . . standards of living . . .

There was only one prison in what remained of England: a special place, knocked up out of two ancient churches, for speculators . . . a place where they could worship money to their heart's content.

The one-a-day train had only a few miles to go; and now, the scene grew weird and fantastic beyond wonderment. With the gradual descent into a once great valley, even the tops of drowned churches and the leafless crowns of trees all but disappeared.

They were in the great cutting that ran for miles into the heart of old London; a masterpiece of human endeavour, carved out of chaos by thousands of men and women, five years it took to clear the debris and half-a-million well-preserved corpses . . . across Surrey, Middlesex, West London, Kensington to where, like a miracle out of mythology, Eros still stood, poised to aim his arrow at the heart.

The pioneers unearthed him in 25 A.C. Five thousand survivors, a multitude for the times, gathered in a great arena to celebrate the event and, though the Southland remained agnostic, it felt kinship with the little god who knew how to survive. As for the other business, Christ on a cross might be a personal misfortune, but it must take its rightful place—second in the disaster table.

Don't argue otherwise with men who'd dug out untold thousands of redemptives with picks and shovels.

Men, women, middle-aged and more, stood in their ragged working clothes, observing a silence for the country's forty-two million dead, six million around them still in the vast necropolis. The crowds on the rim of the man-made crater could look down on the ceremony or up to the shattered tower of St Stephens, the remains of Big Ben, skyscraping chunks of punk architecture and the spare ribs of Paul's floating on a sea of devastation.

One of their number, Len Graddick, made a simple speech and that was all. There were no leaders, civic or otherwise. They were done with leaders, let the rest of the world do what it would.

'Friends, there's not a lot to say. We've had twenty-five years to discover the value of words. When your back's breaking on a ten hour shift, the least said is enough. Maybe that was the trouble. Too many words. You'll remember, most of you, how it used to be. All day and every day—radio—television—newspapers—books— journals—words—millions of 'em, all saying different things more

often than not. No peace, no end to it . . . till the 17th of October
1998 . . . over there—in the East—I should've been home with my
family . . . but I was on a tanker five thousand miles out. Could I
believe it when news began coming over the radio? It was just
words—more words. How could I know they'd about got it right this
time?

'"The World's Worst Disaster." England, Scotland, South Wales
submerged, Denmark disappears, Holland, half of northern France,
most of Belgium—impossible! They've always been there . . . but we
could see and feel the drag of the water pulling us off course to prove
it, the tidal waves right round the world, and the sextant . . .

'Being a British ship we sailed home—to Southampton for
once—no more Liverpool. We struggled through and found . . . and
found . . . silence. Silence and darkness, more than you'd find in the
grave.

'Friends, let's never forget. What we did to the world, the world
repaid with interest. There's no message except this: next time, let's
tread over it, carefully, the way we did over there, excavating every
single body we found in our path.'

The voice of little England. Never to be forgotten. The exhorta-
tions of those early Pioneers, most of them products of a cholesterol
society, pampered and jaded, remained with succeeding generations, though by an irony the words were superfluous.

Because the intensity of the shock stemming from disaster had
bitten into the very genes of a remainder population, was impressed
like a sign manual, transmitted from father to son, from mother to
daughter. Shock, felt but unseen and unknown, showed its profit,
creating a hardier strain, purifying a stock too long contaminated
with the Norman streak of dominance, cruelty, snub-nosed, feudal-
ised superiority; gave England back to what was left of itself.

That much good out of evil-smelling history was somewhat to be
thankful for.

Lucus forgot the need to question, forgot everything but that view
from the carriage window. No time to ask 'what's that, and that,' and
the rest of the jumbled flotsam embedded in the detritus. They
seemed to be traversing a fossilised trench that must once, surely,
have defended a madman's nightmare?

Metrix, too, gazed in fascinated awe, from one side to the other, as
the twin slices of catastrophe unendingly revealed their contents. It

was his first visit to the old Metropolis for many years and, he soon
realised, time had done nothing to soften first remembrance.

Matrix still slept.

Houses crushed, walls torn away to reveal rooms filled with
ghostly furniture, a piano suddenly, little boxes with grey glass,
often still unbroken, and cars, cars, cars. Lucus had never seen so
many, yet all so differently alike, rusting wrecks like the one in the
village garage: a reddish pillar box, oxidised machinery in what
remained of factories: the stern of a cargo ship, a tractor, the
skeleton of a horse, a great barn-like shop with shelves and shelves,
long since stripped of canned goods . . . a whole cemetery of cars,
more houses, crushed, bleached trees against a dun dreary background of rubble, the battered hulk of an aircraft shorn of its wings,
cars, rocks . . . rubbish.

It had its effect of course. To all travellers on that line depression
inevitably sets in. The eye can absorb a great deal and in some
detail, but vision and perception flag until one must, at last, look
away and suffer the inward pangs that go tandem with melancholy
reflection.

Once, they passed the left-overs of what must have been a
school; the boy turned from a glancing view of a jagged blackboard
to find his father studying him with an indefinable expression. He
seemed about to speak but checked himself and gazed instead at
the outside scene, mentally rehearsing the question he might have
asked.

What does it mean to you? I'm that much nearer to all this, not
much, but enough to remember the quiver in my father's voice
when he tried to tell all *his* father had remembered what he'd
heard. He realised that understanding, the effort of comprehending, weakens with the passing years; could regret, unaware perhaps
of the phrase, the acceptance world, where all that is, is, and will be
so for one's natural term. The boy had grown up astride two
permanent yet utterly dissimilar worlds, and surely—he broke from
reverie, cursed himself for his weakness, wanting to delve and
question, and found a release in more everyday matters.

'Wake your mother and ask her to pour some ale and find the
bread and bacon.' Brusquely, as if to snap the spell cast by that
grim passage, and to rid himself of a lingering question still burning
the tip of his mind as Matrix began to fumble at the contents of a
large, plaited straw bag.

Do you realise, son, beyond these walls, millions upon millions of men, women, children, lie buried, yet not buried, perfectly preserved—broken maybe . . . millions?

He shuddered the thought out of existence, knowing he'd addressed the question by no means to Lucus, but to his still incredulous self.

Seasoned travellers called such depression the Lot's Wife curse. They read, or played chess, talked, slept or knitted, but they never looked out of the windows.

The family ate and drank through the last ten minutes of the journey. Metrix, more voluble than usual, talked of everything he could lay his mind to, striving for the boy's attention until even the sightseeing Lucus must let his gaze slide from the passing show to concentrate on a word game his father seemed to have invented on the spur of the moment.

The nearer they came to London, the more crushing the devastation. Considering the substantial nature of many structures existing in all capital cities, the Pioneer gangs were puzzled until hard won experience provided an answer.

The business of excavation became more and more arduous; shifts were cut from ten to eight to six hours as the strongest and weakest toiled to continue the path through suddenly concertina'd buildings and the tangled wreckage of oil rigs, ships, and huge boulders, an incredible mélange rising to a mean height of 60 feet.

Proving the inexplicable irruption had flowered quite consistently with known physical laws. The initial upsurge of mud, being light, had splayed outwards, creating a fantastic umbrella over thousands of square miles on a scale no antediluvian H bomb could have equalled. The heavier material also sprayed outwards but by diminishing degrees, until some simply fell back into the epicentre.

One such explosion would have been enough but it was repeated with scarcely less intensity for some hours till, to the distracted survivors, it surely seemed the entire world must crack apart or be buried by its own entrails.

Thus the obstacles faced and overcome by the Pioneers, that odd assortment of bank clerks, farmers, miners, mechanics, undertakers, printers, landowners from the rich, untouched counties of Hampshire and Wiltshire, baronets and a handful of peers; united at last, class dismissed, for a task devoid of profit or self interest, hardly more than a gesture, though none could have said of what or why.

The task, begun with pitiful resources, their descendants continued, fervently determined to salvage the whole metropolis if not the rest of the inundated country. And so, when the ancient train clanked to a halt in the tiny station called London, Lucus and his parents could gaze for at least a quarter of a mile in all directions. It was not, as Lucus expected, a plain encircled by the petrified flood, but, to his excited eye, there were concentrated more buildings than he'd seen in all his fourteen years. Even Matrix was impressed, while the father, his expression a compound of conflicting emotions, regarded the ancient statue of Eros on its crumbled plinth and the little stone cottages radiating like wheel spokes away from the tiny 'plaza'; London, still a name to conjure with, already it could claim a population of fifteen thousand and growing, day by day, towards the maximum twenty thousand: so said Thinktight.

In the distance they could see gangs of men, ant-like, tearing away at the detritus with picks, shovels, battering apparatus and wood-fired steam shovels, inching the circle outward with an almost geometrical precision. In the immediate foreground, townsfolk jostled them as they bustled from one shop to the next, the goods openly displayed on wooden trestles—and everywhere, signboards swinging in the faint breeze, the butcher, the baker, the candle-maker . . .

How could the newcomers know that, even now, at the north-west tangent, men were beginning to uncover the façade of Selfridges, the store of a thousand dead shoppers?

They could just identify bits of two gaunt palaces, some of the Parliament buildings besieged by whitened statues of ancient Prime Ministers, the lower bastion of the tower housing Big Ben, most of which had fallen at last, weakened by the tilt nothing could stop.

Much of the stonework could now be found in the rows of neat and snug little cottages thereabouts.

They wondered at a bridge running meaninglessly towards a ghastly ruin of freak architecture once proudly disfiguring the South bank of Thames. Now, there was no bank and no river. The Thames had retreated to lower reaches with the drop in sea level, dead at its source till it found strength to run another course, curling in perplexity before taking a way out somewhere on the Dorset coast.

In every quarter of that strange township they heard the sound of hammering as wood wrenched from newly disinterred properties was converted to provide floors, doors and roofing frames for new schools, hospitals, houses . . .

Lucus saw it all with shining eyes and a heart that beat a little faster. After the unvarying pace of life in a Cornish village the present scene discharged such vitality, displayed so boisterous an air of endeavour, that he swaggered along wondering that anyone could be satisfied to live elsewhere.

Besides, he was chattering now to his parents and even to himself when their attention strayed too far, imagine how it must be—always discovering new things. Every blow of the pick would unearth something.

Metrix caught the last rambling words and frowned. They were very nearly at the perimeter westwards. He pointed sternly, with great deliberation, and, fair as he still was, the gesture more than hinted at a patriarch thereabouts. Lucus took the direction and saw there were three men perched on a rough and precarious seeming cradle suspended by ropes from a framework of steel poles and baulks of timber high on the cliff's edge.

The eye deceived might suggest a trio of masons carving a delicate bas-relief for monuments so lightly they handled mallets and chisels. But there was, about their air of studied concentration, an intensity compelling the second glance, and one realised how finely controlled each movement had to be, because the ramshackle cradle scarcely swung by an inch.

Metrix led wife and son a little to one side. At once the boy understood why such care was being taken in that oasis of profound silence.

Above the doubled figure they could see clearly the triangulated collapse of the roof, its steel supporting beam aslant enough to miss the crouching woman, leaving the rising tide of mud to end her agony. A small building, not above 35 feet high.

A typewriter stood on a perfectly preserved table or desk, the chair she sat on seemed moulded to the indistinct figure from which they were tapping the last of the solidified muck, while she, not yet succumbed to the air, a mould rather than the form, appeared also to be tapping away at the skeletal machine, but blindly, as if unaware that death had long since given her time off.

On a small projection close to her feet, was a handbag, its shiny blackness aggressively visible through gaps of incrusting mud.

They watched with the absorption of observers faced with a totally new experience—even Metrix. What they had read about, thought of and discussed so often, was happening . . . forcing them to realise that the bustling little township, trumpeting its population of thousands, was no more than a hole carved from a vast mausoleum of Nature's own handiwork, and the three Pioneers, different Michelangelos, fashioning the very form and features of death from the indifferent earth.

Matrix turned away sobbing a little; for the moment her pity was wide enough to embrace the whole of suffering mankind, her sex revolting at the oldest adage: life . . . is . . . always was, a desperate, senseless struggle in which all must come home to nothing.

Not so Metrix the man and Lucus the boy. They stayed to the end; watched as the figure, still bent to the shape of acquiescence, was eased from the chair, watched as the three workmen, tenderly but with professional skill, lifted it into the cradle, nodded with satisfaction as one of their number placed the handbag at its side before signalling to those above to hoist away.

As the cradle rose slowly with its burden Metrix touched Lucus's arm and pointed to a man on the rim, silhouetted against a deep blue sky. His brass badge glinting with sun, Metrix explained, gave him tremendous authority. He was a talley-man, an office invested with the highest responsibility: recording every detail that could be discovered about every human creature unearthed. A job so skilled and complicated that his son would be apprenticed, and his son's son, and so on till the task was done.

'How long will it take?' the awe-struck Lucus wondered.

Metrix shrugged. 'Three—maybe four centuries, Thinktight reckons. But who knows.'

He added that the Great Book already held a million names.

'Shall we see that?'

'Yes—I expect so. But it's more important you remember what you've seen here—and what I tell you. "Every blow of the pick would unearth something" you say. Aye, all very fine and poetic, and so it does. But don't imagine there's joy in it for those men. They're more severe seeming than the ancient priests—have to be. For they deal in nothing but death and its left-overs. They know all's vanity except the reality of what they're doing.

'They maybe find a grand house, filled with rich and costly goods—and somewhere in the middle of it there's a baby child, dead to suffocation, buried in none but its own pram. Do you think they're not sick of the sight of treasures when there's humanity to be rescued?'

'Rescued?' The boy frowned at his first sight of a two-headed monster called paradox.

'Rescued!' Metrix wanted no doubts. 'We the living pay the respect owed to the dead who once were us—and so—we rescue ourselves through them.' He glanced at his wife who'd wandered off to browse over a pile of rubbish waiting to be carted away. 'Nothing happens in isolation, son. We're a part of an echo of that day. It don't grow fainter while we keep remembrance of it alive . . . because if we do forget, by a single body, what happened in those days, we'll be in danger of making the very same mistake that created the conditions for all this.'

'What mistake?'

'Forgetting the unborn, remembering only ourselves.'

The boy nodded, not in confirmation of what he'd heard, but to show that he'd tried to understand. At which Metrix was satisfied.

The 'facts of life' were as nothing to those he and his generation were bound to pass on to their children. A journey to old London might assume the superficial character of an excursion, a high day of distraction from the year-round matter of scratching out a living; but all men were enjoined by Thinktight to impress on the young ones the almost sacred nature of what was being done, here and in many other parts of the country.

'A sense of pilgrimage should mingle with the holiday mood. Each site is a Mecca which we best approach in a spirit of atonement, penitence and, above all, with a personal determination that mankind must never again raise its hand against itself this side of the Day of Judgment.'

Thus Nestorius.

So much to see: the underground station, perfectly preserved, the concourse with its circle of shops, all as it had been on that day . . . those are ticket machines—you put a coin in there and you could travel to Camden Town—where's that? Somewhere over there . . .

Great flights of metallised stairs—once, Metrix told them, they'd moved as if there were miles of them, rising or falling and disappearing from sight. How could that be? Matrix for one refused to believe it.

'They were called escalators, my dear,' he couldn't think of a better explanation and she remained unconvinced.

'No one denies their technical brilliance,' he added, lamely.

'Didn't do them much good did it?'

They looked at all the little shops, Villiers market, the under-ground cinema, the hotels, more or less restored and converted where that was possible but strangely at odds with the long rows of homely cottages with their neat gardens. Smoke feathered from every chimney. Wood served for fuel, was everywhere for the taking. In one backyard Lucus saw a great hammer beam dominating the woodpile, a curving monster on which an angel's form swallow-dived like an ancient ship's figurehead. Probably from one of the old Parliament buildings yonder, Metrix supposed.

It was time to eat.

They found a half-ruined arcade, cloister-fresh after the sun's heat: sat on a small wooden bench and ate bread, cheese and home grown figs, leaving the pigskin of ale to cool for a while in spite of their thirst. Behind them was the solid, blank façade of what had once been the Ritz Hotel, now a jumble of tenements cobbled together for the Pioneers and their families.

They chewed in the slow, reflective fashion of country dwellers and gazed with diminishing interest at the old London bus, flaunting its new coat of red paint. Not much more than a shell, it stood monumentally and exactly at a fare stage waiting for passengers long since departed.

Matrix wanted to know if they'd seen the old Houses of Parliament. Her man brushed crumbs from his beard and wond-ered, not for the first time, at woman's capacity for absorbing and eliminating information between tick and tock. He jerked a thumb behind him.

'Back there—where I showed you the old clock-face by the tower.'

'But there's no government now,' she objected, as though he'd asserted otherwise.

''Course not—they've no roofs on 'em have they?' he smiled a little to prove it was nothing serious.

'What's that got to do with it?' Lucus looked puzzled.

'Something. They must've told you at school about Lords and Commons. Wanted to abolish the Lords, but they all went. Most of 'em sitting in their chambers, as I've heard called. The roofs fell in.

They all perished. After that, what with one thing and another, people found they could manage well enough without. Now, every year we choose twelve men—each with a staff of five—but the twelve—just for a year.'

He pointed to his left: 'If you walk out a bit, you'll see a fair-sized open space. It used to be a park, but they cleared it for housing. Right in front there's a line of one-storey buildings—the sixty public servants work there . . . that's the government, and quite enough too for running what business we've got with the rest of the world.'

So it was—and so the English were determined it should always be. They lived; and managed, until it wrought a change in the 'national' countenance and character. The stresses and strains of a rusting civilisation no longer showed in people content with a measure of contentment. The psychiatric paradise filled with fissiparous 'personalities' scream-searching for fulfilment, unalloyed happiness, had gone with the deluge. Now, a benighted traveller in time would marvel at the calm, naturally tranquil features of those around him, such as had not shown for two or more centuries.

They gathered up the remains of their simple meal and set off on the last stage of the excursion. A short walk by way of the cottage lane leading back to Eros, then left through a covered passage brought them to where a massive stone building dominated. It might have been a palace with its severe and classical wings flanking and enclosing the expansive courtyard; and it might have appeared that nothing had happened on that fatal day, for there stood the old Royal Academy, even to the statues on the façade, still sheltering in their niches.

Ten years of renovation, of clearing mud and rock, collapsed roofs and floors, jumbled together with a collection of masterpieces on loan from the Uffizi . . .

Here, then, was the Great Exhibition: 'In which,' Thinktight announced, 'is displayed a selection of artifacts commonly used in the last quarter of the twentieth century B.C. No commentary is needed. We leave those visitors who may still be unconvinced to judge for themselves the truth of Nestorius' assertion that it was "the Age of Tarnished Miracles".'

Beautifully mounted, assembled and organised, it presented sophisticated chaos plucked from primeval chaos and shown, as nearly as possible, in original settings. So important had it become, that public opinion favoured its permanent retention as a kind of salutary influence in the national interest. But it remained the Exhibition; no high-sounding title would do.

One simply walked in. No tickets, no entry charge. The programmes were crude affairs: roughly printed, but instructive— and free. A few guides were available to answer questions, but there were no custodians, no security systems (other than those on display) to monitor every move made by the viewing public.

After all, there was nothing worth stealing. Values, priorities, had long since righted themselves and so, crime, in the post-diluvian era, had all but disappeared.

'There's hardly anyone here!' Matrix blurted out, impressed despite herself by the opulence of the place. True, it was so enormous that a thousand people scattered about the innumerable rooms, galleries and corridors still gave the Academy a half-deserted air. Metrix too was a little awed by the size, the grandeur of everything.

Lucus tugged excitedly at his father's sleeve with one hand, clutched the catalogue with the other and, constituting himself the family dragoman, pulled them with accelerating zeal, towards and up the stairway. 'This way! It says "The Exhibition starts upstairs on the left but no particular order need be observed". Come on!' He couldn't wait; boy-like, he bounded up two at a time, then, child-like, turned in perplexity to ask: 'Which way shall we go?'

The parents smiled. Metrix pointed to the left.

Into a 'room', described in the catalogue as a typical living-room of the Nineties.

They gaped in utter astonishment at so small a space holding so much: it seemed to be filled with over-stuffed leatherette arm-chairs and a sofa to match. With a mother and two children, a boy and a girl, all sitting glassy-eyed before a large TV set, sitting, or rather sprawling in those uterine chairs, all with a half-finished bag of crisps in their hands . . . just as they were found.

The father sat at a distance, head bent in an agony of concentration over a table littered with bits of paper. The catalogue explained that the head of the family was filling in 'Football Pools', a form of gambling in which one might hope to win a fortune.

In one corner stood a well-stocked cocktail cabinet.

Through the rear window a car appeared to be parked in the front garden.

So that's how it was. They smiled, a shade pityingly, as former sight-seers might if they'd caught sight of a distant relative in Bedlam. Lucus was glad to move on, giving a litter of Action Men on the thickly carpeted floor only a cursory glance. He'd no idea that in those days boys played with dollies wearing funny clothes.

A Sunday scene showed a man with a bucket of soapy water; he was washing the car. His wife appeared to be cleaning the interior with a tiny vacuum cleaner.

Semi-darkness dramatised the third tableau. The catalogue explained that the two exhibits had been unearthed on the Surrey-Sussex borders. One car was crushed to a right angle, the other had had its side sheered away. A misshapen mass, shrouded in earth, was half way through the windscreen. The two dead Jehus, anticipating the deluge by no more than seconds perhaps, had remained in their tin coffins for more than a quarter of a century.

'If that's what having a car was all about—' Matrix sniffed expressively and passed on, not bothering to give the 'tragedy' another glance.

'It dominated their lives,' Metrix said. But he lingered with the boy to be certain he retained a lasting impression . . .

'Don't you feel sorry for them, Father?'

The man shook his head. 'Why should I? They never felt sorry for themselves or anyone else. A man's car was his Kingdom and a King can't bear other Kingdoms passing him.'

On one side of the next gallery they found the walls and screens papered with soiled photographs. It seemed they had been found, almost perfectly preserved, in steel cabinets excavated from the offices of a press agency.

A thousand records of grisly road crashes, sickening to the point of nausea.

On the other side was a selection of photographs of places with outlandish names: Sachsenhausen, Dachau, Belsen . . .

For those with time and stomach to read, dozens of old newspaper cuttings were displayed, each one a detailed variation of man's inhumanity to man.

They read one, and could read no more.

'It was alleged by the prosecution that the accused ploughed into a group of three au pair girls waiting for a bus, drove on for a hundred yards before stopping. He then got out and swept one girl, impaled by a broken wing mirror off the bonnet, after which he continued his journey.

'The accused was given a six months' sentence, suspended, and banned from driving for a year.'

Lucus turned and found his father staring at yet another exhibit high on the far wall. It was a ghastly parody of Christ's head, made from bits of crashed cars; found, by accident, in the ruins of a cathedral in a place called Coventry. Such an expression Lucus had never seen till now on that mild and gentle countenance. His father's, that is.

'No, my son. I don't feel pity. Only how good it is not to be living in the past. . . . That past!'

They were glad to leave those chambers of horrors: room after room of chromium plated insanity, even to the modelised car victim, unearthed and discovered to be 40 per cent plastic and 25 per cent aluminium. They'd extracted a wad of treasured press cuttings from his wallet: Miracle Man Drives Again! Motorway pile-up victim—A Triumph of Spare Part Engineering. Indescribably mutilated, Mr Bloggs was snatched from the grave and refashioned over a period of three years by a team of surgical mechanics.

'I feel a new man,' quipped Mr Bloggs as he zoomed away in his new Jaguar invalid car.

'He looks like that face they found in Coventry,' said Lucus.


'In Gallery Six you will find seats provided for more comfortable viewing of the exhibits shown.

'To some extent the collection has, of necessity, been chosen at random. For example, the material for a view of average family life would be rare, if not non-existent in the central area of old London, and our collectors were at pains to prospect further afield. Quite unexpected material would be salvaged on these sites, one such proving to be a storage area for brief films which we know were shown between TV programmes. The custom has long since died out in the rest of the world except for some remote areas of the United States of Canamerica.

'The present, continuous selection of twenty representative examples of the "commercial", as they were called, can be shown in less than five minutes.'

Very likely; and time enough to rest one's feet for a spell in cool semi-darkness while one set of bizarre images ran into the next.

Not with soporific detachment, rather, with polite incredulity the family watched a rapid reeling off of unadulterated banality. The vicarage lantern-show of 'savages' and their quaint customs had given Time's whirligig a vengeful twirl.

Example: A little freak wearing outsize spectacles dances into view with the determination of one trying to be funny.

'Hello! I'm the Honey Man! Bzz—Bzz—the funny, honey man. Watch how it's done. Take two hives (he somehow suits the action to the words). Pour them together—and there you are—it's in the jar. Har-har! Have some. It's delicious!'

Winnie the Phew walks solemnly by, grabs the jar and goes off. Funny man looks glum. 'Have some more!' The Phew returns, pinches the last jar and disappears. Funny man grows distracted. Rushes off shouting: 'Try your local superstore—NOW!'

Example: Woman dressed in little but shadows, lies back in bed, reaches out a hand to—a cup of hot tea. Hand sensuously fondles cup, lifts cup to her lips, steam curling everywhere. A masculine voice, deep and vibrant, whispers, possibly from beneath the bed.

'Not just a tea—all the subtle flavours of the East in one packet. Taste the romance in a single sip.'

While the woman's lips close over the rim in a revolting close up shot, the voice below mutters on: 'Surrender to the romance . . . In Gan Green Tea. Knock softly at your local superstore's door and ask, with bated breath, for Gan Green Tea.'

Example: A bloated, very pompous executive type lies in bed, hands clasped behind his head, gazes dolefully at the ceiling. The bedside clock registers 2.30 in the morning. Suddenly his hairy wife turns over sleepily, sits up and says: 'Oh, for goodness' sake, Charles! Buy that six cylindered, supercharged, ten a gallon, maxi-road-holding electronic steering platinum plated JPZ1007 Black Mamba tomorrow and go to sleep!'

Example: Sweetie-pie voices croon a versicle as MOTHER hands round a plate of CREAM cakes to the bilious looking family. Father takes one with a gay smile and pushes his well-fed face into the sticky mess. Daughter chooses one and takes a panoramic bite with a sickly

simper. A small something grabs one and crams the lot into his
wholesaler's mouth at which the family laughs insanely.

Cut to hands grabbing, grabbing, till the plate is empty.

Cut to MOTHER, horror-stricken. Not one left for her!

Voice: from nowhere: Cream Cakes . . . get some more tomorrow.

Example: A pub scene. Music.
Voice: You can always tell a real man.

In walks a weedy little character—surrounded by hard-drinking
men, short back and sides men. He asks diffidently for 'Pint of
Malice, please,' pays for it, takes it, drinks it.

This requires a close action shot of an Adam's apple sliding up
and down as he guzzles. The music accelerates, volume increases
and, wonder of wonders, thanks to Malice, the little runt swells to
giant-sized proportions, bursting out of his shabby raincoat while the
big Burkes diminish to less than pygmy stature.

He brings down his empty glass with force enough to shatter it and
leers round, announcing in a throaty bass baritone: 'Malice!'

A few of the few suffices; indeed it was more than enough for the
family and several other viewers bored by inanities puerile and—
unpleasant. They crowded to the exit hearing but not listening to a
cacophonous outpouring that had some connection with a chocolate
bar.

'So that's what television was all about? No wonder that family
back there looked so scut-eyed,' a verdict from Matrix was always
loud and clear.

'They took it in small doses, I've heard,' said Metrix.

'Have to—wouldn't they?' Matrix sniffed and made no further
comment.

But Lucus wasn't satisfied. 'I didn't understand most of it,' he
admitted.

'Well, it's all about "I want" or "I must have" or "I haven't got it, so
I'll get one". That's how Thinktight puts it. You couldn't have a
proper standard of living unless you bought enough of everything
from the people who set the standards.'

'I see that. But why does everyone look so—so happy?'

'Convenience smiles—everything was for convenience in those
days—even the food. It's a way for saying—"you could be happy like
me—if only you had this lot".'

'Is that why advertising is forbidden?'

'Not forbidden—strictly limited.'

The next room gave a cutaway view of a supermarket, its shelves loaded with dummy packets and tinned food of every kind. They hurried past the dun-coloured shell of a woman, wheeling her infant along the aisle in an oddity on wheels, half pram, half trolley.

The child, in its mud casing, seemed to be in the act of reaching out to some brightly coloured packets of crisps.

There followed a gallery filled with examples of consumer durable goods—'their description, not ours' the catalogue's only comment, terse to the point of contempt.

The variety of gadgets displayed beggars description. It's enough to say that most of them excited laughter—even the electronic pocket calculator. The label beneath it took a more serious view.

'These instruments could be bought quite cheaply as standard articles for the masses, more expensively as silver-plated accessories for the narrower stratum of sophisticates; at any price they served as yet another accretion of prestige through possession. We know now that their introduction was a deliberate attempt to assist in creating a race of mentally deficient cripples, increasingly dependent on the growing power of computer technology. This at a time when the authorities showed "deep concern" at the standards of "numeracy" in their educational system.

'Their use was banned, as you know, in 3 A.C.

'Most exhibits in this section tended, like the car in its effects on limbs and heart action, like the television with its constant assault on the senses, like computers inhibiting the strength of organic powers of calculation, to produce a universal condition bordering on mental and physical atrophy. Political opportunism festered in this situation with consequences we know too well.

'Of course the curious system of economics practised by our forefathers required that nothing should bear witness to the sterility of the system, nothing must be allowed to prevent its destructive course. By the last years of the millenium, countless teams of apologists, called psychologists, were employed by government and industry, to convince the public through every available means of communication that all such goods not only enhanced "standards of living", not only pointed infallibly in the direction of Progress, but were above all, a necessary benefit without which man must inevitably sink into an aboriginal state of ignorance, thus succumbing to a disease very nearly eliminated along with cholera, the plague and other loathsome and contaminant diseases . . . individualism.

'These ampoules, continuing the above theme, contain examples of drugs on which millions became increasingly dependent in their attempts to face the stresses peculiar to the so-called Affluent Age.'

Metrix and his family gazed uncomprehendingly at samples of heroin, cocaine, cannabis, Dextramyoceptalin, name followed meaningless name. Hard drinks and every variety of cigarette were included. Needles and hypodermics of all types and sizes were shown.

It needed the photograph, taken from medical files, to make the point: a drug addict, in the terminal stage of addiction. The kind of contorted monstrosity they used to love in their midnight horror movies . . .

Metrix hurried the boy away before he could quite grasp its meaning and both parents looked pale and anywhere but at each other.

Metrix could not restrain himself. 'I hope, my dear, you'll not go on quite so much about the wonderful times these poor people lived through and how much easier life was then.'

'Well,' as far as she was capable Matrix looked and sounded crestfallen, 'well, how could I know all this?'

'Thinktight tells us,' he reminded.

'Yes, in bits, but—sometimes you have to see for yourself.'

Metrix gave a *quod erat demonstrandum* glance about him.

'Anyway,' typically she remained on the defensive by returning to the attack, 'you knew no more about it than I did.'

He stopped short, frowning angrily at her. 'Woman! You forget I did my stint in the Pioneers long before we came together.' But the show of anger soon passed, for Metrix was a good man, badly harrowed by what he'd just seen. Who could blame him for being disturbed by once dormant memories? Every blow of the pick . . .

'Anyways,' mildly, 'men were most times content with their lot. It's woman's fate to push 'em where they don't always care to go.'

'*Was* their fate, my dear,' timidly enough for Matrix.

Anxious to read true contrition he studied her countenance and seemed satisfied at last with what he saw.

Peregrinations of this kind can be an exhausting experience; they had seen enough, and hardly gave a glance at the gambling section through which they must pass to gain the exit. The betting shop, the 'amusement' arcade, the Bingo parlour and the 'intimate casino' gave a promise of mysteries they could not fathom; nor could they find inclination enough to do so.

It would suffice for Metrix to read aloud from the catalogue.

'Gambling is an indispensable adjunct of most civilisations which, at the highest point of their intricate social organisation, suffer an irreversible reaction associated with inevitable decline and extinction.

'This reaction is characterised by a mood of uncertainty widespread enough to be symptomatic of social decay. This further creates, as the "Entertainment" section demonstrates, a kind of wild hysteria (you will recall the recording of an ancient radio audience and its desperate laughter unsupported by evidence of material worth even a smile). Collective hysteria, like collective violence contributes to the general sense of insecurity and uncertainty, and this, in turn, fosters the phenomenon of gambling, a phenomenon stronger, in its more virulent stage, than the hope of survival.

'This sad fact is exemplified in photograph 784: a crowded betting shop in which the gamblers clearly have taken no steps to save themselves. Only one figure was found near the door.

'During the excavation it was discovered that all the victims held winning slips in their hands.'

There was so much more to see, but they were tired and anxious about the train home. Lucus protested feebly, his curiosity unquenched, but still, a tired youngster uncertain of his limitations.

No, they were wrong. One more room yet must be gone through before they could leave the Exhibition. A high ceilinged chamber hung with bits of heraldry taken, as the catalogue conceded, from Windsor. The furnishings belonged to an exclusive club or a palace. Every article had been painstakingly cleaned and repaired. Ancient photographs depicted the moment of breakthrough by early Pioneers to the ground floor of an edifice crushed and compressed in part by the stupendous weight of the deluge.

The site of this once-famous building had been lost or forgotten for years—nor was much effort made to discover its whereabouts.

In time they unearthed a small group of mummified creatures clutching, in their death agonies, some bent and rusted iron railings; the mud shell of a figure crouching in the remains of a tiny wooden shelter nearby removed all doubts.

Across the forecourt, inch by inch, clearing, not hundreds, but thousands of tons of rubble, up to and through the collapsed façade.

Among the dozens of cadavers dug from an endless series of shattered rooms sat one in solitary state, still enthroned in a half-disintegrated wing chair, drowned by the mud that had rained in from above.

Now, the ancient, blackened figure lay, perfectly preserved, in a glass case, surrounded by most of the objects amongst which it had died.

The Norman conquest was done with at last.

They paused to read the singular inscription.

'We are not actuated by their love of sensationalism in exhibiting these remains. Rather, it is an oblique but supreme reflection of the Twentieth Century mentality.

'Conditioned by two horrifying wars and many smaller conflicts, by a continuous running battle between order and anarchy, by a faithful recording of any act however violent, by the everlasting pandemic of violence on their roads, it became the Age of Violence, an ingrowing canker caused, it may be, by the growing dearth of external aggression.

'This morbid addiction complemented an oddly dualistic attitude to death. While unable to believe in its reality as a personal and inevitable experience, many people were infected with a tainted curiosity about the extinction of others.

'Therefore, it seems fitting that a world in which the remains, sacrilegiously disinterred, of a Pharaoh could be displayed to the vulgar gaze, in which the casketed remains of an eastern princess could be offered as an intellectual peepshow; in which, at last, the remains of several hanged, notorious criminals taken from a prison compound, could be shown in a "special exhibition", cannot reasonably complain if we do as the Romans did and demonstrate to our visitors what was capable of attracting the lost generations of long ago.'

'Let's be going,' Metrix said at last. 'We don't want to miss the train home.'

Matrix hesitated, her eyes still held by the recumbent figure;

shuddered, took off the prized coat, rolled it into a ball and looked about her for a litter bin.

'I want no part of them,' she said, quite simply.

Metrix smiled, knowing the journey had been worthwhile.

No, they didn't want to miss that train. Nor would they ever want to return. Lucus, of course, must come back to do his year's service with the Pioneers. But he too would be glad to rediscover the simple peace and contentment enfolding his village world, even wonder, perhaps, why it should be necessary to reclaim more of a way of life already flaunting enough of its barrenness, its grubby obscenity.

One last exhibit caught Lucus's tiring attention as they came to the exit. A great painting in oils almost covering an adjoining wall, showed signs of salvage from the old Parliament House.

It depicted a woman receiving the Roman salute from hundreds of 'MPs' as they were called. Above her was a flag, a Union flag with a white circle bearing a strange, black and crooked device.

They read the inscription.

'The blessing of the renewed flag for the inauguration of the one party state.'

'What's that?' Lucus wondered, almost in his sleep.

Metrix's jaw tightened at remembrance of Nestorius' words.

'A little before this time men, sapped by luxury, drained to the dregs of their former self-respect, craved the rule of women who, it is known, are more ruthless, more tainted by malevolence in pursuit of their objectives, especially where these are of an evil and vindictive character. In a land of the blind the creation of a one party state ruled by a virago was but a matter of time.

'After the Catastrophe it was decreed: No woman would ever again be free to soil the natural law that divides while uniting the sexes. No woman would ever again have the power of death over men, for was it likely a loving mother would be ready to fall in the first ranks of those she sent to war?'

'But who was she?' Lucus insisted.

'That, my son,' Metrix said with a strangely meaningful look at his wife, 'is another story.'